Mac sensed Stacy was hurting inside

He could feel it in the way she held her body, see the darkness in her eyes. Still, he felt she shouldn't be left alone tonight to brood over the day's happenings. While he wanted nothing more than to make love to her, he wouldn't rush her into it. Not when there was yet so much standing between them. Right now, he just wanted to hold her in his arms and help keep the hurt away. For now, he'd take what he could. And be there when she needed him.

"This is like another world," she murmured. "I almost feel as if we don't belong. That only lovers should stay here." Her jaw flexed. "We're imposters, Mac. We want to become lovers, but the timing never seems to be right for us. It's as if fate wants us to suffer for some past misdeeds. My past misdeeds."

ABOUT THE AUTHOR

Linda Randall Wisdom is a well-known name to readers of romance fiction. Long-term service in personnel, marketing and public relations gave her a wealth of experience on which to draw when creating characters. Linda knew she was destined to write romance novels when her first sale came on her wedding anniversary. She lives in Southern California with her husband.

Books by Linda Randall Wisdom
HARLEQUIN AMERICAN ROMANCE

Don't miss any of our special offers. Write to us at the following address for information on our newest releases.

Harlequin Reader Service
901 Fuhrmann Blvd., P.O. Box 1397, Buffalo, NY 14240
Canadian address: P.O. Box 603,
Fort Erie, Ont. L2A 5X3

SINS
OF THE
PAST

LINDA
RANDALL
WISDOM

Harlequin Books

TORONTO • NEW YORK • LONDON
AMSTERDAM • PARIS • SYDNEY • HAMBURG
STOCKHOLM • ATHENS • TOKYO • MILAN

For Bob,
who still keeps the romance
alive and well
in our marriage

Published January 1990

First printing November 1989

ISBN 0-373-16325-8

Prologue

It was a typical downtown police station in the middle of the night; brightly lit, redolent of anger and human suffering, noisy and very impersonal.

Frank "Mac" McConnell stared down at his torn uniform shirt pocket, then at the cause of another shirt's demise. For a kid, Stacy Markham was more than a handful. He'd lost count of the number of uniforms she had torn over the past couple of years. He wondered if she did it as part of a game: if you get arrested, make sure the cop's uniform isn't left intact.

He looked at her, a teenage girl sitting up straight and tall in a scarred metal chair. Brown hair hung to her waist in tangled waves; her black sweater and leather miniskirt were obviously not bought off the rack, and the narrow gold rope chain circling one slender ankle was very definitely the real thing. He idly wondered if she had stolen the anklet at one point in her criminal career.

"Stacy, my girl, we've got to stop meeting like this," he told her in his rough, gravel-voiced drawl, handing over her purse to a policewoman waiting nearby. "This is the third time this month I've picked you and your friends up, and I'm sure your father must be tired of bailing you out of here. I know I'm tired of picking you up. It would serve you right if your old man let you stick around here for a while and discover what real life was all about.''

"Hey, man, you've got nothin' on us." A boy in his late teens sneered as he was roughly pushed into a chair and handcuffed to the arm.

"Chad, my boy, you're not even funny anymore." Mac sighed. "Someday we'll have enough to send you away for a very long time."

The boy grinned, the expression more evil than humorous. "That's what you think, pig. You better start watching your back."

Mac yawned dramatically. "I'm real scared," he said in a bored voice.

The barest hint of a smile touched Stacy's lips, as if she found Mac's remark amusing. She stood up when the policewoman laid a hand on her arm, and allowed herself to be led away.

"Poor kid," Gary Watts, Mac's partner, murmured, coming up from behind.

Mac turned his head, the expression on his features showing disgust. "Poor kid, my ass. We all should have it so rough. Her father makes more in a couple months than we do in a couple years. Although I can't imagine he enjoys calling in favors in order to keep his darling little girl out of jail. Maybe if she spent some time in a jail cell, she'd think twice about running around with that gang and raising so much hell." He spoke of a group of wealthy kids who got their kicks by breaking into homes and taking off with small items. Stacy Markham, daughter of prominent corporate attorney Jonathan Markham, was well-known as one of the ringleaders. To date, not one of the lawbreaking teenagers had spent more than an hour at the police station. Their deeds were immediately hushed up, thanks to their influential parents, who viewed the episodes as nothing more than childish pranks.

The policeman was still toiling at his paperwork when Stacy's father arrived. Mac felt he knew Jonathan Markham well; after all, he had arrested the man's daughter enough times during the past two years. He'd once joked to Gary that he and Markham should be on a first-name basis by now. The tall, elegantly dressed man approached Mac and held out his hand.

"Officer McConnell, we meet again." He offered a coolly polite smile.

Mac nodded and accepted the man's hand in a brief shake. "Stacy will be brought up in a few minutes."

The other man looked around the room, disdain for his surroundings clearly etched on his thin lips. "You'd think with her upbringing she would prefer being anywhere but here," he muttered, making it sound as if the station were only one step up from hell. "I swear, that girl never learns. If I had my way, she'd be shipped off to a boarding school that wouldn't put up with these kinds of stunts, but her mother won't allow it. She feels I'm too hard on her, as it is."

Mac privately thought that applying a board to an appropriate part of Stacy Markham's anatomy would be more beneficial, but he prudently left that idea unspoken. Since Jonathan Markham was a good friend of the mayor and police commissioner, Mac knew it was better to remain silent.

When Stacy appeared, Jonathan Markham looked at her with the same kind of disgust he'd displayed toward his current surroundings.

"You just don't learn, do you?" he said in a fierce, low voice, grabbing her arm. "Do you realize I was called away from an important dinner because of you? At the rate you're going, I'm not going to be able to cover up these stunts of yours, and I'll lose my chance to run for the state supreme court. So help me, if you screw up this opportunity for me, you'll be shipped off to a European boarding school until you're forty.''

She looked up, not one shred of emotion in her hazel eyes. "Then I guess I should be flattered you came for me, Daddy dear. But then you've worked so hard all these years to get to this point. You don't dare allow anything, including your *darling* daughter's little high jinks, to ruin it for you, do you? So what if Mom and I don't see you except on Thanksgiving and Christmas—as long as you get elected to the state supreme court! No wonder she drinks. Your career is all that matters to you—not Mom, and certainly not me. We're just outside trappings to make you look the part of the perfect family man."

Jonathan Markham whipped his head around, as if afraid the remark would be overheard by the wrong ears. "I suggest you remain quiet." His cold voice held a warning.

Her smile was equally arctic. "Yeah, we can't have the world know all our secrets, can we? Your daughter is a thief and your wife's a lush."

His eyes snapped with temper. "You should be grateful I was willing to come down and get you."

"Just don't expect any heartfelt thanks for coming to get me, okay?"

Mr. Markham dragged his daughter away, reprimanding her the entire time without raising his voice, although fury was evident in every tense muscle in his body.

"There's something about that guy that leaves a bad taste in my mouth," Gary commented, walking up to stand beside Mac.

Mac looked at him. "Come on, Gary. Jonathan Markham is putting up with a kid who doesn't appreciate what she's got. How many fathers are willing to bail their kids out every time they get into trouble? You know as well as I do, a majority of the parents we deal with blame us for their kids getting into trouble. There's Mr. Conners, who's obviously on drugs. He says it's our fault his kid rips off car stereos to pay for his own drug habit. Not to mention Mrs. Anderson, who usually shows up drunk and with her latest lover, and screams at her daughter for getting picked up for prostitution. I guess we should be thankful Markham doesn't blame us for his daughter running around with that punk kid, playing Bonnie to his Clyde. I'll tell you one thing. If I was him, I'd lock her in her room until she was thirty. All she's going to do is get into more trouble, until she's locked up in a place where Daddy can't help her.''

"Yeah, but do you notice all he talks about is how she's forced him to leave some meeting or important dinner and how she's screwing up his chances? I just bet he doesn't give her one ounce of attention at home. No wonder she gets into so much trouble. The way she talks, the only time she sees her old man is here,'' Gary argued. "And word has it her mother's an alcoholic, and prefers to stay in her room all day with a bottle and daydream. That kid has no idea what a real home life is like.''

Mac chuckled. "Look at this. The guy's been a father for all of three days, and he's already an expert on teenagers,'' he joked. "I can't wait to see you in about fifteen years and see if you can be so philosophical.''

Gary looked toward the front door, where father and daughter had recently exited. "At least my kid's going to know I'm there for her when she needs me,'' he murmured.

"I TELL YOU, I wasn't there!'' Stacy Markham said days later. Her hazel eyes blazed furiously with anger as she tried

vainly to pull away from Mac's inflexible grip. He guided
her to an empty chair. "Why won't you listen to me?"

"Probably because I've heard this story a thousand times
before," Mac said wearily, pushing her into the chair. "The
whole setup smacks of your gang's style, sweetheart, and
where they are, so are you."

"I was at a movie, damn you," she said through gritted
teeth, her entire body tensed for a fight. "And I wasn't
anywhere near the Loudons'. I haven't seen any of those
kids for almost a month. Okay?"

He didn't bother looking at her as he pulled a pen out of
his shirt pocket. Luckily, this time his clothing remained
intact. "What did you see?"

"Lethal Weapon 2."

"Can you prove it?" He wasn't convinced.

"Yeah, I'm sure the ticket seller is going to remember
me."

"Did you save the ticket stub?"

"Give me a break!" She took a deep breath.

Mac shrugged. "How about the names and addresses of
the people sitting around you?"

Stacy shut her eyes. "Yeah, sure. In fact we became such
good friends, we're meeting for cocktails tomorrow night."

He hid his grin as he grabbed a nearby phone. He had to
give her credit; she was never at a loss for words.

Mac shook his head as he dialed the call. As usual, he got
Mr. Markham's housekeeper and left a message that he had
given so often, he felt he could recite it in his sleep. He
pulled out the report forms and began filling them out. He
had no need to ask Stacy for pertinent information; he knew
it all.

More than three hours later, Stacy was still waiting in the
same chair. Her coltish body was hunched, jean-clad legs
ending in black high-heeled boots crossed at the ankle.

"Hey, Mac, call on line #2," one man yelled above the sea of voices.

"Officer McConnell," Mac snapped, cradling the receiver between chin and shoulder.

"Officer, this is Amy, Mr. Markham's housekeeper." The woman's voice sounded hesitant.

"Yes. Were you able to track down Mr. Markham?" he asked absently. "We've got a kid impatient to get out of here. I guess she doesn't like us."

"That's just it." Now she sounded downright embarrassed, Mac thought. "Officer, Mr. Markham will have things taken care of in the morning."

"What exactly did he say?" Mac asked in surprise.

"He said that perhaps a night in jail with some hard cases might straighten her out, so she'd stop embarrassing him with her pranks," the housekeeper went on. "And if she continues on this course, he doesn't even want to know about it." She paused. "I'm sorry."

Mac looked at Stacy. She was trying very hard to look indifferent about the situation, but all the while was watching the front door.

"Yeah. Thanks." He hung up and rose to his feet. While he wasn't fond of the rebellious girl, he wasn't happy with the task ahead of him.

Stacy looked up when he approached. "Don't tell me—he's at an important dinner party and he doesn't want to leave," she drawled, mimicking her father's speech.

"No, kid, it appears he's decided you should have the opportunity to check out our plush facilities." He grasped her arm. "Come on, I'll drive you over to Detention."

Her head snapped up. For a split second she looked stunned. "You mean he's not coming?"

"Nope. It appears you've pushed him too far this time, and you're going to have to pay the consequences."

Varied emotions flew across Stacy's young face, then it hardened, losing all vestiges of youth.

"Isn't it funny—the one time I'm really innocent and need him, he isn't here," she muttered. "But then he never has been. Why should I expect anything different this time?"

"Hey, you call wolf too many times, no one's going to come to your rescue." He walked her outside to the patrol car.

Mac's last sight of Stacy was of her unsmiling features and bleak eyes as she was led away by a juvenile officer.

"Maybe you'll learn something this time," he murmured, walking out of the building, instantly putting her out of his mind.

"Looks as if we're going to lose our steadiest customer." Gary dropped a raised donut in front of Mac.

He didn't look up from the newspaper he was reading. "Who?"

Instead of replying, Gary turned the pages of the newspaper and pointed to a particular article.

"Jonathan Markham died from a stroke yesterday," he explained. "Hell of a way to spend Thanksgiving, isn't it? It says he collapsed during dinner."

Mac's gaze skimmed over the article. He shook his head. "It says his wife is prostrate with grief and can't be reached for comment. Nothing said about Stacy. She probably ripped off the family silver and took off for Mexico with her punk boyfriend."

Gary shook his head. "It's really something. He had everything a man could want, and now he's dead."

Mac looked down at the watch his wife had recently given him for his thirtieth birthday, and thought of the gold Rolex he had seen on Jonathan Markham's wrist. "Yeah, money can't buy everything," he murmured. "Oh, well, I'm sure it won't be long before we see the lovely Ms. Markham again."

"Hey, old buddy," Gary said, "show some faith. Maybe we won't."

Chapter One

"My little snookums is just so traumatized from that horrible attack, Stacy!" the tiny silver-haired woman exclaimed, stroking a champagne-colored, sour-faced Pekingese with her chubby, bejeweled hands. "I've always sheltered him from the harsher elements, and for this to happen—well, he isn't the same since that terrible episode. I felt just terrible when I called that other service. I know it was very naughty of me, acting like a spoiled child when you told me that Irene was no longer working for you. And unfortunately, my poor little Tito has had to pay the price. I do hope you forgive me." Her faded blue eyes pleaded with the younger woman.

Stacy swallowed the laughter that was bubbling up in her throat and managed a sympathetic smile. "I understand your distress, Mrs. Coffman, and you can be assured there is nothing to be forgiven. After all, the Kramer agency offered you their best. It was only natural you would want to try them. You had no idea one of their employees would upset Tito so much. I'm just glad you felt comfortable enough to discuss this with me." She sipped her tea from the fragile Limoges china teacup and set it on the equally delicate saucer.

The fluttery woman, dressed in a blue print silk dress, smiled. "That's because I know how conscientious you are, Stacy. And I have to think of my little baby boy." She stroked the long, soft fur. "Not to mention all those horrible robberies happening in the area. If someone broke in and upset my baby, I don't know what I would do. You see, Ronald is planning a six-week buying trip to the Orient in the near future, and would like me to go along with him. I have to know that Tito will be in good hands while I'm gone. That's another reason I asked you to come for tea. I do hope you have someone as wonderful as Irene."

Stacy nodded, keeping down her excitement and listening as her client outlined what was known in the trade as a job order. "I have someone in mind who would be perfect to look after Tito," she told Mrs. Coffman. "Maura is a student at UCLA and very reliable. We've had nothing but praise about her from some of our other clients. She also adores dogs, and certainly would never allow anything to happen to him. Would you like me to have her stop by?"

The woman beamed. "Oh yes, please do."

Stacy stood up, smoothing her deep bronze trumpet skirt that furled teasingly around her knees. "I'll take care of it the moment I reach my office and give you a call." She walked to the front door accompanied by the older woman. "Be sure to let me know the date you'll be leaving, so we can set everything up."

"You're such a dear to care about my baby, Stacy," Mrs. Coffman said, tittering. "Now you drive carefully, and thank you so much for coming."

"I will." She reached her red Mazda and opened the door. "Goodbye, Mrs. Coffman."

During her drive from the ornate San Marino home to downtown Pasadena, Stacy mentally calculated the fee for a six-week job and laughed out loud.

"Thank you, Mrs. Coffman!" she crowed. "May you take more six-week trips!"

When Stacy opened her house-sitting service a few years ago, she knew she would be competing with well-established firms, but with a combination of hard work and quick wits she was now beginning to show a tiny profit. In a jubilant frame of mind, she headed for the Foothill Freeway.

"I'm SURE Ms. Harris will be here any moment, Detective McConnell," the receptionist ventured warily, watching the man standing by the window.

"I'm in no hurry," he assured her with a slightly crooked smile. "I should have called before stopping by, but as I was in the area..."

Janet nodded, her flaxen braid flopping over her shoulder. "One of our clients asked her to stop by her house," she explained, trying again to relax under the man's unreadable gaze.

Mac nodded and turned back to the window, idly noticing a fire-engine-red Mazda roaring into the circular parking lot and slipping easily into a space. His first glimpse of the driver was a pair of long, slender legs sliding out of the open car, a hint of gold glinting around one trim ankle. A gust of wind caught the hem of the deep bronze shirt, and the wearer hurriedly grabbed it to keep her modesty intact. He couldn't miss the laughter on her face as she stood up, tucking the cream-colored, long-sleeved blouse into the skirt's waistband and settling the narrow strap of a black leather purse over her shoulder. At first the ends of a black bow fluttering against the cream silk and the flirty skirt made him think she looked like an old-fashioned school-marm, even though her hair was short and shaggy instead of in the sedate chignon that would really go with the look. He watched her cross the parking lot toward the building until she disappeared under the covered walkway. He felt disappointment that he hadn't got a closer view of her.

"Janet, Mrs. Coffman's poor little Tito was attacked by a Pomeranian while under the care of one of Kramer's people, so she's asked to be forgiven, and wants us to find her someone for six weeks!" the woman in the schoolmarm's outfit said, breezing into the office. "Six weeks. I love it!"

Mac turned slowly and found his attention focused exclusively on the newcomer. The outfit might have been strictly modest, but the froth of lace visible through the semisheer blouse was far from it. And to think he had tried to get out of this assignment!

"Stacy." Janet spoke hurriedly. "This is Detective McConnell. He's here to talk about the robberies. He's been here for about an hour." She gestured toward the tall, dark-haired man standing by the window.

Stacy's bright expression dimmed as she turned to face the man. At that moment she felt the past roaring toward her with a vengeance.

"Ms. Harris." The man spoke in a low, gravel-voiced drawl that betrayed too many cigarettes—and probably too much whiskey. It was a voice Stacy couldn't have forgotten in a thousand years.

Nightmares weren't supposed to happen at three o'clock in the afternoon, Stacy thought hysterically. They should creep into your subconscious at midnight, when the moon was full and creatures of the night roamed the earth to haunt the unsuspecting.

So why was she standing there, staring calmly at the man who had been the cause of bad dreams for so many years? She swallowed, hoping the saliva would moisten her throat enough to allow her to speak. He might not have been wearing the blue uniform she remembered so well. His shaggy black hair and heavy mustache were now liberally sprinkled with gray, and his craggy features showed his forty-odd years, but she doubted she would ever forget this man if she lived to be a hundred.

"Detective McConnell, I apologize for keeping you waiting. Won't you come into my office?" She was relieved that her voice had only a trace of huskiness, considering the acute distress running through her body. She knew manners dictated that she offer him her hand, but she would have preferred being shot at dawn by Emily Post for her rude behavior rather than touch him. She waited until they were both seated in her small office. "Now how may I help you?"

The tall man settled back in the powder-blue chair.

"First of all, let me explain that this is purely routine, Ms. Harris," he began, pulling a notebook out of the pocket of the battered brown leather jacket that topped equally battered jeans. "I'm sure you've read about the rash of burglaries sweeping through Pasadena, San Marino and Arcadia."

Stacy nodded. "Anyone who reads the paper is aware of them." She resisted the urge to toy with the bow at her throat. Instead she kept her hands in her lap, out of sight. They were so tightly clenched that she doubted they would ever return to their normal state. Her stomach rolled at an alarming rate, and she only hoped she could get through this meeting with a serenity she certainly didn't feel. Afraid that body language would give her away, she slowly placed her hands on top of her desk, the picture of cool composure.

Mac's questions were innocuous at first. He asked how long Stacy had been in business, how many employees she had and how she garnered her clients.

"According to what we've already learned, two of the victims, the Winslows and the Carters, have used your house-sitting service during some time in the past eighteen months," he commented.

Stacy's lungs expanded in a painful rush. "I believe so, although they don't use me exclusively." She remembered each telephone call in vivid detail. She had lost those two clients because they wanted to blame someone, and she was the perfect scapegoat. After talking with two other agencies, she'd discovered that they had also been blamed for something beyond their control.

Mac studied her intently. After years of experience, he could size up a person right away. Stacy Harris's hairstyle was simple, the top and sides fairly short and brushed away from her face to leave a wisp of bang on her forehead, the back layered, covering her nape in loose waves. On its own her medium brown hair probably wouldn't have rated a second glance, but the golden streaks woven through the heavy strands gave it a life of its own. Her hazel eyes reflected many colors, blue, green, even a deep amber, but all they showed now was a polite coolness. A tiny scar bisected her left eyebrow. Her skirt and blouse showed off a nice figure, but nothing he hadn't seen before. Still . . . there was something about her that nudged at his memory. Unfortunately for him, he had never been good with names and faces, a weakness that had prompted him to take a course on how to boost one's memory a few years ago. He figured she was in her late twenties. Something about her manner said she hadn't lived an altogether easy life.

What was this something that was gnawing at the fringes of his memory? He couldn't seem to bring it into focus. She certainly didn't look like the kind of person he met in his line of work. But then years of working in Narcotics and Vice had him meeting people from all walks of life—most of them not the kind one takes home for Sunday dinner with Mom. He was surprised to think that the young woman sitting behind the old-fashioned walnut desk owned the small, but apparently flourishing house-sitting agency. He'd expected someone older. The detective half of his mind wondered where she had gotten the financial backing to open an office in a building whose high rents were well-known. Her manner was correct and her clothing and makeup were unpretentious, nothing to indicate she came from money, but something about her manner transmitted a different message. She was also very much on the defensive in his presence. He sensed that he had something to do with it.

"It seems a majority of the victims use a house-sitting service," Mac went on. "Here are people who are rich as Croesus, who have security systems to rival the White House, yet they still pay someone to stay in their house. No offense, but you have to admit it doesn't make sense."

Stacy smiled faintly. "None taken. Some of my clients only employ outside household help, and while their alarm systems are state-of-the-art, they still like a personal touch. Also, not all of my employees stay in the house. Sometimes they only go in to water plants, make sure everything is in order. They see to it that the cleaning crew does its job, and take care of the pets if the owners don't want them put in a kennel."

He nodded, recalling the few times he'd gone on vacation. All he did was stop the paper and mail. "Are your employees college students, housewives or a little of everything?"

She answered, although she was certain he already knew what she would say. He was the kind of man who checked everything out ahead of time. "Many of my employees are retired. Some are college students, although those usually only work for me during the summer."

His eyes widened slightly. "When you say *retired*, are you referring to the over-sixty-five set?"

"Just because they've arrived at retirement age doesn't mean they're infirm," she said, a bit more sharply than she'd meant to.

He held up his hands in self-defense. "Hey, no disrespect intended. I'll be there before I know it. I'm just here to check every angle I can, Ms. Harris."

Stacy nodded. She felt as if her entire body were tied in knots. Deep down she wanted to scream at him, order him to get out of her office and just leave her the hell alone!

"We'd like your permission to talk to your employees," he went on.

"Interrogate them, you mean."

His brow lifted at her sharp tone. "Well, we have dispensed with the rubber hoses in the past few months, but we still have plenty of other methods that seem to prove effective. My favorite is the rack."

Stacy bit her lip. "I'm sorry, Lieutenant, it's been a long day, and I'm afraid I'm not at my best. Naturally we'll do whatever we can to assist you. Janet, my receptionist, can pull whatever files you need."

Mac couldn't stop staring at her. Her reply was all he'd hoped for, so why did he feel as if she wanted to say something else? He noticed her fingertips rubbing the small scar just above her left eyebrow. He'd bet everything she only did that when she was nervous. What was she afraid of? Did she have something to hide? Could she be the one behind the robberies? No, his cases were never solved this easily, and he wouldn't be that lucky this time.

Stacy steeled herself not to fidget under his sharp-eyed regard. "Is there anything else you'd like to know at this time, Detective?" she asked politely.

Mac shook his head, flipping his notebook closed. "No, I think that's it for now. We'll be in touch within the next few days." He stood up and offered his hand. "Thank you for giving me your time, Ms. Harris."

Summoning a smile, she stood up and gingerly accepted his large hand, feeling faint calluses slide across her palm. It took every ounce of courage not to snatch back her hand and rub it down her leg.

Stacy watched the police detective walk through the reception area. When he stopped to have a word with Janet, Stacy dropped into her chair and picked up the business card he had handed her when he first walked into her office. Detective Frank McConnell, Pasadena Police Department. The man's too-rugged features, gravelly voice and name were all a part of a past she preferred to forget.

She wanted to laugh out loud with relief. He hadn't recognized her! It had been, what, twelve, thirteen years since their last meeting, when she had been a fifteen-year-old rebel? Her lips tightened, and her stomach rolled over as she recalled the last occasion she had seen him. That was a time she didn't want to think about.

"Stacy, you okay?" Janet appeared in the doorway. "You look as if you're going to faint."

"Chalk it up to not eating since last night, Mrs. Timmon's vitriolic call this morning, my visit with Mrs. Coffman and now the police." Stacy sighed. "I had planned on doing some work, but I think I'm going to head on home instead. It's been a horrible day." She picked up her purse and draped the strap over her shoulder. "In fact, why don't you call the answering service and close up now? If there's anything important, they can always reach me at home."

"I won't argue with that." In short order the young woman made the necessary call and had her purse under her arm. The two left the old-fashioned office building and walked toward their cars.

Stacy's first inclination was to drive home, crawl into bed and pull the covers over her head until this was all over. Instead, she turned her car in the opposite direction. She knew that if she wanted to rest tonight, she would have to talk things out. And there was only one person who could understand.

The small, Spanish-style house in nearby Arcadia had been a haven for her many times over the past few years. She parked in the driveway and walked up a low ramp that covered a portion of the four steps leading to the front door. Not bothering to knock or ring the bell, she used a key to unlock the door.

A gray-haired woman, wearing a simple cotton dress, appeared in the living room as Stacy entered. "Stacy, how nice to see you," she said in a pleased tone. "Amanda's going to be thrilled you stopped by. She's out on the patio, enjoying some afternoon sun. Why don't you go on out? Dinner will be in an hour. Care to stay?"

Stacy sniffed the air. "Roast beef? You're on, but first I'm going to steal a cup of coffee."

"You go on out back. I'll bring some to you."

Stacy nodded and headed toward the rear of the house. She slipped out the screen door and paused to watch the woman seated in a wheelchair at the concrete edge.

"Darlin', I always told you not to stare. It's not lady-like," said a melodious Southern voice. "I swear you never remember anything I've taught you."

Stacy laughed. She crossed the patio to the older woman and bent to drop a kiss onto her cheek. As always, she smelled the scent of violets. It helped to reinforce the feeling of security that was still so new to her.

"Sit." Amanda Harris gestured toward a nearby cushioned patio chair. Smoke-gray eyes regarded her sharply. "How long do I have to wait before you tell me what's troubling you?"

Stacy rolled her eyes. "Don't you ever stop acting like a shrink?"

"Honey, I've been a doctor for too many years to be anything else," she reminded her. "And you know how much I detest that nasty term."

"Yep, sounds like a shrink to me." This was an old argument between them.

"A psychiatrist."

"That's still a shrink as far as I'm concerned," Stacy teased, looking up when the housekeeper brought out a tray, holding a china coffeepot and two cups. "Thanks, Alice. You don't know how much I need this. Are we having buttermilk biscuits with your roast beef?"

"Are there any other kind?"

"What's happened?" Amanda asked Stacy after Alice left. The psychiatrist sensed trouble in the woman whom she considered a daughter.

Stacy wrinkled her nose. "Don't you have enough with all your patients, without having to try to work on me? If it would make you feel better, you could always talk like a mother, telling me I'm not eating right, my clothes don't fit my image or something like that. And like any other well-mannered daughter, I'd smile and nod my head and promptly forget everything you told me," she told Amanda.

"You haven't eaten right for years. You aren't sleeping well, judging from those nasty circles under your eyes, and I still want to know what happened today, so don't try to change the subject." While the older woman's voice was musical, her tone was also remarkably firm and brooked no nonsense, which made her an excellent doctor dealing with troubled children. Even an automobile accident that had claimed her husband's life and cost her the use of her legs five years ago hadn't stopped her from keeping up with her busy schedule.

"Due to the burglaries going on, a police detective came by to see me," Stacy said quietly, sipping her coffee and setting the delicate china cup on the table.

Amanda nodded, well aware of Stacy's aversion to the law. After all, her husband had counseled Stacy, as well as acting as her foster father.

"His name was Frank McConnell."

"I see."

Stacy rolled her eyes and exhaled a gust of air. "Great, use your famous doctor's words," she said sarcastically. "What shall we delve into next? My feelings on seeing him again? And what I think of the police in general?"

"I think you've already given me your impression. As for the former, that's been covered quite nicely." Amanda smiled.

Stacy lifted her head, staring at the woman's serene expression. Her silver-frosted black hair was pulled back in a classic chignon, baring a delicate face that belonged on a cameo. Amanda might be in her sixties, but her porcelain skin and serene manner led many to think her much younger. Even her navy shirtwaist dress with white trim around the collar and cuffs gave her the appearance of the Southern gentlewoman she was. But Stacy knew a great deal of inner strength kept Amanda going during her days of pain and frustration over her physical limitations.

"How did you put up with me all this time?" she wondered aloud. "I was such a terror that I still don't understand why you were willing to take me on."

"And you think you've improved all that much? You still give me moments, you know." Amanda chuckled. "Now let's get back to your visitor. How did you feel when you first saw him?'' Her doctor's manner clicked on, and Stacy knew better than to ignore it. She knew she wouldn't be allowed to leave until she gave an honest answer.

"Shocked, surprised, angry," she replied without hesitation. "I wanted to order him out of my office. I didn't want to look at him and remember the past, but I had no choice but to sit there and allow it to wash over me."

"He didn't remember you?"

Stacy shook her head. "It shouldn't have surprised me, since it's been so long, but it did. After all, we saw each other frequently for over two years. But still, it was a long time ago," she said wryly. "You know, I hated that man for so many years, but when I saw him I couldn't dredge up that blackness that I had lived with for so long."

"There was never a reason for you to hate him. You just felt it was easier to blame him for what happened."

Stacy's eyes blazed. "Oh, yes, there was a reason," she said fiercely, lost in the past. "He could have seen that my father didn't give a damn about me, and that my mother didn't know I was alive, because she cared more for her brandy. But instead he saw me as some punk kid, deliberately trying to ruin her father's career with her crazy stunts." She jumped up and paced the concrete floor.

"Your father didn't know how to love, Stacy. He had his eye on the supreme court, and that was all that mattered to him," Amanda said gently. "Your acting like Public Enemy #1 only made him look like the victim, instead of the father who could only see one thing. That was why people saw you—the neglected daughter—in the worst possible light. You allowed them to."

"Yes, and all his ambition didn't save him, did it?" Stacy heard acid dripping from her words. She wrapped her arms around her body to ward off the inner chill that ran through her veins. Then she spun around to face the woman who had loved her more than her natural parents ever had. "When will it all end, Amanda?" she cried. "When can I live a normal life?"

"When you allow it to end. And you had been doing exactly that until you ran into your policeman again," she reminded her.

Stacy sank to the ground in front of Amanda, laying her head into her lap, as she had done so many times before when the hurt had grown so great that she didn't know if she could survive it.

"I want it all gone now," she moaned.

Amanda's fingers combed gently through the hair that had been ruffled from the late-afternoon breeze. She knew all she could give Stacy now was her love, something the young woman still desperately needed.

"What if he eventually remembers who I am? The agency will come under even closer scrutiny because of my past. They may even close me down on suspicion alone." Stacy gnawed at the problem the way a puppy gnaws at a bone.

"Darlin', your records were closed when you reached your majority," the older woman explained, her hand now gently rubbing Stacy's forehead, erasing the lines of strain. "Your past can't be used against you. It's the law."

Stacy shook her head. She had dealt enough times with the law in the past to know differently. She told herself that as long as she didn't have to deal with Detective McConnell anymore, everything would be all right. Funny, she didn't remember him looking so—for lack of a better word—battered, as if he'd lived and worked hard these past years. Deep lines were etched in his face, and his hair and mustache were liberally sprinkled with gray, but there was something about him that tugged at her. She should have been put off immediately, just because of her past association with the man. Yet there had been something comforting and reassuring in his manner when he talked to her. If she cared to think about it, there always had been. He hadn't treated her as rudely as some of the other officers had treated both her and her friends.

Stacy squeezed her eyes shut. Instead of the neat rows of Amanda's rosebushes, she saw a younger McConnell, wearing a patrolman's uniform and looking down at her with a pained expression. Returning to the present, she listened to Amanda's softly spoken instructions to clear her mind and breathe deeply until she felt calmer. By the time Alice came out to announce that dinner was ready, Stacy felt more relaxed than she had in a long time.

THE DARK SEDAN slowed down and parked across the street, a few houses up from Amanda Harris's place. The driver settled back in the seat with a Styrofoam cup of coffee in one hand and a cigarette in the other. He had first thought about going over to Stacy's office, but had decided that he preferred waiting here, to see if she would go home or return to her office, as she was prone to do many evenings. He had followed her enough in the past to know her habits. He also had to admit he worried about the cleaning crew, which didn't keep the strictest of timetables. He couldn't afford to be seen by anyone. Not yet. He smelled his victory coming soon, but wasn't going to rush. He intended to savor watching little Miss Rich Bitch Stacy Harris suffer for her sins. She always seemed to land on her feet. Now he intended to sweep that rug out from under her.

IGNORING the loud and mostly profane talk rolling around him, Mac studied the notes he'd taken at the three housesitting agencies he had visited that day. It had already been a long one and was far from over. The idea of eating a greasy hamburger or a cold taco on the run turned his stomach into knots. He had hoped this kind of crazy schedule would have been behind him by now. But then he'd been the one who didn't want to sit behind a desk all day.

"Nothing really adds up, Mac," observed Dean Cornell, his partner, perching his lanky frame on the edge of Mac's desk. Several years Mac's junior, Dean had been working with Mac for over two years. "Although I do think your hunch about the house-sitting services being behind the robberies is on the mark. They certainly have the edge."

"Monday I want to go through their files and see how their people are screened," Mac told him. "Then we'll double-check anyone who's even remotely suspicious."

"One of the owners could be the leader, you know," Dean pointed out, shrugging off his brown leather jacket.

"Yeah, but if we dig around, they may back off long enough for us to get a lead." The image of Stacy Harris invaded his brain for just an instant. Especially the picture of the lace peeking through the fabric of her blouse. And here he thought he was getting too old for such thoughts! Funny, why did he want to visualize her with long hair? And why had she looked at him as if he was the devil himself when he had entered her office? That was another puzzle he'd have to work out. Mac enjoyed working at puzzles; no matter how long it took, he always figured them out.

Mac studied the front of Dean's T-shirt and rolled his eyes. The white print on the navy cotton boldly stated Feel Safe Tonight. Sleep with a Cop.

"You're losing your touch. That shirt is only remotely sick," he commented.

Dean grinned, his teeth flashing white under his beard. "I just like to assure the ladies I'm a great guy. Hey, why don't you forget that stuff and come out with me for a beer?"

Mac shook his head. "Thanks, but I think I'm going to go over this a bit more before I leave."

Dean sighed theatrically. "You work too hard, boss. You should be out whoopin' and hollerin' instead of stuck here."

"No, thanks, I'll leave that up to you."

He nodded as he stood up. "Okay, Dad, I'll do you proud."

"That's what I'm afraid of," Mac said dryly.

"Don't wait up for me." Dean waved a hand over his shoulder as he left.

Mac wished he could remember the last time he'd had a Saturday off. After another hour of looking over his notes he pushed himself away from his desk and rubbed his eyes, which were burning from all the reading he had been doing. He knew he probably needed glasses, but who had the time to make an appointment to see an optometrist, when houses kept getting robbed? Even now he wanted to make a couple of stops before he left the station.

An hour later, Mac carried a six-pack of beer up a walkway. The town house he wanted was at the rear of this large complex.

"Mac, hey, good to see you!" Gary, his ex-partner, clapped him on the back. After a shoot-out that had left him with a steel pin in one leg and minus a lung, he'd retired from the police force and now worked at a desk job in a well-known security firm. "Come on in."

Mac looked around the living room, which was homey with photos of Gary's son and daughter and his wife's pottery. "Where's Marilyn?"

"She and Joanne are attending some mother-daughter thing at school." Gary eyed the six-pack with delight. "They should be home about ten. You better stay long enough to see her, or she'll never forgive you."

For the next hour, the two men sat in the kitchen, drinking beer and eating potato chips Gary had brought out. Other times in the past Mac had discussed his cases with his former partner; this was the reason he was here tonight.

"I have a hunch one of these house-sitting services is behind it," he told Gary. "The trouble is finding out which one."

"Any one in particular bother you?" Gary drank deeply of the brew.

Mac shook his head. "Nope." His finger traced the rim of the aluminum can. "Although one person has me intrigued."

"Male or female?"

"Female."

Gary grinned. "About time a woman caught your interest. You've been working so hard lately, you tend to forget you're human."

"Hell, Gary, I'm forty-three going on sixty some days. She's twenty-eight and certainly not going to give me a second look," Mac said with disgust. He leaned back in the chair, wearily raking his fingers through his hair. "There's just something about her that bugs me."

The other man looked interested. "Bugs you good or bugs you bad?"

"Don't know," he admitted. "It's just a crazy hunch of mine. I know, I'm not making any sense. Who knows, maybe I'm finally having my midlife crisis. I'm probably more than ripe for one." He was disgusted with himself for not sounding like the hotshot cop he was supposed to be. "I just feel that I may have met her some time ago, and you know how bad I am with names and faces."

Gary chuckled. "Do I? The joke around the station was if we didn't see each other every day you'd probably forget me, too. I thought you took a course to help that."

"I did, but it hasn't helped with this lady." He sounded disgusted with himself. "They say one of the first things to go is the mind, and I'm a perfect example of it."

"What's this mysterious lady's name?" Gary got up and retrieved another beer can from the refrigerator.

"Stacy Harris. She runs one of the house-sitting services I visited today. Does the name sound familiar to you?" Mac reached across the table and grabbed a handful of potato chips. "I know you've been away for a while, but you never seemed to forget a name."

Gary's mind clicked away like the computer his friends said it was. "I need more than just her name, if you want any input from me. What does she look like?"

Mac shrugged, trying hard to look nonchalant and sound as if her description wasn't all that important. "Short brown hair with blond streaks in it, hazel eyes, twenty-eight years old, tall, slender, great legs, nice looking. There's something about her attitude, as if she's lived longer than her years." He dug into his jacket pocket and pulled out a folded sheet of paper. "I got a copy of her Department of Motor Vehicles photo," he explained. He handed the paper to Gary, who unfolded it and studied the grainy picture. "Not an excellent likeness, but it will give you an idea. I don't know why, but there's something about her that really bugs me. As if I should know her. Plus the way she looked at me, as if she knew me and wished I'd go far, far away."

Gary stared long and hard at the photo. "Who do you think she is?"

Mac's laugh was rusty. "Hell, if I knew the answer, do you think I would be here? You're the one who could tuck information away in that brain of yours as if it was a computer. I figured if I met her through my work, there was a chance you might have, too."

"Sure, who else could you find to help you drink this six-pack?" Gary chuckled. "Mac, old buddy, if you'd just stop and think this over very carefully—" he picked up a pencil, drew lines around the woman's head, then sat back "—you'd remember our favorite kid as well as I do, so I don't know why you're asking me. She used to love tearing your uniforms off that beat-up body."

Mac's nerves tingled with awareness as he looked again at the picture. The woman's hair was now much longer, and the bits and pieces began to fall into place. "Well, what do you know? No wonder she looked so spooked when she first saw me. I must have been the last person she wanted to meet again."

"Yeah, I'm sure you're right there. You and I busted this kid and the gang she was in on a regular basis. Except back then her last name wasn't Harris. She and her boyfriend were the Bonnie and Clyde of Pasadena."

Mac nodded, inwardly wincing at the word *kid*. "Yeah, you're right. It was Markham then. Damn," he breathed, remembering a young girl, furious with the world. Then he recalled another time when she'd looked bleak, even accepting her fate as she was taken to a detention home, because her father had decided it was time she be taught a lesson. She'd learned one, all right. Another girl had deliberately picked a vicious fight with Stacy that night, and if Stacy hadn't been quick on her feet and willing to fight back, she would have lost an eye. Instead she'd ended up with a scar across her eyebrow. He wondered why she bothered keeping such a grim reminder.

Within a short period of time, Jonathan Markham had dropped dead of a stroke during Thanksgiving dinner, and Stacy's mother had been hospitalized because the alcohol she'd consumed over the years had finally eaten away most of her mental processes. Mr. Markham's will had stated that custody of Stacy be given to friends of his: Dr.'s Russ and Amanda Harris, even if his wife was still alive. He must have known Laura Markham was beyond helping anyone, since she couldn't even help herself. Mac finally remembered that the new family had later moved to Santa Barbara.

Mac recalled the young woman he had met that afternoon. No wonder she had looked at him with a combination of fear and hostility. She probably viewed him as nothing more than the enemy. He'd certainly been that about thirteen years ago. He would have laughed at the irony of their meeting again if he could have found the least bit of humor in it. Instead he muttered a curse under his breath.

"This could put a whole new slant on your case, Mac," Gary added in a low voice. "If somebody digs too deep and comes up with her real name and her past, she'll be in a pack of trouble she might not deserve. She was a kid back then, but that doesn't mean people will look at it that way, especially those who were victimized by the kids she ran with. They'll only want to paint her in the worst light, and, considering her past, it won't be difficult."

Mac suddenly felt very tired. "No kidding."

Chapter Two

Stacy liked to use her weekends to catch up on all the household tasks that built up over the week, instead of rushing through them in the evenings, when she was usually too tired to do more than warm a meal in the microwave. After a quick breakfast of coffee and scrambled eggs, she sorted her laundry and threw the first load into the washer.

"Where do some of these stains come from?" she muttered, rubbing detergent into an unidentified spot in her favorite blouse. She only hoped that whatever the stain was would come out.

She was in the middle of mopping her kitchen floor, not one of her favorite chores, when her doorbell rang.

"Ugh!" She made a face as her bare foot hit a small puddle of cold, sudsy water. She had to grab the counter before she slipped. "Coming," she called, quickly rubbing her foot dry with a dish towel and hurrying across the living room. When she pulled the door open, her welcoming smile froze as she stared at the tall man standing before her. "Detective McConnell. What a surprise."

He inclined his head in acknowledgment of her formal tone and he looked with frank male interest at the woman standing in the doorway. She wore a pair of once-gray shorts with damp splotches on them, and a sweatshirt with a faded Rose Parade emblem on the front. Today her scent was ammonia-laced floor cleaner, not a beguiling floral perfume. He admired her poise. He knew only too well that most women didn't want anyone to see them in any other than mint condition. His wife had even hated him to see her without her makeup.

"Is this an official call, Detective?" Stacy's feminine half wished she didn't smell like the inside of a Lysol bottle.

"In a way. May I come in?"

She nodded and stepped back, her hand outstretched to indicate her desire that he be seated. Once he had chosen the couch, she sat down in the easy chair. She decided that giving him her time was more than enough, and didn't bother offering him coffee. She was, however, grateful that Amanda wasn't present to chide her for her lack of manners.

Mac looked around the small living room. He noted that the delft-blue couch with soft, rose velvet pillows plumped against each arm and the blue, rose and cream plaid easy chair were of excellent quality. From the damp kitchen floor he'd caught a glimpse of, he realized he had caught Stacy in the midst of her weekend housework. He thought about making up a story to explain his official presence, then just as quickly threw it out. He studied the woman sitting nearby, mentally comparing her to the girl he once knew.

"You're sure not the rebellious kid I used to bust," he said quietly, leaning forward, his laced fingers hanging over his knees. "I'm glad to see you've done so well with yourself."

He knew! Unwilling to reveal even the slightest bit of weakness in front of him, she kept her smile ice-cold. "I wondered how long it would take for you to remember me.

After all, we used to see each other enough times for me to wear your class ring.''

With more years of experience behind him now, Mac now saw Stacy's cockiness as a mask to hide her fear, rather than the essential manner of a coldhearted girl.

"I went by your office. I didn't think it would be closed today.''

"Saturdays aren't usually all that busy, and the answering service calls me if there's a problem,'' Stacy replied. "As for any questions you may have, I'm afraid I couldn't help you today, since I don't have immediate access to my files.'' She didn't bother to offer to go to her office. As far as she was concerned, if he wanted them, he could wait until Monday morning, when she would hand him over to Janet.

Mac knew she wanted him gone, but found himself wishing he could stay. The quiet colors in the room made it restful, more a retreat than a living area. Was that what she needed now? He wouldn't blame her. His own job didn't afford him a lot of rest.

"You have a nice place,'' he commented.

Stacy shrugged, hearing the specter of Amanda prodding her to be more polite. "Since it appears you intend to stay a while, would you care for some coffee?''

His lips curved into that odd crooked smile under the heavy mustache. "If you drank the sludge that passes for coffee down at the station, you'd be grateful for the real stuff anytime you can get it. Yes, thank you.''

Stacy found herself smiling, too. "You might change your mind after you try mine.'' She uncoiled her body from the chair and stood up, motioning him to remain seated. "I just mopped the floor, and I wouldn't want you to slip on a wet spot. My business isn't so successful that I can afford a lawsuit just now.''

Stacy measured out the ground coffee and water and switched on the coffee maker.

"Do you take anything in your coffee?"

"Just black, thanks." He looked around the room, able to study it more fully without Stacy watching him. A medium-sized, pastel-striped vase sat on one lamp table and a ceramic ashtray on the coffee table. Two lithographs of swirls and odd shapes that somehow blended with the room hung on the wall. Still, he didn't see anything that gave him the slightest hint of what lay inside Stacy Harris. The information he'd dug up on her stated she had lived here for a little over three years, after moving out of the home of Dr. Amanda Harris, her foster mother from her teen years, who presently lived in Arcadia.

Mac got up and walked over to the sliding glass door that opened onto a minuscule patio. He fiddled with the lock, which proved to be so flimsy that he knew he could easily break it with a firm twist of the hand.

"You really should have this lock repaired," he advised. "Actually, a new one would be better. This thing is so pitiful, it wouldn't keep a rabbit out."

"I've lived here for three years, and there hasn't been one robbery in the complex." Stacy walked in, handing him an earthenware mug before curling up in a chair.

"There's always a first time."

"You cops always so cynical?"

Mac smiled as he sipped his coffee. "Yeah, they teach it the first year at the academy. Cynicism 101. You should see the instructor. He can put the fear of God into anyone."

Stacy studied her visitor over the rim of her mug. "Now that we have the small talk out of the way, why don't you tell me why you showed up on my doorstep this morning?"

"The lady is blunt."

"The lady has a kitchen floor to finish mopping, two loads of laundry ahead of her and furniture to polish, along with grocery shopping." She ticked off each item on her fingertips. "The lady's time is very valuable to her on the weekends." She surprised herself with her direct behavior and mentally patted herself on the back.

"Okay, you made your point." Mac chuckled, amused to see her acting so spunkily. "The truth is, I came by to reassure you that while I remembered you, I want you to know it doesn't have any bearing on this case. Your past is just that—and no one's business."

Stacy shifted in the chair, at a loss for words. Whatever she had expected him to say, it wasn't that. "Thank you."

Mac, also searching for the right response, stared into his coffee. "But you're still worried someone will find out that Stacy Harris is actually Stacy Markham, daughter of Jonathan Markham and the coleader of a teen gang of thieves."

"Wouldn't you be?" she demanded, feeling the raw pain in her breast at the mention of her father's name. "I'm not like other people who knew since the age of ten what they were going to do when they grew up. It's only been recently I've found my niche, and it took me a long time to get my business off the ground. I'm just now beginning to show a small profit. If news of my past comes out in the same breath as those robberies, I may as well close up."

"Stacy, your records were sealed when you reached your majority," he reminded her. "They can't be used against you."

Her laughter had a harsh note to it. "Maybe so, but that doesn't stop someone with a long memory remembering me, just as you did. Maybe I don't have the kind of record some of those kids had, but it's still enough to make people stop and think twice before considering my agency. We both know if someone is persistent and knows the right people, they can find out anything they want.''

Mac finished his coffee and stood up. ''This is probably a good time for me to leave.'' He carried the cup into the kitchen, rinsed it out and set it in the sink. He turned to find Stacy standing in the doorway.

''A man who knows where a dirty dish belongs,'' she commented sardonically. ''My, my, what is the world coming to?''

''When you live alone, you either learn to pick up after yourself or resign yourself to living in a mess,'' he explained.

''Last I remembered, you had a wife.''

''I did, until she found someone who made more money and didn't wear a gun to work,'' he explained quietly.

Stacy had the grace to flush. ''I'm sorry. That was very rude of me, not to mention none of my business.''

''Don't worry, it's old history,'' he replied. ''Is it all right if someone comes by your office on Monday to discuss your employees?''

''Anything that will help solve the case faster is fine by me.'' She moved back to allow him to pass and followed him to the door. ''My secretary, Janet, can answer any questions your men might have. Goodbye, Detective.''

He walked outside, then turned. ''You've grown up into quite a lady, Stacy Harris,'' he said quietly. ''I'm glad for you.''

Her eyes darkened with past pain. ''What a shame others were unable to see that I've done so well, contrary to popular opinion back then.''

Mac shook his head, realizing she was talking about her father. The years hadn't eased her bitterness toward the man. ''Sometimes things aren't meant to be, but that doesn't mean a person can't show the world that they can pick themselves up and make something of themselves. Well, I'll be going now. Take care, Stacy.''

Stacy remained in the open doorway, watching him walk down the path. As she studied him from head to toe, especially lingering on the flat buttocks covered with tight denim, she found herself smiling. What she saw wasn't the man she remembered—wearing a neatly pressed uniform that usually had a torn pocket or sleeve, thanks to her. This man wore aged jeans, a chambray shirt and leather jacket, and ended up looking more like a thug than a police detective. He wasn't handsome in the conventional sense. His features were too battered for that, and the heavy mustache lent him a dark air. Still, if she were caught in a dark alley, she knew she would want him on her side. She closed the door and returned to her work, but found herself wondering what he did with his free time, and if he had someone special to spend it with.

She had just finished mopping the floor and begun another load of laundry when her doorbell rang again.

''Perhaps I should start doing my housework in the middle of the night,'' she murmured, then exclaimed with pleasure at the sight of her visitor. ''Timothy! What a surprise! Come in.''

The elderly man entered and sat down on the couch. ''I heard the police are talking to house-sitting agencies about those horrible robberies,'' he said in a quiet voice. ''Is everything all right?''

''Everything's fine,'' Stacy assured him. ''They're just talking to all of us, in hopes of finding a clue to all those robberies.''

He shook his head. ''It is so sad,'' he murmured. ''Do they think a house-sitter is behind the robberies? Is that why they question you?''

She shrugged. "I don't think they have any concrete ideas just yet, so they're checking out every possibility, although a majority of the owners of robbed houses use sitters on a regular basis."

Stacy saw Timothy peer at her through his bifocals. He had worked for her for almost eighteen months and had come to treat her as a beloved granddaughter. For the past six months, their relationship had escalated from one of employer to employee to one of close friendship, especially since Timothy lived in the adjoining apartment building.

"I thought I would see if you would like to go out for a bite of supper this evening," he told her.

She sighed. "It sounds wonderful, but I have so much housework to do that I'll be lucky to get a portion of it done by tomorrow night. I'm sorry, I wish I could."

He stood up slowly. "I am sorry too. I am available to work if you need me."

Stacy walked with him to the door. "I'll tell Janet first thing Monday," she assured him. "I'll warn you now. If the police decide a house-sitting agency could be behind the robberies, we'll all be out of business in no time."

He smiled, touching her cheek with his fingertips. "I would not worry. The police will learn the truth very soon."

Stacy smiled back. "I certainly hope so."

STACY SAT AT HER DESK reading the morning paper with mingled dismay and anger. "I can't believe they would do this!" she exploded, jumping up and carrying out the paper to the reception area. "Janet, look at this!" She tossed it in front of her secretary. "I'll be lucky if my present customers pay their bills, after they read this trash!"

Janet scanned the article. "We're not the only agency named," she told Stacy. "It does say the police are talking to all the house-sitting agencies in the immediate area."

"And how many are there? Three, four, five at the most? Nothing is even mentioned that they're also talking to the local security firms," Stacy ranted, walking back and forth in jerky strides. "It certainly doesn't look promising for any of us, if people believe this. This article about the robberies and how the police are talking to the house-sitting agencies makes it look as if one of us is guilty! Why don't they just barge right in and make their arrests and make themselves look good? Then maybe we'll all have some peace!"

An embarrassed-sounding cough startled Stacy out of her tirade. She turned and found two men standing in the doorway. One was conservatively dressed in slacks, tailored shirt, tie and sport coat. The other wore a carbon copy of what she privately called Mac's thug look.

"Janet, meet the police." She swept her arm toward the men in the doorway. "They'll want to look through our personnel files." She looked at them. "Janet can answer any questions you may have, gentlemen." She walked into her office and pointedly closed the glass door with a click.

The better-dressed detective whistled softly. "I thought Mac said she was going to be cooperative," he commented to his partner.

"Trust me, she *is* being cooperative," Janet informed him tartly, holding up the newspaper. "She just didn't expect you people to start pointing fingers at all of us, before collecting your so-called facts. We've had three clients call and cancel this morning because of this article!"

The other man, who looked as if he belonged on a horse instead of catching bad guys, shrugged. "Hey, what can I say? You'll have to go after the reporter on that score."

Janet looked him over from the toes of his scuffed cowboy boots to his sheepskin-lined jacket and dark full beard. She eyed his T-shirt that read Trust Me, I'm a Cop with distaste.

"Obviously your mother doesn't dress you any longer," she observed.

He grinned. "Are you kidding? She gave this to me for my birthday."

Janet stood up and walked over to a file cabinet and pulled open the three drawers. She narrowly missed bumping the knee of one of the men, who stepped back quickly to avoid injury. "The top drawer holds our client files, the second our active employee records, the third our inactive. They are in order, so don't mess them up. Have fun."

The bearded man, who introduced himself as Dean and his partner as Craig, smiled his thanks, looking the secretary over with a more than disinterested eye and sneaking a quick peek at her stocking-clad legs. "What constitutes an employee becoming inactive?"

"If they haven't worked for us in the past year, if they quit or were fired or died," she said dryly.

"Have there been many people terminated?" Craig asked. He was a nice-looking dark haired man, probably in his early thirties, Janet judged. He pulled a notebook out of his jacket pocket and opened it.

Janet thought for a moment. "No, not many. I think three or four."

"For what reasons?"

She smiled as the telephone rang. "You'll find their files in the bottom drawer with all the gory details. All I ask is that you put them back the way you found them and not make too much noise. This is a place of business, you know." She returned to her desk and picked up the phone. "Good morning, Harris House Sitters. This is Janet. Oh, hi, Mrs. Morrison. Yes, Stacy's in. Hold on a moment." She pressed the red Hold button and buzzed her boss. "Stacy, it's Mrs. Morrison."

Stacy didn't view that as good news. She stared at the blinking light for a moment, and took several deep breaths before picking up the phone. "Good morning, Mrs. Morrison. How are you today?"

"I would be better if I hadn't read that article in the paper about the robberies, and how the police are talking to the house-sitting agencies," the woman said bluntly. "I'll be honest with you, Stacy, it has me worried. It says the police are investigating you."

Stacy closed her eyes, willing the headache to go away. "They're investigating all the house-sitting agencies, domestic agencies and security firms to see if there's a link, Mrs. Morrison," she explained. "I'm sure the police would tell you it's standard procedure."

But the older woman wasn't about to be pacified. Instead she informed Stacy in her usual forthright way that she would be making other arrangements when she and her husband made their annual jaunt to Europe next month.

"I'm sorry to hear that, Mrs. Morrison." Stacy clenched her jaw to keep the frustration from spilling over into her voice. "Goodbye." She waited until she knew the other woman had hung up, then slammed down the receiver.

As the morning passed, Stacy received several more calls. She tried to explain that she was doing everything in her power to ensure that their houses would be taken care of as they had been in the past, but it was difficult when the press had all but accused house-sitting services of masterminding the crimes. Luckily, not all of her clients were as suspicious as Mrs. Morrison. Some cautiously agreed to keep using her, but she still felt that her time was growing short. By the end of the morning she had a throbbing headache, which threatened to destroy her sanity.

Needing to get away from her desk, Stacy stepped to Janet's desk, opened the bottom drawer where the aspirin were kept, and tapped two tablets into her palm.

"Mr. and Mrs. Cameron won't be needing our services for the present," she said quietly, heading for the water-cooler and pouring herself a cup.

Janet turned to the two detectives. "Whatever happened to people being presumed innocent until proven guilty?" she charged. "Do you realize how hard Stacy has worked to get this agency going? It took a lot of twelve- and fourteen-hour days of planning the right advertising to attract employees and clients alike. She used to sleep in this office more than she slept at home!"

"Janet," Stacy wearily intervened, finishing her glass of water. "It's not their fault. Newspapers report the facts, and the readers make their own conclusions."

"That's a far cry from what you were ranting and raving about earlier," Dean remarked.

She managed a wan smile. "I got it out of my system. It doesn't help when your best clients decide you just might not be trustworthy. Talk about a nasty way of learning who truly believes in you. Too bad, those numbers are few. At the rate things are going, I may as well close up now. But I've always been hardheaded. That's probably why I used to get into so much trouble," she murmured, glancing down at her watch, then at her secretary. "Janet, why don't you go on to lunch? There's nothing here I can't handle."

"Aren't you going to eat anything?" the secretary asked in a worried tone, knowing her boss's habit of skipping a meal if she remained in the office.

"Maybe later. I have some paperwork to do."

The two men exchanged glances.

"Would you mind if I joined you?" Dean asked Janet.

Janet eyed him suspiciously. "Are you planning on interrogating me?"

"Only to find out what kind of food you like." He smiled winningly.

She still appeared uncertain.

"Go ahead," Stacy urged, murmuring, "If nothing else, you'll get a free lunch. If he does start questioning you about our work, you can always walk out—just ask for a doggie bag first."

Janet reached for her purse and slung the strap over her shoulder. "Okay, but let's go where no one knows me," she declared, walking out the door.

"I know a great place for chili dogs," Dean could be heard saying as he followed her out.

"I see I have a big spender here," Janet retorted.

Stacy eyed Craig, who was jotting down a few notes on the typing paper Janet had given him earlier. "Is this your divide and conquer strategy?" she couldn't help asking. "Your partner works on my secretary, and you work on me?"

He grinned. "No, you're perfectly safe. Actually, my wife doesn't work very far from here, so I thought if you didn't mind my using your phone, I'd call her and see if she could meet me for lunch."

"Go ahead." She turned away as he made a quick call and arranged to meet his wife in twenty minutes. Stacy's eyes flickered over the files. "Does everything look all right, or aren't you allowed to say anything?"

"It's not a state secret," he assured her. "We're just looking through your employee files to see if there's anything that doesn't fit. Possibly an employee termination that could have left an employee furious with you for firing him or her."

Stacy's eyes narrowed. "One, we screen our people very carefully. I'm certainly not going to take just anyone off the street and place them in a home filled with priceless antiques. Two, the few terminations we've had didn't involve anger on either part."

Craig nodded. "I'm sure you're very careful. We were already told how meticulous you are with your people, but sometimes it could be one small piece of information that appears all right to you, but looks suspicious to us. Sometimes you need that objective party, seeing something you don't."

Stacy felt a tight knot coiling inside her. "Such as Mrs. Gordon, who came over here as a war bride in 1944? Is that what you're talking about? You're right. I wish I had picked up on that in the beginning. After all, she might be a spy."

He didn't take offense at her sarcasm. "A little overreactive, but the general idea. We aren't trying to put you out of business, Ms. Harris. We're just trying to find a lead. Believe me, I'm no happier being here than you are having me, but sometimes it's this kind of legwork that pays off for us."

Stacy nodded, feeling calmer. "You've told me more than you probably should have, haven't you?"

"Not really." He glanced down at his watch and stood up. "Would you like me to bring something back for you? A hamburger, hot dog, salad?"

She shook her head. "No, thanks. I'm going to finish this paperwork up and run out for something."

Enjoying her time alone, Stacy shut and locked the front door and switched on the answering machine they kept; she preferred to use it to screen calls when they were very busy or eating their lunches in the office. While busily reviewing the previous week's work sheets, she half listened to the phone ringing and the answering machine picking up the call. Stopping for a moment to see if it was a call she should take, she returned to her work when she heard nothing more than a dial tone. She shook her head, thinking that a lot of people didn't like talking to answering machines and hung up whenever they heard one.

It couldn't have been more than fifteen minutes later that Stacy heard a noise at the front door. She glanced out, noticing a shadowy figure standing in front of the large pane of frosted glass. For a moment she didn't say anything. The unknown visitor's actions bothered Stacy. She didn't recall hearing anyone knock on the door, although she had been busy and might not have noticed if someone had. She remained silent, watching the doorknob twist back and forth a few times.

Finally she called out. "Hello, can I help you?" She stood very still in the doorway to her office, watching the shadow freeze, then seem to drift away. Stacy continued to watch the front door, finding herself unable to move. She strained her ears, but could hear nothing. She moved to the window and looked down, but saw no car leave the parking lot and no one walking away. She didn't know why it bothered her, but she wrapped her arms around her body in the hope of stopping the chill that was threatening to overtake her. Her first thought was that she should tell the two detectives about the episode. Then she dismissed the idea. Perhaps the person hadn't heard her and decided the office was closed for the lunch hour. She'd just wait to see if anyone came in this afternoon who mentioned coming by earlier.

But no matter what Stacy tried to tell herself, she still couldn't shake the idea that her visitor wasn't there to apply for work—or to look for a house-sitter.

HE CURSED SOFTLY as he left the building by the rear door. He had called the office first, and when he heard the answering machine click on he'd assumed the office was closed for lunch. He'd thought he would have no trouble getting in, thanks to the extra passkey he'd filched late one night. Damn! Why hadn't he watched from across the street to make sure she had left?

Still, he wasn't going to worry. He had a few other ideas up his sleeve on how to unnerve Stacy Harris before he dragged her down into the mud. By the time he finished with her, she wouldn't have a chance in hell of recovering.

Chapter Three

"I want you all to tell me you've come up with some brilliant detective work and have the name or names of the people behind the robberies. Right?" Mac looked at the men assigned to assist him with the case.

"Right, boss," Craig drawled, lifting his coffee cup in a toast.

"Actually, the butlers got together and pulled off the robberies. We were afraid to tell you because it sounded too conventional," Dean told Mac with a straight face. "One of the maids knows a good fence."

Mac rolled his eyes. "Okay, very funny, guys. Now what do we really have?"

Kevin, one of the other detectives, spoke up first, looking through his notes. "Thompson Security's employees go through a security check that puts the government to shame. They go through a pretty stringent background check that tells the agency everything they would want to know, and probably a few things they don't care to know. I wouldn't be surprised if they know the color of an employee's underwear on a given day. Yet five of their clients were hit in the beginning. The men on duty during those times will be coming in tomorrow for questioning. Sloane Security Industries is equally strict with their people. If we find our burglars among them, I'll be very surprised."

Mac nodded. "They were just a hunch. I have an idea we're going to find the link with one of the house-sitting services." He turned to Dean and Craig. "What did you find out?"

The two men opened their notebooks.

"Stacy Harris runs a very tight ship," Craig replied. "Her checks on prospective employees are pretty thorough, but they're not infallible. We found a couple names that didn't seem right, so we're going to run them through the computer. We also stopped by Kramer's House Sitters. Now that guy was something else." He grinned. "He didn't appreciate us going through his files. At first we were threatened with all kinds of lawsuits dealing with invasion of privacy, but he soon calmed down when I explained to him we could always come back with a search warrant. There were a few suspicious facts in his files, so we made copies, which didn't make him too happy."

Dean spoke up. "Stacy Harris wasn't too happy in the beginning, either. She had read that article in the paper and acted as if we were zeroing in on her." He laughed. "You'd think she had something to hide. 'Course, while we were there, she had several clients call in and cancel her service, which didn't make her day or mood any better."

Mac had read the same article with his morning coffee and felt nothing but disgust for the journalism trade for making the police's job even more difficult. "You really can't blame her. That article did sound as if we were going after all the house-sitting agencies with a vengeance. Even I'd feel a little paranoid."

The three men looked at him with surprise. Mac McConnell had never felt empathy for a suspect before. They all considered him the typical hard-nosed cop.

"Let's run the list of names through the computer and see if anything comes up," Mac decided. "It would be great if our burglar would crop up from that, but we all know we won't be that lucky. Between the press—and the police commissioner—on our asses to solve this, we will hold a moment of prayer in hopes the case will be solved within the next five minutes."

The other three men laughed and combined their notes.

"Do you think I'll be able to get out of here within the next hour?" Dean asked, finishing his cup of coffee, which was now ice-cold. He grimaced at the bitter taste.

"Hot date?" Mac quizzed, familiar with his partner's active social life.

"He's taking Stacy Harris's secretary out," Craig told him. "This guy moves faster than the speed of light when a pretty lady is around. Personally, I'm surprised he didn't go after the boss. She sure isn't bad looking."

Mac's smile froze. "I'm surprised you didn't, Dean," he remarked, working hard to sound normal.

"Stacy may be a good-looking lady, but she also has a king-size chip on her shoulder. She sure doesn't seem too fond of cops. I'll stick with the cuddly ones." Dean set his coffee cup down. "At least Janet will be, as soon as I wear her down with my charm and savoir faire." He glared at the men hooting at him and throwing napkin wads in his direction. "Hey, I'm not just a pretty face, you know."

Mac leaned back, thinking about Stacy. He knew exactly why she didn't like members of the police force, and figured it was time that Dean understand why, if he was going to have to deal with Stacy from time to time.

He leaned forward and lowered his voice so he couldn't be overheard.

"What I'm about to tell you can go no further." The intensity in his voice indicated how serious the subject was.

Dean didn't crack one joke. "You got it."

"Stacy Harris is Stacy Markham Harris. Thirteen years ago she was part of a teen gang who got their kicks breaking into houses in San Marino and Pasadena. Her father was a well-known attorney, who constantly pulled strings to keep her out of jail, until he got fed up one night and let her sit it out, for what turned out to be the first charge she was innocent of. Not much later he died of a stroke, and because her mother was mentally incompetent to handle Stacy, Stacy was put under the guardianship of family friends, Russ and Amanda Harris. She was a pretty mixed-up kid back then and had a pretty nasty reputation."

"Are you trying to say that she might be behind the robberies because of her past?" Dean muttered. "Mac, you know very well her records are closed and can't be used against her."

He shook his head. "That's not it at all, but this could all come out, and I wanted you to hear the truth from me."

"How do you know so much about her?"

"I used to arrest her on a regular basis back then," he explained. "I later realized what I thought was a spoiled rich brat in the need of a good spanking was actually a scared little girl, needing love and attention. Her old man was one of the coldest men I'd ever met, and he treated Stacy like dirt. Considering what happened years ago, she's come a long way, thanks to her guardians, I'm sure. She's no longer a rebellious kid, but a young woman who's been able to start her own business and make something of herself."

"And you don't think she's a part of the robberies?" Dean guessed.

Mac shook his head. "I'd stake everything on her being innocent of all this."

"And whether you know it or not, you're showing some interest in the lady. Be careful, old buddy," Dean warned. "You might have to stake your badge."

By the time the men had filled out the proper reports and requested computer checks on the names they deemed suspicious, they all announced they were more than ready to go home. When Kevin asked Mac if he'd like to come by for dinner, he accepted, since he was in no mood to return to an empty house. Sometimes he wished he had sold it after Carol had left him, but an accountant friend had told him it was an excellent investment and that he would be better off keeping it. He should also consider himself lucky that Carol hadn't demanded her fifty percent of the house's value. But she had been so eager for her divorce that she'd wanted nothing from her marriage. All she'd wanted was to settle down with her insurance executive husband, who, she'd stated coldly, didn't need to look like a hoodlum to go to work and raise children in a safe atmosphere. Mac had heard that their house had been burglarized twice in the past two years and that her husband had been mugged a few years back. So much for so-called safe jobs. He sighed as he stared at the tall pile of paperwork on his desk. He decided that eating at Kevin's house sounded much better than staying here and settling for a greasy hamburger. He reached for his jacket and turned his back upon the work that he knew would still be there the next day.

Replete from a delicious dinner of beef Stroganoff, and after listening to Sharon's gentle teasing that he needed a wife, Mac returned to his house. The two-bedroom bungalow in Sierra Madre, a tiny town nestled against the San Gabriel Mountains, wasn't a mansion, but it was comfortable and offered him solace from the emotional wear and tear of his work.

After pulling a bottle of beer out of the refrigerator, he walked into the tiny den and settled down in a worn easy chair. Not caring to watch television, he turned on the radio. Unfortunately, the soft music didn't cure his restless feelings.

He reached for the phone, knowing he was doing something against his better judgment, but he couldn't help himself. He dialed the number before he changed his mind, and listened to it ring ten times before he realized it wasn't going to be picked up. He depressed the button and tried another number; this time he received an answering service, asking if they could help him. Without saying a word, he hung up and leaned back in his chair.

Where was she? Just from the little things she'd said, he doubted she had a steady man in her life or dated that much. Why was that? She was a lovely woman and had a lot to offer a man. Did it have something to do with her father? Had his neglect of her ruined her feelings toward the male sex? Did she think they were all coldhearted machines like Jonathan Markham?

"Old man, you're definitely going off the deep end," he said out loud. "You're thinking about a woman who could very well end up to be a chief suspect in an important robbery case. Do yourself a favor, and let Sharon set you up with one of her friends, as she's wanted to do for so long."

When the phone rang, he jumped. Mac was irritated with himself for being so lost in his thoughts that he was caught off guard, even by something as innocent as that.

"McConnell," he said crisply into the receiver.

"Why isn't your progress report regarding these robberies on my desk, McConnell?" a loud, abrasive voice boomed in his ear. "I expected to see your report by the end of the day."

"Probably because it hasn't been done yet, Captain," Mac replied. "And there was really nothing concrete to report."

The other man's retort was obscene. "I'm getting flack from everyone on this, McConnell, and I want these characters arrested ASAP. Understand? You screw this up, and I'll have your head for breakfast."

Mac nodded, more than familiar with the routine. His superior had strong political aspirations, and the man knew that the best way to become known was to get his name into the paper. Right now, catching the people responsible for the robberies was perfect.

"I also want you to keep a close eye on Stacy Harris," Captain Henderson went on.

Mac bristled. "Any particular reason why?"

"The lady used to be Stacy Markham, part of a gang of thieves running in the Pasadena, San Marino area about twelve years ago. I'm certain you already knew that, since you arrested her several times back then. I'm wondering if she hasn't decided to revert to her old ways."

"What you're talking about is a closed record," Mac said in a hard voice. "It can't be used against her."

"Maybe not, but it doesn't mean that she's as squeaky clean as she appears to be. Now I want to see results on this right away, or you can see your promotion go down the drain...again." With that he slammed the phone down.

"The reason my promotions don't come across is because I don't play the game your way," Mac groused. When he replaced the receiver, he was no gentler than his boss had been, and muttered every description he could think of for the man. None of them were kind.

"Next thing we know, he'll declare Stacy armed and dangerous," he grumbled, rummaging through the coffee table drawer for a pack of cigarettes. He lighted one. When the phone rang five minutes later, he picked it up. He wasn't surprised by the caller's message.

The thieves had struck again.

"WHY SHOULD WE worry about acting like model citizens, when our parents don't care what we do?" asked Maria, a dark-haired girl in her mid-teens with liquid brown eyes and waist-length dark brown hair. "My dad comes home drunk more nights than he comes home sober, and my mom sits there and cries all the time about how it's all us kids' fault. Why? Because she had seven of us? Hey, I didn't ask to be born, or to get hit by my dad, just because I happen to be there."

"Did running away help?" Stacy asked.

The girl shrugged. "You know just as well as me."

"Do I?"

"Hey, we've all done stupid stuff," drawled Cal, a boy with a Mohawk and multicolored stripes painted across his cheekbones, looking extremely bored.

Stacy smiled. "And you don't, do you, Cal?"

He grinned. "Me, I'm perfect, remember? Hey, the cops never had anything on me."

She continued smiling, remembering the sullen boy with a penchant for shocking his elders with dirty language and equally obscene habits when he first came to the teen shelter. "That's true. You have the role of an obnoxious kid down to a fine art."

The other four in the group all laughed and threw taunts at Cal, who took them good-naturedly, Stacy observed. Before he'd always been spoiling for a fight. Those were the evenings when she'd felt more like a referee than a counselor for troubled kids.

"It ain't right that our parents could care less, while we're supposed to learn how to be responsible adults," Maria interjected. "Aren't they supposed to be—whaddya call it?—role models for us?"

"That's so we can take care of them, when they're so hung over or so stoned out of their skulls they don't know which end is up," muttered Joe, one of the other boys. "They don't give a damn about us."

Stacy held up her hands. "Look, guys, all I'm here for is to be your sounding board, not to turn you into responsible adults or show you how to get better grades in school. We meet here so you can talk about your problems at home or school and perhaps, between all of us, we can come up with some answers. You're here because you don't want to end up like your parents or friends, and I respect you for that. But remember one of our first rules."

"No fighting among ourselves," the five laughingly intoned.

"Right. Now, who's next?"

By the time Stacy got home that night she was so tired that she felt as if she couldn't think straight. After grabbing a can of Diet Coke out of the refrigerator, she wandered back into the living room. She frowned when her gaze fell on the coffee table. She would have sworn the ashtray was on the other end when she left. Feeling uneasy, she looked around the rest of the room. Nothing else appeared out of place. She shrugged it off; being overtired had apparently fueled her imagination. She dropped onto the couch and forced herself to relax after her wearing evening.

It had been Amanda's suggestion that Stacy do what she could to prevent teenagers from suffering from the same fate she had by working as a volunteer in various halfway houses one or two nights a week. Stacy had worked with this particular group for several months now. At first they had been suspicious of her—until she told her story without any embellishments. She wanted them to know she understood what they had or were going through. The best way to do that had been for her to make them understand that she wasn't there just because it was the thing to do, but because she sincerely wanted to. But emotionally these evenings were also very draining. Listening to the kids, some barely into their teens, forced her to relive her own past, and there were nights when she would wake up sweating. She would be convinced she was back home in San Marino, with her father coldly informing her that she was ruining his career aspirations with her crazy stunts, and her mother floating around the house all day like a ghost. Stacy recalled that her mother could only appear animated if she had enough brandy in her to numb the pain of her empty and loveless marriage.

Wanting a hot bath and bed, Stacy went into her bedroom and took off her jeans and sweater. When she worked at the shelter, she made sure to wear clothing that wouldn't put off the suspicious teens. From past experience she knew coming in wearing designer labels put off kids who didn't always have a lot of money.

After her exhausting evening, it took a while for Stacy to fall asleep. Then something disturbed her. Her inner self was convinced that someone was standing over her. She shot up in bed, breathing hard to control the rapid beating of her heart. Her fingers were shaking as she reached over to switch on the bedside lamp. Nothing was there.

"Just a nightmare," she muttered, pushing her hair away from her face. "Nothing but a nightmare." So why didn't she feel convinced?

STACY WAS ON THE GO from the time she got up until she reached her office. She grabbed her morning newspaper on the way out her door and stopped for a box of donuts before getting into her car. Janet was already there, talking on the telephone and looking very frustrated.

"Yes, I'll be sure to tell her when she comes in." She hung up and looked at her boss. "Don't ask."

"I won't." Stacy set the box down on the desk and headed for the coffee maker. "How was your evening out?"

Janet blushed. "Very nice," she mumbled, rummaging through the box. "Didn't you buy any chocolate ones with peanuts on top?"

"If you look closely, you'll find three, and they're all yours. I figured we'd both need all the help we could get." Stacy came back with her coffee and picked out a strawberry-frosted French cruller before opening the paper. One of the lead articles immediately caught her eye. She read it swiftly and swore under her breath when she finished. "There was another robbery last night," she muttered.

"Oh, no," Janet moaned. "Anyone we know?"

She nodded. "The Nicholas family."

Both women remembered the family as clients they had dealt with several times.

Stacy closed the paper and tucked it under her arm. "I have an idea the police will be coming by sometime today to talk to us," she said quietly. She walked into her office, forgetting all about her coffee and donut.

Mac appeared in the office a little over an hour later. A subdued Janet looked up from her typing for long enough to tell him to go on in.

"Detective McConnell," Stacy greeted him solemnly. "Please, have a seat."

His eyes settled on the newspaper that lay centered on her desk. "The Nicholases were cleaned out completely," he said, taking the chair across from her.

"So I've read." Stacy's eyes were bleak. "And because they use our service exclusively, you're here to check us out again."

"Is it possible for me to go over their file?"

She nodded. "Janet," she called. "Would you bring in the Nicholas file, please?" Then, turning to Mac, "Would you like some coffee?"

"No, thank you."

Janet appeared in the doorway a moment later. The expression on her face wasn't encouraging. "Stacy, I can't find it."

"What do you mean, you can't find it? It must have been out yesterday." Stacy felt a chill running through her veins.

She shook her head. "I know, and I don't understand it, but it isn't where it belongs in the file cabinet." She turned to Mac. "I'm not trying to put you off. It just isn't where it belongs." She looked at her boss. "I'm going through all the files, in case one of the detectives misplaced it." She shot Mac a look of apology, then walked away.

"Files get misplaced," he said, hoping to reassure her.

"In all the time Janet has worked for me, we have never had a misplaced file," Stacy replied. Suddenly a vision of the shadow standing in front of the frosted glass door the day before flashed before her. She quickly banished it, deciding that she was growing paranoid. No one had appeared later in the day, so she had decided the person might have changed his or her mind. "She keeps the files in such meticulous order, I'm afraid to go digging through them," she said with a tight smile.

"What are you afraid of?" he asked abruptly.

Stacy looked startled. "Afraid? I'm not afraid of anything."

"A minute ago you looked frightened of something. Perhaps there's a good reason the file is misplaced," he went on ruthlessly.

She shot to her feet, leaning forward to slap her hands on the desk top. "Now wait a minute," she said through gritted teeth. "From the very beginning I have been more than cooperative with you and your men. You barge in here, demand to go through my files, and act as if I'm trying to hide something. In fact, for all I know, your men may have put the Nicholas file back in the wrong folder when they were going through the client files. If you have something concrete to accuse me of, go for it. If not, just sit out there and wait for Janet to find the file. Now, if you'll excuse me, I have work to do." She stared at him long and hard, hoping he would get the message.

Mac stood up slowly. "There are no accusations, Stacy," he said quietly. "We're checking all possibilities, including their gardening service, the caterers they used for their last party, even Mrs. Nicholas's psychic."

Stacy's expression didn't lighten. "Ah, yes, Madame Zora. Knows all, sees all," she intoned. "You'll love her."

"Why don't I feel secure with that?" he muttered, hopeful she was over her short burst of temper. "Stacy, I'm not trying to pin anything on you, but we need to cover all bases. Maybe something will come to you, or we'll see something in their file that will give us a lead."

"Whatever happened to finding that all-important fingerprint, scrap of clothing or perhaps a bloodstain on the carpet?" Stacy knew she sounded sarcastic, but she was past caring. She had put herself under so much pressure the past few days that sleep was becoming elusive and her stomach was in constant turmoil.

"You've been watching too many TV shows," he chided. "We should get so lucky. This gang is very clever. They obviously wear gloves, are familiar with the home's security systems and know exactly when the owners aren't home—whether it's just for the evening or on long trips. They're in and out in no time, and no one sees anything out of the ordinary.''

''Maybe Madame Zora will look into her crystal ball for you and find your burglars,'' she suggested, her tone still brittle.

Mac smiled. ''Maybe she will. I'm seeing her this afternoon. I'll be sure to ask her. Stacy, I don't want to turn into your enemy again.''

She found herself mesmerized by his smile. How could a man, who certainly wasn't good-looking in the usual sense of the word, smile as if there were no one more special than herself? She remembered him as a younger man, with a cigarette-raspy drawl and crooked smile that flicked up the ends of his mustache, but the years had etched his face with more than character and lines. They had given him a face people couldn't easily forget. She suddenly found herself wishing they had met under different circumstances.

''That was a long time ago, and I'm adult enough to recognize those feelings as those of an angry child,'' she said. ''If I appear upset, it's only because I know if this goes on much longer, my past will come out, and I'll have no choice but to close down my business.''

''Stacy, no one will learn anything from my office—and especially not from me,'' he assured her.

She looked a little skeptical, but knew she would have to trust him. Especially now. She needed Mac as an ally.

''Stacy, I found the file.'' Janet appeared, holding up a bright blue folder. She held it out to Mac, who smiled his thanks and said he would look it over in the reception area.

Janet walked farther into Stacy's office as Mac left, leaned over her boss's shoulder and murmured, "It doesn't make sense."

Stacy looked puzzled. "What doesn't?"

"The folder. I found it in the inactive drawer."

Stacy didn't feel as worried about it as her secretary. "The detectives just put it in the wrong pile yesterday."

Janet shook her head. "No, I made sure they put everything back in one drawer before they continued on to the next one. I was afraid something like this would happen, so I kept a close eye on them." She hesitated.

"And?" Stacy prompted, certain the woman had something else to say.

"I'm sure it's just my imagination, but I was certain I locked my desk yesterday—and it was unlocked this morning."

"Maybe you were thinking more about your dinner date than about locking it," she teased.

Janet didn't think it funny. "I make sure that desk is locked every night, Stacy. I swear there are mornings I come in, and things look out of place. I want to blame it on the cleaning crew, but I can't remember that happening before, and we've used them ever since we moved in here. It's almost as if someone comes in here at night and looks around, but doesn't take anything. It's really weird."

Stacy thought about her own feeling that someone had been in her apartment with the same result—nothing had been taken. Could there be some kind of strange connection? Was someone using her files to find prospective victims, with the intent of planting some kind of evidence in her office or apartment? The thought frightened her, even as she tried to dismiss it as fancy.

"It might not hurt for us to start double-checking each other at the end of each day," Stacy said quietly. "Believe me, this is no reflection on you, Janet. I understand your feelings, and I get a little paranoid every now and then, too. In fact, why don't you call a locksmith about coming in and changing our door and file cabinet locks? See if someone can come in as soon as possible. I think we'd both feel a little more comfortable then."

Janet nodded. "I'll make some calls." She began to move toward her office.

Stacy grasped her arm and stopped her. "Wait until he leaves," she suggested. "There's no reason for him to know about this."

Janet studied her face, plainly looking for answers to unspoken questions, but Stacy was a past master of hiding her feelings.

"All right," Janet murmured, beginning to move away.

"Here you are." Mac reappeared and handed Janet the folder. "Nothing much in here, I'm afraid, but thanks for taking the time to look for it." He glanced at Stacy. "I'll talk to you later."

She smiled wryly. Now why did she view that statement more as a threat than a promise?

The two women were subdued for the rest of the day. Luckily, a locksmith was able to come in that morning and by noon they were the owners of new door and file cabinet keys. Feeling more assured, they took a longer than usual lunch hour and returned to work.

When they closed up at five, Janet watched Stacy lock her desk and the file cabinet in her office, and Stacy watched Janet do the same in her area.

"Maybe you should keep on seeing Dean. It would be a perfect way to get police protection," Stacy joked.

Janet's face reddened. "We're going to a concert Saturday night, unless something comes up with his work."

"And to think you were so rude to him in the beginning."

"He did turn out to be very nice," Janet admitted, walking to her car. "Of course, I've gone out with other guys who start out like a dream come true and turn into first-prize jerks."

"Tell me about it," Stacy agreed. "See you tomorrow."

She thought about stopping by to visit Amanda, since she wasn't eager to go home, then silently berated herself for allowing her imagination to work overtime. Besides, if she did see Amanda, the older woman would easily guess something was bothering her; the last thing Stacy wanted to do that evening was to talk about something that was probably just in her head. Before she could change her mind again, she stopped off for some chicken and drove home, with the intent of settling down with a book and her meal.

Stacy had barely finished her dinner when the doorbell rang. She looked through the peephole and was surprised to find Mac standing outside. She was tempted not to open the door, but suspected he knew she was there.

"Again?" she asked, pulling open the door.

He stepped inside without waiting for an invitation.

"We have to talk, Stacy," he said without preamble.

She stiffened. "About what?"

"Why you and your secretary were acting so uneasy this morning. I don't think it had anything to do with the loss of business." He sat down on the couch, looking prepared to wait. "What happened to upset you?"

Stacy closed the door. "My, you do have an imagination, don't you? Does it come with the badge?"

He smiled. "Do I? Stacy, over the years I've gained a sense about people. Instead of acting guilty, like a suspicious character might, you're acting fearful about something. I think we should discuss this. So why don't you sit down and start at the beginning?'' he suggested.

Her eyes blazed. "I have nothing to say."

Mac settled back. "And I'm not leaving until you do. Take your choice."

Stacy closed her eyes and counted to ten under her breath, swearing when she heard him chuckle. "I hate stubborn men," she muttered.

"Stubborn women give me a pain, too. Sit down, Stacy, and let's talk."

Reluctantly she sat down and faced him. "Fine. You want to hear a story, that's just what you'll hear. I'm growing paranoid in my old age, because it seems things have been moved around in my apartment and in the office, during my absence. I had a locksmith come in and change the locks in the office, even though I'm sure it was only my imagination. But I preferred reassuring both myself and Janet. End of story. Are you happy now? Now I have a book I want to finish, so if you don't mind…'' She looked at the door and back at him.

He wasn't moving. "I believe you."

Stacy's mouth dropped open. She had not been prepared for such easy acceptance. "You do?"

Mac nodded. "Why not? I have to get a lead somewhere, and this could be it. Why don't we discuss this further, and see what we can come up with? I'm certainly open to any ideas you have."

Stacy curled up in her chair and studied him long and hard. "All right," she said finally. "We'll discuss this. And when we're finished, I'm throwing you out." She smiled sweetly.

Chapter Four

"Who do you think is going through your files?" Mac leaned back in the chair, his ankles crossed.

Stacy looked helpless. "I don't know, but I can tell you that I think someone's been in my files at work, and for all I know, someone might have gotten in here." She leaned forward. "Wouldn't it make sense that the thieves might break into house-sitting agencies and find names and addresses there?"

"Why?"

"Why not? My high fees don't necessarily allow just anyone to use my services, and anyone who knows that could go through the files and find out clients' addresses, and sometimes even their schedules," she argued.

Mac continued playing the devil's advocate. "Wouldn't it be easier for the thief to work for an agency or run one, instead of bothering to break into them for the information? And none of the other agencies have reported any kind of break-in."

Stacy tightened her jaw. "Maybe no one has noticed, or like me, it's just little things that don't seem right, and most people don't want to feel as if they're paranoid. I know I've been feeling that way. I'm afraid I'll start jumping at the slightest sounds or strange shadows next."

"Which is why you didn't say anything to me," he concluded.

"I didn't say anything, because I didn't think you'd believe me."

Mac sighed. "All because of thirteen years ago?"

She laughed bitterly. "Of course. You didn't believe me back then. How would I know you would now?"

He closed his eyes, feeling incredibly weary—and not because he hadn't had more than a few hours' sleep in the past two days. "Your past record spoke too eloquently, Stacy. As it was, we caught up with your old buddies the next day, and your coleader tried to say you were in on it. The only thing that saved you from implication was the fact we found the other kids' fingerprints at the scenes—and not yours."

Stacy rubbed her temples with the tips of her fingers. "Logically, I know I can't blame you. I certainly didn't do anything to improve matters back then, did I?"

"Nope."

Her head shot up and she glared at him. "You certainly didn't have to agree so quickly, not to mention so cheerfully."

Mac sobered. "Stacy, your agency has all too lenient security measures, and your way of checking references isn't infallible. For all you know, some of your people could have records. They may not have been checked out thoroughly. You're lucky nothing has happened before."

"If they did have a police record, they couldn't very well be bonded, could they?" She smirked knowingly.

"Believe me, it can be done if someone wants in badly enough. If a person knows the right people, fake social security and driver's license numbers can easily be secured."

Stacy wilted. "Then what am I supposed to do?"

"Run more than one check. In fact, we'd like to double-check all your employee's fingerprints."

"They were fingerprinted when they were bonded," she reminded him.

He nodded. "I know that. So before you get on your high horse, screaming about your being singled out, I'm going to let you know that we're doing this with everyone, even the companies that already have very strict hiring procedures."

She nodded. "I'll have Janet make the calls tomorrow and try to get everyone together for you. If you don't mind, it might be easier doing it in the office than going to their homes."

He took pity on her. "Stacy, how many clients have you lost since all this started?"

"Not all that many," she bluffed. "We're doing fine."

Mac wasn't about to be put off. "How many?"

"Six." The word was barely audible.

"I can't hear you."

"Six! What do you want me to do, shout it from the roof?" she demanded. "I'm not alone in this—everyone else is losing clients. And while the police are screwing around, trying to figure out what's going on, we're taking the heat."

"You're not alone on that score," he murmured, thinking of his superior's vitriolic telephone call.

"Don't you have any leads at all?"

"I really can't discuss the case with you, Stacy," he said gently.

The lights in her eyes dimmed, leaving them flat and empty. "Because I'm your prime suspect?"

"We have no prime suspects," Mac lied, thinking again of Captain Henderson's call.

Stacy suddenly felt very cold. "Someone remembered me, didn't they?" Her voice grew harsh. "Didn't they?"

He nodded reluctantly. "My superior, Captain Henderson, remembered your previous name. I don't know how, since he wasn't working this area at the time."

"Even taking Russ and Amanda's name didn't help," she murmured, feeling very sick. "I feared this would happen. I guess I didn't expect it to happen so soon. I'm sure he can't understand why you haven't arrested me immediately, since I have such a nefarious past. After all, who better to know all the ins and outs of the victims than someone like me? Right?"

"Can it, Stacy," he growled, leaning forward, flexing his hands. "You're overreacting."

"I feel entitled to." Her tone was frosty now.

Mac suddenly grinned, the expression warming his rough features. "Ah, the lady of the manor finally comes out. You do that pretty good. What do you do for an encore?"

Stacy stood up, furious enough to want to hit him. "I believe the time has come for me to throw you out, Lieutenant McConnell."

Not at all offended, Mac stood up as well and sauntered over to the door. He looked back as he opened it. "Be very careful with that attitude of yours, Stacy," he warned. "It got you into trouble once before. I'd hate to see it happen again."

Her eyes narrowed. "Is that a threat?"

He shook his head slowly. "No, just some friendly advice. You got a raw deal back then. I don't want to see it happen again. A lot of pressure is being applied to wrap this up as quickly as possible. If you antagonize the wrong people, they're not going to waste any time hauling you in and letting you take the blame."

Her insides churned with terror, but on the outside she remained impassive. "Then you don't think I'm behind the robberies?" While she sounded calm and self-assured, she knew that the frightened teenager still lurked beneath the surface.

"No, I don't."

"Why?" She had to hear his reasons for believing in her innocence.

His smile was slow in coming but nonetheless sincere. "Because you're not so stupid as to cast suspicion on your own agency. You're a smart lady. You wouldn't screw your life up again. Not when you're doing so well." His hand gently cupped her cheek in a brief caress, then he turned away and left, quietly closing the door after himself.

Stacy stood there, pressing her trembling fingers against her lips. "Well, what do you know," she murmured.

"THIS IS the way I see it," Dean mused, leaning back in his chair, propping his booted feet on top of the desk that stood back-to-back with Mac's. "It's definitely an inside job. We just don't know who's doing it."

Mac shot him a dry look. "Very good. Did you think that up all by yourself?"

"Sure did. I'm a clever guy." He stretched his arms over his head and yawned. "Man, do you ever wonder what it would be like to get a full night's sleep?"

Mac eyed his partner's latest T-shirt offering. Heaven Doesn't Want Me, and Hell's Afraid I'm Going to Take Over.

"We've got to talk about a dress code in here," he muttered, going through his growing pile of notes.

Dean laughed. "You should talk. I remember some of the stuff you wore when you worked undercover. You looked like you belonged more in East L.A. than most of the inhabitants did."

Mac grinned, remembering that time only too well. "Yeah, but we busted that gang good."

"Hey, guys, the Page house was broken into again!" someone called out amid a chorus of groans. "Whoever gets her this time, raise your hand."

Mac and Dean looked around, noticing that everyone conspicuously kept their hands down, just as they were doing.

Kevin spoke up. "The woman is right when she called herself the perfect victim. The last time, which happened to be a week ago, they took all her small appliances and stereo equipment. What was left for them to take this time?"

The detective who'd taken the call was trying hard not to laugh. "Her freezer in the garage was broken into, and they took a hundred pounds of meat, her lawn mower and the weed eater."

"Oh yeah, a real biggie," someone snickered.

In the end, lots were drawn, with the loser going out to tackle the new case.

"At least it doesn't have anything to do with ours," Mac muttered.

"No way it could. The lady's jewelry was taken the first time around." Dean munched on a candy bar. "Besides, I heard she's a real ditz. Rich and gorgeous, but a ditz. I just hope we can get out of here before it's our turn to go out to see her. By the way, I'm going out to the Harris agency tomorrow, to talk to some of her employees. Anything in particular you want me to concentrate on?"

Mac shrugged. "Anything and everything. Who knows? Maybe one of them will crack, and you'll have a confession and get Henderson off my butt."

"We should have stuck with busting drug dealers," Dean told him. "Better yet, we could have gone over to Homicide, where no one talks back to you." He grew more animated as he spoke.

Mac shook his head, smiling at his buddy's eagerness. "Fisher is in charge over in Homicide, remember?"

"Oh, yeah. I guess he hasn't forgiven us for that time, has he?"

"No, I don't think so." Mac ran his fingers through his hair. "I am so tired, I can't see straight, and my stomach isn't about to take on another cup of that battery acid they call coffee."

"What do you say to our going out and getting a real meal?" Dean suggested. "You know, in a sit-down restaurant, where a cute little waitress takes your order and you've got real silverware instead of plastic, real plates and cloth napkins. How about it?"

Mac admitted the idea sounded wonderful. "What you talk about sounds great, except I can't imagine the kind of place you're talking about letting us in, dressed the way we are." He gestured toward his chambray open-throated shirt and worn jeans.

"So we change first. Come on," Dean urged. "It'll do us good to be out among civilized folk again."

"I don't think there's any such animal."

"It's been so long since we've been out like this," Amanda pronounced, looking around the restaurant. Wearing a black silk dress with silver jewelry and her hair pulled back into a French twist, she looked as regal as any queen. She smiled at Stacy, who sat across from her. "I'm glad you were free tonight."

"We haven't done this since the last concert," Stacy replied, nodding when the waiter asked if she'd like ground pepper on her salad. She leaned across the table. "You should be proud of me. I didn't fall asleep once," she whispered dramatically.

"You always were a heathen when it came to classical music." The older woman was unperturbed by her foster daughter's teasing. "Have the police found out anything new?"

"If they have, they aren't letting anyone know it," Stacy told her.

"Have you seen your detective again?" Amanda asked slyly as she dipped into her salad.

"Please, don't ruin my meal," Stacy begged. "The man is not mine, and I sincerely doubt any woman in her right mind would want him." *Liar,* her brain scolded. *The man is sexy as all get out, and if you care to admit it, you wouldn't mind seeing him outside of an official capacity. And you have the feeling he wouldn't mind, either.*

"You're protesting too much, my dear," Amanda said serenely. Seeing the younger woman's expression, she knew it was time to change the subject. "Tell me, how is your work at the shelter going?"

Stacy beamed. "Wonderful, and I don't care if I sound as if I'm bragging. The kids are great, even when we're yelling and screaming. I'm glad you suggested I work there."

"I knew you especially could relate to them, and I felt it would help you, too."

"I hate smart women," Stacy muttered, but she was smiling. Her eyes caught something just over Amanda's shoulder and her smile disappeared. "Wonderful, I can't even have a meal in peace."

Amanda raised an eyebrow and casually looked over her shoulder at the two men who were being seated at a table near them. When the younger of the two spotted Stacy, he smiled and nodded. Out of the corner of her eye, Amanda noticed Stacy didn't respond, but she didn't look away, either.

"Someone you know?" she asked, already certain of her answer.

"Unfortunately," Stacy mumbled, concentrating on her salad.

"Why, Ms. Harris, imagine seeing you here," a friendly male voice sounded from above.

Stacy glanced up slowly. While Dean had spoken, it was Mac's dark gaze that caught her attention.

"Hello, Stacy." He spoke in a low voice that wrapped itself around her senses like a fur coat.

"Mac." His name came out on a husky, almost breathless note. "Amazing! I didn't know you even owned a tie." She scanned the navy sport coat, pale gray shirt and navy-and-gray-striped tie. "You almost look civilized."

He grinned. "I'll take that as a compliment."

"Anastasia." Amanda's tone expressed mild reproof. "Don't you think you should introduce us?"

Mortified that she could lose herself so easily, Stacy quickly introduced the two police officers.

"So you're the horrible men harassing my daughter." Amanda's smile took the sting out of her words. "The least you can do is join us, so I can find out what exactly you plan to do with her. I've always wanted to be a spy, so you won't mind if I ply you with wine, do you?"

"I'm sure they already have plans. In fact, they're probably meeting someone," Stacy said rapidly, her eyes sending orders loud and clear to both men. *Go away!*

"Actually, we're here on our own. Thank you, ma'am, for your kind offer," Dean said, taking the chair next to Amanda. He noticed her wheelchair and shot a quick glance at Mac.

"You're quite welcome." Amanda's attention focused on Mac after he and Dean had given the waiter their dinner orders. Within moments she had taken stock of the policeman, and her smile said that she liked what she saw.

Mac smiled back. "I can't say I envied you taking Stacy on, Mrs. Harris. She seems to still be a handful."

"Dr. Harris," Stacy corrected in a clipped tone. "Amanda is a psychiatrist. Stick around. We're bringing out the inkblot test next. I'd love to see what your results would be."

"Pardon me, Detective." Amanda cast Stacy a look of mild reproach. "I'm afraid I subjected her to a classical concert this evening, and she doesn't do well listening to Mozart."

"I know some psychiatrists have specialties—do you?" Dean asked her, curious to hear what the older woman would have to say.

"I work with children," she explained. "Most of them have been physical and sexual abuse victims. Others are drug addicts, and I once worked with an eight-year-old arsonist."

"She talks lightly about her work, but she's one of the top five experts in the country." Stacy spoke with more than a touch of pride. She smiled warmly at her former foster mother. "She also donates a great deal of time at a couple of the teen shelters." She shot Amanda a warning look, silently asking that no word of her also working at one of the shelters be given.

Mac watched Stacy as she spoke. He'd thought she was lovely before. In these surroundings she was beautiful. The amethyst-colored, long-sleeved silk jumpsuit with a deep V neck draped softly across her breasts. An emerald-cut amethyst pendant nestled just above the faint hint of cleavage. Her earrings and solitaire ring matched the pendant. He didn't have to ask if the jewels were real, or if the perfume she wore was French and expensive. He reminded himself that she was out of his league, but it didn't stop him from wanting to be with her.

"Tell me, Doctor," Mac drawled. "Do you think it's Freudian when a girl tries to tear a guy's clothes off every time she sees him?"

Amanda's eyes sparkled with merriment, and Stacy looked mortified.

"It depends on the woman and the man, not to mention the circumstances," the psychiatrist answered.

"That must have been something to see." Dean chuckled. "Too bad no one got pictures."

"I was only trying to escape police brutality." Stacy bit out her words, trying not to notice when Mac shifted in his chair and his leg brushed against hers. How could she be so attracted to him? Of course, judging from various covert glances from some of the women diners, she wasn't the only one.

"Amazing how I was the only one to end up with bruises," he murmured.

Stacy returned to her veal before she could say more than she should.

"All these robberies going on must keep you very busy," Amanda commented.

"A bit." They all knew what Mac said was an understatement. "But that's how we earn our pay."

Amanda nodded. "Do you think any more will happen?"

"If the thieves are as greedy as we think they are, they will," Dean said, hungrily eying his filet mignon and baked potato.

"So you believe there's a gang?"

Mac glanced at Stacy, whose head was downcast during her foster mother's questioning, as if her only interest were in her dinner. "That—or one very clever person."

"And Stacy is one of your suspects." Amanda spoke the words as a statement, not a question.

"That's probably why they so easily agreed to join us," Stacy interjected. "Ten to one they've been tailing me, and they thought if they caught me off guard, I'd confess to everything."

Mac turned to Amanda. "Defensive, isn't she?"

"I can't blame her. Can you?" She looked him squarely in the eye.

"Look." Stacy held up her hands in a request for silence. "I don't get out very often for a nice dinner, and I really would like to enjoy this one. So why don't we dispense with the subject of the robberies and my somewhat villainous past? All right?" She looked around the table at the other three.

Mac nodded. "She's right. To be honest, Dean and I decided to go out to get away from our work, and I'm afraid we're not doing it very well. My apologies, Stacy, for intruding."

She flushed at his quiet-voiced sincerity. "I just don't want Amanda to start worrying anymore than she already does," she mumbled. "No matter what she claims, she still isn't as well as she pretends to be."

"She feels better if she can think of me as a frail little old lady," Amanda explained to Dean. "All right, we won't discuss business. Instead, tell me about yourself. Obviously you aren't married."

"Who says I'm not?" Dean asked in a teasing tone.

She had the expression of a woman who knows all. "No married man would dare go out on a Friday night without his wife. Especially not to a restaurant like this, and not if he wanted to go home."

Dean nodded. "True. Nope, I'm single, have good habits and I can cook, as long as it's hamburgers or hot dogs. I'm great at picking up take-out food. I was paired up with this guy a couple years ago, and as long as he behaves himself, I'll stick with him.''

''Were you ever shot in the line of duty?'' Amanda questioned him the way she questioned her patients; there was no way of avoiding an answer.

Mac chuckled. ''Yeah, buddy, tell the lady.''

Stacy's eyes widened. While she knew a police officer's job wasn't the easiest in the world, she hadn't thought too much about the danger involved. Somehow the idea of Mac being shot and possibly killed didn't sit well with her.

For the first time that evening Dean looked uncomfortable.

''Don't tell me you faint at the sight of blood,'' Amanda teased lightly. ''I've heard of it happening.''

''Only his own.'' Mac grinned. ''We busted a drug ring a year ago. That ended up in a shoot-out. Dean got nicked in the arm, but didn't notice it until afterward. He took one look at the wound and was out like a light. No one has ever let him forget it, either. It will probably come up at his retirement dinner. It's things like that they like to remember.''

''And nothing fazes you?'' Amanda turned her attention to Mac and eyed him.

''Not so far. And in answer to your other questions, I'm divorced, no children, and I've been with the police department long enough to trust my instincts.''

She looked long and hard at his face; whatever she saw there, she must have liked, because she only gave a brief nod.

After dinner, which the women completely refused to allow the men to pay for, the four left, with Dean pushing Amanda's wheelchair. They chatted companionably.

"Your partner and Amanda seem to be getting along very well," Stacy remarked to Mac, who walked slowly by her side after helping her on with her coat.

"She said she worked with kids. That's probably why." He appeared lost in his own thoughts. "Sometimes I think Dean's thirty-eight, going on twelve. His idea of relaxing is playing with his yo-yo."

"And how do *you* relax?" She looked up at him, unaware that her eyes were glittering under the lights and that her face was pleasantly flushed from the wine they had drunk with dinner. She had only imbibed one glass, because she was too wary to drink any more in the company of two police officers.

Mac stopped and half turned. He said nothing, looking down at her upturned face. Words weren't needed just then. His gaze wandered over the brilliant-colored silk that curved where it should and nipped in where it should, her waist accented by a gold cobra chain belt with jeweled cabochons decorating the clasp. It was as if he could look beneath the soft fabric to even softer skin.

Stacy could read all too much in his face and eyes, as if he was allowing her to do just that. Caught under his spell, she couldn't turn away. She was aware of the heat from his body, even though the air was cool. He was an uncivilized being, dressed up in civilized clothing. The man was even more dangerous than she'd thought in the beginning.

Stacy dragged her gaze away from him and managed to smile at the parking valet as he approached her. She handed him her ticket and gave a description of her car.

"I thought you drove a hot little Mazda," Mac commented.

"The Thunderbird is Amanda's. My car is too difficult for her to get in and out of, not to mention that her wheelchair won't fit in the back," she explained as a dark blue sedan was parked in front of her. "Well, all in all, it was a nice evening." She held out her hand.

Mac clasped it between his own, aware he'd have to be careful because of the two observers standing nearby.

"I'll be in touch," he said quietly, then moved away to say his farewells to Amanda.

"Come by and see me if you're ever in the area, Mac," Amanda told him. "My housekeeper makes wonderful coffee and even better coffee cake."

His smile warmed his rough features. "I just might take you up on that."

"Please do." She nodded toward Dean. "He's already told me he'll be by in the morning for breakfast."

"She wants to see my yo-yo tricks," Dean confided. "Besides, I never turn down a home-cooked meal."

"Amanda, you're a very rare woman," Mac told her, taking her hand and noticing the faint scent of violets. After meeting Amanda, he realized, he knew what was meant by "a genteel Southern woman." "I'm glad Stacy had you during those dark years."

She smiled. "And I'm glad she has you now."

He stepped back, startled by her words, but Amanda said nothing more. It was apparent that she had said what she wanted, and would now just sit back and wait.

Mac stayed in the background while Dean assisted Amanda into the car and said good-night to Stacy. The latter looked at Mac, but remained quiet as she climbed into the driver's side and drove away.

"What did Amanda say to you?" Dean asked as they waited for Mac's car.

"Nothing."

He ignored the other man's abrupt tone. "Wait a minute. She must have said something to get you turned inside out."

Mac pinned Dean with a sharp look. "She said nothing."

Dean knew that if he wanted to remain in one piece, he should drop the subject.

"THEY CERTAINLY AREN'T of the storm-trooper mentality," Amanda mused.

"Hmm?" Stacy was trying to figure out the odd expression in Mac's eyes, while making sure she remained in the right lane.

Amanda was used to her selective hearing. "You heard me."

"Yes, they were charming as hell."

"Anastasia."

Stacy winced at the faint reproof. Amanda never had to raise her voice with her. Just that deep Southern accent and the faint sorrow in her tone were more than enough to send guilt racing through Stacy.

"Sorry. I guess I'm just a little uptight."

"Because you still consider them the enemy, even though you're very attracted to Detective McConnell," Amanda stated.

Stacy's head whipped around for a second before she returned her attention to the road.

"Where did you get such a ridiculous idea?" she squeaked.

"Body language. The way you two looked at each other and pretended not to look at each other. It was only too obvious to a trained observer." Amanda shifted in her seat.

"He only sees me as a logical suspect, nothing more," Stacy said.

"If you say so."

Not wanting to hear any more of Amanda's hunches, Stacy begged off staying for coffee, saying she wanted to get some paperwork done before going to bed.

As she drove home, she mulled over Amanda's words and wondered if that wasn't, after all, one of the problems she had been battling lately. Yes, she had to admit she was attracted to Mac. But the past kept intruding upon the present, marring any fledgling feelings she might have for him.

Stacy quickly parked her car in the carport and locked it before heading for her ground-floor apartment. As her high heels clicked on the sidewalk, she felt a prickling sensation, as if someone were nearby—and that someone were no friend. She forced herself not to look around, but turned her key ring in her hand, so that the sharp end of the key pointed outward, and kept her pace even. Just before she reached her door, she noticed a dark shadow standing next to it. She hesitated for a moment, wondering if she shouldn't open her mouth and scream loudly for assistance. She wondered if she'd receive any.

"Stacy." The warm, gravel-voiced drawl stopped her dead in her tracks.

"You frightened me," she accused, now able to move forward.

Mac stepped out of the shadows. "I took a chance you wouldn't stay long at Amanda's."

"Don't tell me. There's another robbery, and they think I did it while I went to the ladies' room, right?" she suggested wearily, brushing past him to insert the key into the lock.

He grasped her arms and turned her around. "That's not why I'm here, and you know it."

He slid his hands up and down her arms in a light caress, then anchored them on her hips. They stood facing each other, he looking down, she looking up. Stacy tentatively touched Mac's shirtfront, feeling the heat of his body under the soft fabric. As if her hands had a will of their own, they circled his waist, grazing his shoulder holster before meeting and clasping.

She tipped back her head, her features barely visible in the dim light. "Do I?"

"Yes." He lowered his head and captured her mouth before she could utter a protest. By then she had no desire to.

Chapter Five

He crept back into the safety of the shadows and watched the couple embrace. He'd thought the timing would have been perfect. Walking down the dimly lit path late at night, she would have been the perfect victim of a mugging. Actually, all he had intended to do was run past her and knock her to the ground—just frighten her—give her something new for her nightmares. So how had he missed someone waiting for her at her door? He tamped down his anger and silently moved away. He was in no hurry. She would still get hers. He'd make sure of it.

MAC'S ARMS were looped around Stacy's waist, hers circling his shoulders as they clung together, bodies meshed. His mouth moved over her face, his mustache a soft brush against her skin as he tasted and savored her. Their harsh breathing echoed in the silence, but they heard nothing; the sense of touch was too important just then. His fingers tunneled through her silky hair, grasping her head to hold her still for his marauding mouth and teasing tongue. She warmly reciprocated the kiss. Her silk-covered breasts, framed by her open coat, rubbed against his shirtfront in a sensual caress.

"Why did you have to grow up to be so lovely?" Mac growled against Stacy's moist lips, nipping the corners and drawing her lower lip into his mouth. He wished he could deny his attraction to her—especially because this case was rapidly involving her—but for once, he wanted to do something just for himself.

"Why couldn't you have turned into Kojak?" she moaned, pressing even closer. She needed the reassurance of his presence. That he had come to her, not as a cop but as a man, heightened that sense and warmed her from the inside out.

He chuckled as he nuzzled her ear, gently biting the stud earring. It sent shivers down her spine. "I'm a cop. He was a cop. The way I see it, that's a pretty good comparison."

She pulled back slightly. "No, you're not overweight and bald."

"I'm glad."

Stacy shook her head in the hope of clearing the fog from her brain, but all Mac had to do was run his hands down her back in a leisurely manner, and her thoughts could only center on one thing: standing there and allowing him to do that for the next fifty years.

"This is dangerous, Mac," she said huskily.

He flashed her a crooked grin. "Why, are you armed?"

She stepped away, relieved—and disappointed—when he dropped his arms. "I realize our being together like this could cause you a lot of trouble. After all, you're investigating a case I'm a suspect in. If your superiors knew you were here, you'd be in a lot of trouble."

"That wouldn't be anything new, Stacy. I'm always in trouble."

Stacy turned to unlock the door and pushed it open. Mac reached around her for the light switch he remembered seeing there. He held her back, indicating that he would walk in first.

"No one's been here," she told him in a low voice.

He turned his head. "How do you know?"

Stacy smiled weakly, aware her answer wouldn't make much sense. "I just feel it."

But Mac wasn't other people, and he knew only too well about that sixth sense. His had kept him out of trouble and saved him from a bullet more times than he cared to remember.

"Nothing looks out of place?" He moved forward, switching on a lamp.

"No."

After shedding her coat and hanging it in the small closet near the front door, Stacy entered the kitchen. "Would you like some coffee?"

He followed her. "Sure." He leaned against the counter, watching her fluid movements, admiring the way the silk slid across her skin. He'd seen women wear jumpsuits before, some showing more skin than this one, but none had looked as good as this one did on Stacy. Deep down, he knew she was right; he was wrong in being here. But that didn't stop him from accepting her offer of coffee or thinking about the way she'd responded to his kisses.

"Dr. Harris is quite a woman," he commented, desperately needing to discuss anything that would keep his mind off what had happened a few moments ago. If he didn't, he would take her into his arms again.

"Yes, Amanda is that. She's also very impressed with you and Dean. Believe me, she isn't easily impressed." She filled the pot and poured the water into the coffee maker, switching it on.

A faint smile touched his lips. "What about the boys you dated? Did she do an interrogation that rivaled the one we went through?"

Stacy was opening a cupboard to pull down two mugs, when Mac moved up behind her and grabbed them first. "No, Russ did that. He felt I should only date someone who passed his idea of the ultimate question and answer test. He prepared one for my dates when I started getting asked to dances and parties. Luckily, Amanda found the test and had a long talk with him. I would have been mortified if he had given it to anyone. Believe me, after reading it, I knew my social life would have been a definite zero," she told him, recalling the time with fondness.

"Do you remember any of the questions?" He set the mugs on the counter next to the coffee maker.

She made a face. "The most memorable ones? Have you ever been the cause of an automobile accident? Have you ever been arrested? Do you drink alcohol? Do you take drugs? Are you considered mentally stable? Are you planning to do something worthwhile with your life?" She laughed and nervously rearranged the canisters. "Russ wanted me to have a normal teenage life. It was a shame that it wasn't to be."

Mac leaned over and grasped her hands, keeping them tightly within his own. "Stacy, I'm not here as Detective McConnell," he told her, gently shaking her hands to capture her attention. "I'm just Mac, a guy you shared dinner with. A guy your mother invited over for coffee. Okay?"

Sadness briefly touched her eyes and lips. "My real mother is in a sanitarium. Did your probing into my background tell you that? Her drinking destroyed her. She's nothing more than a brittle shell that can break under the least amount of stress. I go to see her about once a month. She wants to be back in San Marino, overseeing a household, but it isn't possible. She's too unstable. You know, I can still remember when we were all happy and Mom didn't drink. By the time I was twelve, our liquor bills had almost doubled, and he was hardly ever home, unless he needed to show off his cute little family. Mom would dress in a designer gown and jewels, and smile and say the right thing, and I would be dressed up and paraded out as the perfect daughter. I really fooled him, didn't I?'' Bitterness laced the last words.

Mac pulled her into his arms and held on to her tightly, resting his chin on top of her head. "No one has a perfect family, Stacy," he murmured. "Besides, you survived, didn't you? You didn't start drinking like your mother. Oh, yes, I noticed how you barely touched your wine at dinner."

"I was afraid to drink in the presence of the cops, you fool." Stacy almost choked. "And you know very well one of the reasons I survived was because of you. I was told that you were the one who started the paperwork rolling, when the kids admitted I wasn't with them. That you insisted I be released immediately, even when *he* said the kids were probably lying and I deserved to rot in there. He didn't even care that I was injured and came *so* close to losing an eye." She gestured and breathed deeply through her nose. "Sorry. I tend to get a little manic on certain subjects."

Such as her father, Mac silently observed. She couldn't bear to mention him by any name, he thought, still holding her in his arms.

"The...ah...the coffee's finished." Stacy pulled away and moved toward the coffee maker, quickly pouring two cups and handing him one. "Sorry I went a little nuts there. I guess the moon is in the wrong position for me." She led the way back into the living room and seated herself on the couch, pulling off her black pumps and dropping them onto the carpet.

"Or I bring back memories better left forgotten," Mac said, taking the chair across from her.

Stacy thought about his words and reluctantly nodded. "I've learned to be honest these past years," she said wryly. "Amanda would tell you it's best for these memories to come out."

Mac leaned forward, cradling the mug between his palms and studying the dark brew. "Yeah, and I'm a real old one."

She heard something new in his voice . . . as if there were something he had to accept, whether he wanted to or not. She sensed it had to do with her.

"You make yourself sound as old as Methuselah," she said lightly, taking a wild stab that that might be what had suddenly changed his mood.

His smile held no mirth. "Probably because I am."

"What are you, forty-four? Forty-five?"

His lips twitched. "Forty-three, if you have to know the truth."

"It was the third question on Russ's questionnaire." Stacy tucked her feet under her. "Mac, why did you come here?"

He shrugged and drained his coffee. "Hell if I know," he muttered.

She had to continue probing. "And now you feel you made a mistake in coming, right? Because I'm a suspect? Is that why you kissed me? Was it to be the beginning of your own brand of interrogation?"

Hurt had colored Stacy's question, Mac realized. He looked up, staring at her long and hard. "When I'm with a suspect, I ask questions. When I'm with a lovely woman, I usually want to kiss her, if not more. Does that answer your question?"

She didn't look away from his intense gaze. "You still didn't answer my question. What am I where you're concerned?"

He took a long time in answering. "I guess that's what I'm still trying to figure out."

"We all have our ghosts, Mac," she said softly. "I had a father who refused to love me, and a mother who forgot most of the time that I even existed. For many years I was convinced I had killed him, as surely as if I had used a gun on him, because I deliberately picked an argument with him, told him things he didn't want to hear, and ten minutes after he began yelling at me, he had his stroke. There are times I feel as if I still haven't come to terms with that. And you once said your wife had trouble dealing with your work, and obviously wanted you to find a job that made more money. I've heard there are women who are fascinated with a man wearing a badge. I'm sure you haven't lacked for feminine companionship," she probed delicately.

His crooked smile did things to her equilibrium. "If you're asking whether there's a lady in my life, no, there isn't."

Her lashes swept down to hide the smile in her eyes. "Then I guess I should feel flattered to find you on my doorstep so often."

"Only because my ex-wife won't let me within ten feet of her precious house in Sherman Oaks."

She eyed him slyly. "Any reason why?"

"It seems she thinks it's my fault that their house has been burglarized twice and her husband was mugged a while back."

Stacy giggled. "She blames you for that? Why? Were you the mugger?"

He stretched his legs in front of him, crossing them at the ankles. "You see, she left me because she didn't feel living with a cop was safe. She thought living with an insurance agent was.''

Stacy covered her mouth with her hands, vainly trying to hold back her laughter. ''Oh, yes, she's definitely in safe hands!'' Her laughter bubbled up, and she doubled over, howling with mirth. When she could finally regain her composure, she turned once more to Mac.

''I have a feeling you don't laugh like that too much,'' he commented.

''I guess I should apologize for laughing at your wife's expense.''

He shook his head. ''Our marriage was over a long time before our divorce.''

A silence fell as they looked at each other, feeling something warm and intense flow between them.

''Then it appears we're both free and clear, doesn't it?'' Stacy whispered.

''Yes, it does.''

''STACY. STACY. Yoo-hoo! Earth to Stacy. Come in, Stacy.'' A hand was waved back and forth in front of her face.

She started. ''Oh, sorry. I was thinking.''

Janet shook her head. ''Honey, you weren't thinking. You were in outer space. I got hold of everyone but Timothy. I left a message on his answering machine.''

Stacy nodded. ''Good, thanks.''

Janet placed several message slips in front of her boss. ''I've scheduled them to come in at one, so you can talk to them before the blue-coated Mafia show up.''

She smiled. ''That's unkind, Janet. After all, you're dating one, remember?''

''Not anymore,'' she declared fervently.

''What was wrong with Dean? He seems really nice.'' She decided it was prudent not to mention the dinner she'd enjoyed with the two men, even if her mother had been present.

"I guess I feel more comfortable going out with your run-of-the-mill stockbrokers and accountants," Janet admitted. "It's more than a little unnerving to realize your date is wearing a gun, even if he's good-looking and so sexy he makes your mouth water. I don't know. I guess I always felt as if he was going to swing the light around in my face and start questioning me. No, thanks. I'll stick with the human species of the male sex."

Stacy smiled, understanding that the very serious Janet would have trouble with a man who appeared casual about everything. "He is more than a little off the wall."

"You got it there." Janet took the seat across from Stacy. "What are we going to do?"

"Janet, I appreciate your offering to be a part of this, but I'm not going to allow you to be sucked under because of me." She laced her fingers together and placed them on the desk in front of her, idly noticing the chipped polish on one nail. A part of her brain recalled a manicure appointment for the next day, while the other part was appalled that she could even think of something so mundane when her life was slowly falling to pieces.

"This has nothing to do with you personally." Janet was clearly trying to reassure her. "They just need someone to blame this on, and because we're the newest agency around, we're the most logical in their eyes. No one wants to blame an agency that's been around for as many years as the others have. I'll tell you something. I can't wait until you prove them wrong. And I want to be there to see you rub their noses in it, too."

Stacy smiled at Janet's unwavering loyalty. "I thank you for those words, but I want you to know that if you decide to find another job, I'll understand."

Janet shook her head. "Stacy, didn't you ever stop to think, even once, that I might be the one behind the robberies?"

She didn't hesitate in her answer. "Not even once."

Janet cocked her head to one side, eying her curiously. "Why not?"

"Because if you had any money stashed away, you wouldn't be driving that Volkswagen of yours that's ready to fall apart at any moment. You'd give in to temptation and at least buy yourself a car that's a little newer."

"Honey, the Model T is newer than my old rattletrap," Janet drawled. Her comment was enough to break the tension, and they both burst out laughing.

"Let's splurge on lunch. If we're going to have to face those people, we may as well do it on a full stomach," Stacy suggested.

"That kind of work isn't listed in the secretary's manual," Janet said primly.

"Neither is most of the work you do around here." Stacy studied the message slips. "Mrs. Coffman, hmm? I thought she liked Maura."

"She did. She thought Maura was just wonderful. It appears Tito didn't. He expressed his displeasure in the best way he knew how."

Janet obviously found it difficult to keep her face straight, and Stacy, who had just started to drink her coffee, began choking until Janet placed a well-aimed thump between her shoulder blades.

"You're kidding?"

"Ask Maura about it when she shows up this afternoon. She said that Mrs. Coffman offered to pay her dry cleaning bill." Janet bit her lower lip, but finally couldn't contain her laughter. Stacy soon joined in.

It was a few moments before both women were able to compose themselves.

"I think we needed that." Stacy drew a deep breath, looking through the other messages. "Would you do me a favor? Call Mrs. Lawrence back and tell her that yes, I can be there tomorrow at ten."

Janet nodded.

"Otherwise, it's business as usual."

Now left alone, Stacy looked down at the files littering her desk. Some were there waiting for employee evaluations. After every job, Stacy sent an evaluation form to the client regarding the house-sitter and asked for suggestions to improve the service. Many of the comments she received were helpful, but unfortunately, more were not. Still, she considered it good business to consult the client as much as possible.

"Stacy, Mr. Kramer is on line #1," Janet called out.

She nodded and picked up the receiver. "Good morning, Warren. What can I do for you?" she said. Warren Kramer was one of her major competitors.

"It's what we can do for ourselves," the man boomed over the phone. "The cops were just here again to fingerprint my people. They're acting as if we're all criminals. I'm not going to put up with this kind of treatment, and if you're smart, you won't, either."

"Warren, we have no choice but to go along with them, if we don't want to make it harder for ourselves." She wondered to herself with more than a touch of whimsy why she hadn't tried that advice when she was younger. It was a good thing the man didn't know she was speaking from experience!

"I've talked to a few of the others, and we decided to get together and figure out a plan."

"A plan for what?" she questioned.

"For getting the cops off our backs." He sounded frustrated that she wasn't grasping the problem.

"Where are you planning to meet?" Stacy asked. Even though she couldn't imagine anything good coming from the meeting except the airing of anger, she wanted to hear what the others thought about what was happening.

Warren named a nearby restaurant. "I talked them into allowing us to use their private dining room around seven."

"All right. Warren, have you talked to any of the others? Because I won't come unless they do, too," she stated.

He mentioned several names. "They'll all be there, Stacy. I know how conservative you are, so I called you last. I figured if you knew the others had agreed, you would, too."

She ran her tongue across her dry lips. "Yes. Well, I'll see you then." She hung up and drummed her fingers against the desk top. She wasn't looking forward to the meeting. But she had to go. Otherwise it would look as if she didn't care about what was going on.

By the time noon arrived, she was more than ready to leave the office. The idea that her business could be shut down at any moment, if the police so desired, was making her crazy. Thoughts of Mac had also intruded on her morning—thoughts of him holding and kissing her—but what bothered her most was the fact that she had responded so wholeheartedly to a man who might prove to be her enemy. She was determined to take the time during lunch to shore up her defenses before he showed up later.

"To say I'm not happy with the way this investigation is heading is an understatement," thundered William Henderson at Mac and Dean. He was a corpulent man, who hadn't worked as a street cop for many years. "What we began with was nothing more than a few break-ins. That should have been wrapped up right away. Fingerprints alone should have given you clues. Your contacts on the street should have had information about the items being fenced. But you came up with zip. And I don't want to hear the crap that loose stones can't be traced as easily as jewelry. We've got some influential citizens screaming their heads off, and here you don't have one damn clue! What the hell is going on? Mickey Mouse could do a better job than you clowns!''

He continued ranting and raving as Mac and Dean stood there, knowing they could do nothing more than listen. Any defense they might come up with would only be loudly shouted down.

"I want some action soon, do you hear me? Or so help me, I'll take over and get this settled. Then we'll see where you two end up." His glare indicated that their "meeting" was over.

"Tell me again. What did we finally decide to do with that guy?" Dean mused, as they returned to their desks.

"No self-respecting monkey would have been his ancestor." Mac's lips were tightly compressed with the fury he'd had to hold in. He picked up a book and set it down very carefully, the anger setting his body aquiver. "He wants to settle it? Fine, let him go out there and see what he can find out. We've got a thief or thieves who wear gloves, know the layouts of these places like the back of their hand and take only the items that can be fenced with little problem—jewels that can be taken out of their settings, small valuables, nothing that can be easily traced. So we're left looking into every unlikely corner, and all he can do is scream that we're not doing our job. Fine. Let him solve it, and more power to him." His eyes still glittered with rage, Dean noted.

Dean leaned forward and grasped his arm, feeling the bunched muscles under his hand. "Hey, simmer down," he soothed in a low voice. "Don't let him win, Mac. He wants nothing more than to find an excuse to toss us off this case.

He doesn't like typical street cops, because he thinks our work should be all tied up in neat little packages with pink ribbons. And we know it can't be done that way, even if he refuses to realize that."

Captain Henderson appeared in the doorway of his office, still glaring at the two men. The many voices stilled as everyone waited to see what would happen next.

"And find something more suitable to wear, Cornell!" he yelled. "I'm sick and tired of those smart-ass T-shirts you wear. You're supposed to be a professional here. Dress like one." He walked back into his office and slammed the door behind him.

Dean stared down at his chest. "What's wrong with my shirt?" he demanded.

Kevin laughed. "What's wrong? Anyone who wears a shirt that says I'm Not Completely Worthless . . . I Can Always Serve As a Bad Example has a problem." He looked at the two men with sympathy. "How many layers of skin did he tear off this time?"

"Enough," Mac growled, breaking a pencil between his fingers. "I'm going to nail the bastard doing this to the wall, and I'm going to drag Henderson down to the cells, to see him in full, living color. Then I'm going to punch him out."

"Which one?" Dean asked, sounding interested.

Mac pushed away from his desk and stood up. "Both." He stalked out.

"Does all this have anything to do with that Harris broad? He's been acting kinda funny since that first time he saw her. He's practically ordered us to go easy on her, but he hasn't given us a reason. Do you know why?" Kevin asked, surprised by the usually easygoing man's abrupt mood shift.

Dean also watched Mac leave, equally surprised by his partner's quick temper. "Yeah, I know why," he murmured. "But as he's acting like a time bomb ready to go off at any moment, I don't think I'm going to go after him. I like my head just where it is."

"I'M SURE you're all aware of the local robberies, and how a good many of the victims are clients of ours," Stacy began, standing before the twenty people assembled in the waiting area. "I thought I should let you know that the police are investigating not only the agencies but the people working for them."

"You mean us?" inquired Harold Stevens. He was a retired army officer, who worked for her because he said it made him feel useful, since he had no family.

She smiled at the gray-haired man with the iron manner. "Yes, although I think you're the safest of all of us."

"What is going to happen?" Lora Wilson asked with a worried expression on her face. "I'm entering law school next year, Ms. Harris. I can't afford any problems with the law."

"They're trying to make it as painless as possible, which is why I asked you here today." She looked into each face, noting that some looked worried, others angry at this kind of intrusion, others just plain curious. "Two detectives will be here to question you and take your fingerprints." She held up her hands as the voices began arguing loud and strong. "I'm asking you to please cooperate to make it easier on all of us. We'll prove our innocence that much faster."

"Who do they think they are to treat us like criminals?"

"I thought a person was considered innocent until proven guilty in this country!"

"I'm not going to put up with this."

Stacy had to raise her voice to be heard. "You have no choice. Please, calm down and listen to me. By cooperating with the police, we're showing we have nothing to hide. I'm asking—no—I'm begging you to help me on this, because if you don't, they'll probably close me down."

The silence in the room was heavy as the group digested her words. None could ever remember her begging them before and they were humbled.

Harold was the first to speak. "Don't worry, Stacy, we'll be so cooperative, they'll probably worry about that!"

Lora was next. "I guess I may as well learn the way the police think if I'm going to have to work with them eventually."

Stacy felt her body relax. "Thank you," she murmured. "Those of you who can't stay can schedule another time with them. I made that understood, just as I requested they see you here instead of going to your homes."

She turned when the door opened and Mac and Dean entered. She couldn't help but notice that both were dressed more formally than on the other occasions when she had seen them in an official capacity. For a brief moment she met Mac's eyes, then it was as if a shutter was pulled over his face, blocking all expression. She wasn't the woman he had kissed so hungrily the other night. She was nothing more than the owner of a company he had come to investigate further. It hurt.

"Gentlemen," she said formally, offering her hand to Dean first. In no way was she going to let her injured feelings show. Her smile was brief and extremely cool. "I thought you'd prefer using my office. The files for the people present are on my desk." She ignored the small case Dean carried. "They've all offered to stay now and get this over with."

Mac nodded, his mind obviously on the business at hand rather than on the woman standing before him. "Thank you, Ms. Harris. We'll try to make this as brief as possible. I'm more than aware you have a business to run."

Her reply was sardonic. "How kind of you."

Stacy remained in the waiting area, talking to the others and unobtrusively watching Mac and Dean. They worked smoothly as a team. She grudgingly admitted they didn't take long with each person, and no one seemed offended by the questions they asked.

"You're right. It was pretty painless," Harold told her when he was finished. He hesitated, then went on. "I told them that the Lawrences' security system wasn't as good as they claimed it was, and how it shorted out more than a few times when I was staying there. Even a ten-year-old child could have broken in. I know the Lawrences might not like my saying it, but I prefer saving this agency to protecting their sensibilities," he added gruffly.

Stacy smiled. "They yelled the loudest when they were robbed, claiming no one could have gotten through that system without prior knowledge. They deserve that the truth be known. Don't worry about it."

Harold chuckled. "None of us liked that monster of a cat of theirs, anyway." He patted her shoulder awkwardly. "If you need anything, call me, you hear?"

She nodded, grateful for his concern. "I will. Thank you."

It was early evening before the two men finished. Stacy glanced at the clock and realized she would have to skip dinner if she wished to make Warren Kramer's meeting on time. She'd already sent a protesting Janet home. Stacy sat in the secretary's chair reading a magazine as the last person left. She stood up, waiting for the policemen to leave as well.

"Thanks for your help," Mac told her as they walked out of her office.

"It really made it a lot easier for us," Dean added, glancing from one to the other.

"I wanted this over with as soon as possible," she said in clipped tones. "Cooperating seemed as good a way as any. Now if you don't mind, I have an engagement."

"I'll take this on down," Dean muttered, exiting quickly.

Stacy ignored Mac as she picked up her purse and brief-case. "Is there anything else?" Her tone indicated that she hoped for a negative response.

"I'm just doing my job." He bit out the words, still smarting from his superior's earlier tongue-lashing, not to mention Stacy's formal manner when he'd walked in. He knew he hadn't acted like the friendliest of men, but that didn't stop him from hoping she'd offer him a warm smile to make the task easier. Instead, she was apparently going out on a date. He hated himself for feeling jealous when he'd ordered himself to stay away from Stacy, except on of-ficial business. He was driving himself crazy, and his lousy mood was making matters worse for everyone else.

"I can understand that." She spoke softly. "That's why I wish I could say last night didn't matter and as far as I'm concerned, it didn't happen. The only trouble is, I can't. Can you?"

He took several deep breaths. "No, I can't, either. But I'll have to, if I'm to get my job done. Have fun on your date." He walked out without a backward glance.

When Stacy looked up, she realized her hands were trem-bling. She didn't know whom she hated more for her reac-tion; Mac or herself.

Chapter Six

"Why can't we lodge some kind of complaint with city hall for harassment?" Madge Clark, longtime owner of a prestigious agency, asked the group seated at a round table.

"I asked my lawyer about that. He said there's been no real harassment, that the police are only doing their job and that we should cooperate with them to the fullest extent," Warren Kramer replied, downing his glass of Scotch. "We're the ones losing business because of all of their nosing around. I had two more longtime clients call me today and cancel. I can't afford to lose any more business."

"None of us can," Stacy said. As the youngest in the group, she tried to remain in the background, preferring to listen to the others first. But so far she hadn't heard anything encouraging.

"Then you haven't had those Huns invade your office files and talk to your employees, making them feel like criminals," Madge grumbled. "I even had a few of them quit, because they didn't like what was going on."

"The police were in today, talking to my people and taking fingerprints," Stacy replied. "But they were courteous and did everything possible to calm everyone."

"Stacy, you don't understand what's happening here," Warren said, as if speaking to a child. That irritated her no end. "Of course, since you're still new at this and your business isn't as large as the rest of us, you might not be losing as much business as we are."

"I understand this very well, Warren," she retorted sharply. "I'm hurting just as much as you are, if not more. All I know is, if we don't like the way the police are handling it, we should find the person responsible, instead of sitting here complaining about it."

"She's right," agreed Ron Thompson, head of Thompson Securities. "What we're doing here is bitching and moaning because we're losing business, but we're not looking at the reason for that loss. Someone is out there robbing our clients, and their method of operation indicates they're familiar with the households. I hate to say this, but that means the thief has to be working for one or all of us."

"That sounds so logical it's scary," commented Hank Leonard, owner of another security company. He spoke softly, looking from one to another.

That effectively silenced everyone.

Stacy sat quietly, worrying the stem of her wineglass, wishing there were something, even peanuts, to nibble on. It had been a long time since lunch. By now her stomach was cramping with the immediate need for food. She didn't want to be the first to suggest breaking up the meeting, but decided she would, if no one else did within the next thirty seconds.

Madge spoke up. "Look, we aren't accomplishing anything. Does anyone have any ideas on what we can do? Or shall we just sit back and hope the police catch the thief, before we all go out of business?"

"I think our best hope is to keep an open communication with the police and ask them for the same consideration," Stacy replied. "So far, they've been honest with me."

"Because of your pretty little face, my dear." Madge's words had a decided bite to them, Stacy realized.

Hank chimed in. "Still, she's right. I've been open with the detectives who've come around, and they've been more than fair. Sure, it might be because I was a cop down in San Diego years ago, and I understand what they're going through. Their leads are slim to none. It's not easy to arrest someone who doesn't have the courtesy to leave even a thumbprint at one of the crime scenes."

"Maybe we should put an ad in the paper—'Mr. Thief, next time you rob one of our clients, would you leave a strand of hair or a fingernail clipping, so we know you're a real person and not a ghost?'" suggested Stacy.

Warren shot her a dirty look, but she merely smiled back.

"Look, if you want to sit here and come up with nothing, feel free, but I haven't had my dinner yet, and my stomach is reminding me that lunch was a long time ago." Stacy stood up and grabbed her purse.

"You're acting as if this isn't affecting you one bit," Warren grumbled, looking at her suspiciously, she thought.

Assuming a stony expression, she stared at him for a moment. "Warren, my dear, it's affecting me more than you'll ever know." She slipped on her coat and left the room.

"Very nice," Hank complimented her, catching up as she exited the restaurant. "For a kid, you've got a good head on your shoulders. Come on, I'll walk you out to your car."

"It's not difficult to stand up to a jerk like Warren." She dug her hands into her coat pockets as they walked through the parking lot. "That doesn't take any talent."

"Still, you've got a lot of chutzpah, kid. You broke into a pretty established business in this area and did good. And you do volunteer work." He smiled at her astonished look. "I play basketball down at the shelter a couple nights a week. A couple local cops and I coach basketball and get some games going. Cal talks about you a lot."

She laughed. "Yes, I'm sure he's more than generous with his praise."

The older man chuckled. "He says you're one hard-nosed broad. For him that's a real compliment. I've heard good things about you from some of the others. You should be proud of yourself."

"I would, if I didn't get any new ones in the group." Stacy stopped by her car and dug her keys out of her purse. She looked up and smiled. "Thanks for the escort, Hank."

"My pleasure. If we're all to survive this, we can't battle each other. Also, if you have any problems, please feel free to call me." He offered her his hand.

She accepted it. "I will. Thank you."

After running the engine for a few moments, Stacy turned on the heater, allowing the warm air to wash over her. She had an uncomfortable feeling that she was being watched. Feeling uneasy, she made sure the doors were locked and left the parking lot at a faster speed than she would normally use. Still hungry, she decided against fast food and thought about stopping by Amanda's, since she wasn't far from there.

When Stacy pulled up in front of the house, she hesitated when she saw a strange car parked in the driveway. Then her stomach began growling again, and she decided she would just playfully ask for a handout and leave.

"Well, look who's here!" Alice exclaimed, greeting her with a warm smile.

"I have an ulterior motive." Stacy leaned forward with a mysterious air. "It's called hunger." She pasted on a pleading look.

The older woman chuckled. "How would some leftover fried chicken sound?"

"Like heaven." She stepped inside, then froze when she heard Amanda's laughter, coupled with the familiar sound of a man's low voice.

"Stacy, is that your voice I hear?" Amanda called out. "Come in."

Dragging her heels the way she used to when she was little, Stacy entered the box-shaped living room, where Amanda sat with Dean.

"Well, well, well. Now you're interrogating my mother." Stacy's eyes glittered with anger. "Very good, Detective."

"Dean is here for dinner. I know you might find this difficult to believe, but your name hasn't come up once," Amanda told her in the tone of voice that never failed to leave Stacy feeling as if she had mortally wounded the older woman.

"Amanda's been telling me about her work," Dean interjected. "And the book she's been urged to write for the last few years."

"And she keeps turning the offer down." Stacy silently ordered her tense muscles to relax as she sat down in a nearby chair. "What kind of pie did Alice bless you with tonight?"

He sighed dramatically. "Blueberry with French vanilla ice cream. I asked her to marry me, but she said she was busy Saturday."

A glimmer of a smile touched Stacy's lips. "I'm surprised you're not out catching bad guys," she commented. She looked up as Alice brought out a tray and set it in front of her. "Oh, no, I'll just munch on this in the kitchen." She didn't want to admit that she preferred not to be around what she thought of as *the enemy* when she didn't have to be. After the last couple of hours, she desperately needed to relax, but even Dean's charm couldn't allow her to do that.

"Even cops take a night off, and when I called Amanda to see if she'd like to go out for dinner, she suggested I come over instead. I have never been one to turn down a home-cooked meal—one that hasn't come out of a microwave oven," he admitted, stretching his long, jean-clad legs in front of him.

"Why aren't you home, taking it easy, instead of doing heaven knows what and only coming to see me for Alice's cooking?" her mother chided.

Stacy wasn't about to discuss the meeting in front of Dean. "I haven't done any grocery shopping lately," she confessed, picking up a chicken breast and biting into it hungrily. "And I knew Alice wouldn't turn down my most pleading look."

Amanda looked at her, sensing there was more to it, but she knew that Stacy wasn't about to go into her reasons for her unexpected arrival in front of company.

Stacy managed to stay for more than an hour after she finished eating, listening to Dean talk about some of his more hilarious experiences with the police force. She smiled and laughed at the right places, but inside she wondered what Mac was doing that evening. She didn't want to consider either the idea that he might be spending the evening with a woman or how much that idea bothered her.

"I should get going." She stood up. "Janet has a dental appointment in the morning, so I'm going in early."

Amanda's eyes were soft with concern. "Go to bed early," she advised. "You're obviously not getting enough rest."

"Have I ever?" Stacy responded lightly, leaning down to kiss her cheek. "I'll call you tomorrow. Broadway has a sale starting Saturday. Perhaps we can hit it first thing. Detective Cornell." She nodded at Dean, who promptly stood up.

"I'll walk you out," he offered.

She shook her head. "No, that's all right."

"Hey, it's late and very dark out there." He wasn't about to allow her to refuse, no matter how gracefully, she realized.

"And this is one of the safest neighborhoods around. I'll be fine. Good night." She hurried out of the house to her car. Stopping at the door, she dug out her keys, cursing her stupidity in not getting them out while she was still inside the house. When a dark-colored car roared down the street straight at her, she barely had enough time to run around to the other side of her own car. But the strange car still swerved toward her with a deadly aim. She leaped onto the lawn, feeling the air rush past her.

"What in the hell?" Dean was by her side immediately, his hands swiftly moving over her to insure nothing was broken. "Are you all right?"

She gasped for air, unable to form words. "Yes." The word came out as an expulsion of air.

"She's okay," Dean called back to Amanda and Alice, who were at the door.

"What happened?" he asked, turning his attention back to Stacy.

She shook her head. "I don't know. I was getting my keys out of my purse when I guess I heard something. A car just seemed to appear out of nowhere." She was grateful for Dean's helping hand as she stumbled to her feet. Unable to let go of his comforting grip, she hung on to his arms. She had to take several deep, calming breaths before she could speak again. "Dean, it was deliberate."

He stiffened visibly. "Are you sure?"

"Yes—no—I don't know!" she almost wailed.

"Dean, bring her in," Amanda called out.

"No, please, I just want to go home," Stacy told Amanda. But in the end she did re-enter the house, so that Amanda could see for herself that Stacy was unharmed.

"I'm going to follow you home," Dean told her, following her back outside.

For once Stacy wasn't about to argue. In fact, she was glad of the sight of the Jeep in her rearview mirror as she drove.

"I'm also walking you to your door." He appeared at her side the moment she stopped her car.

"You won't get any arguments from me this time." She managed a weak smile. "I guess I'm still a little shaky."

"You have a perfect right to be." Dean dropped a hand onto her shoulder. "Come on, let's get you inside."

Insisting on taking further precautions, Dean looked through Stacy's apartment before allowing her to enter.

"Why don't you change into something else, while I fix you a stiff drink?" he suggested.

She chuckled. "You're as stubborn as Mac. You're not happy unless you take charge."

He grinned. "I learned it from him. Go."

Stacy quickly changed into a robe and went back into the living room to find a glass of wine sitting on the coffee table. She curled up on the couch.

"Now that you've calmed down, do you still think this was deliberate, and not just some kid or drunk not seeing you?" Dean asked.

"Yes." Stacy didn't hesitate.

He nodded as he took in her reply. "Why?"

"I can't give you a definite reason. It was just something I felt." She paused. "For a moment, when I ran onto the lawn, I thought the car was going to drive right up after me."

"Except I showed up."

Stacy leaned forward to pick up the glass and sipped her wine. "If that person wanted me badly enough, they wouldn't have cared." Her voice was barely audible. "I'm right, aren't I?" Her tone hardened as she stared at him over her glass. "Aren't I?"

Dean nodded reluctantly. "Yes. I think this was just some kind of scare tactic. Otherwise, as you said, the driver might not have cared that I was a witness."

"Why would someone do this? Because of the robberies?" Stacy wanted to know, then answered her own question. "That's why, isn't it? Somehow, I know something about the robberies, and the person is afraid it will come to me."

Dean shook his head. "I don't know, Stacy. I wish I did. Did you see anything at all?"

"Nothing." She sighed. "I can tell you it was a dark sedan, but the way so many models nowadays look similar, I couldn't tell you if it was a Ford or a Chevy."

"Okay." Dean seemed to know when it was better not to push. "If you're feeling better, I'll be on my way."

"I do and thank you. Just one thing." She looked at him steadily. "There's nothing to report." Her meaning was very clear.

"Stacy, no matter what . . ." He groaned when he caught the stony set of her face. "Okay, I get the hint. Still, make sure everything is locked up tight, and if you hear anything, even if it's only a mouse sneezing, call either me or Mac." He pulled a business card out of his jeans pocket and scrawled on the back. "These are our home numbers."

"I don't want Mac to know," she argued, tucking her hands under her arms so that she couldn't accept the card.

"Tough." He pushed the card into her robe pocket. "Now, finish your wine and get some sleep."

"I'm going to tell Amanda that no woman in her right mind would want you," Stacy groused, following him to the door.

"You're right, but let's leave the lady with an illusion, okay?" He grinned. "Now, lock up. Good night."

"No wonder I never liked cops. They don't listen to you," she mumbled, slamming the door after him and slamming the dead bolt.

HE STOOD in a darkened doorway, watching Dean leave and Stacy close her door after him.

How did she manage to have the cops around her so much? he fumed. She wasn't getting suspicious, was she? No, there was no way she could even think of him. Not after all his careful planning.

Still, when he bore down on her, he saw the fright in her face and that pleased him. He was doing exactly what he set out to do. All in all, it was a good night.

WITHIN FIFTEEN MINUTES Dean entered his tiny, cluttered apartment. He rummaged through piles of clean and dirty clothing that lay on the floor near his sofa bed. It still lay open to reveal rumpled sheets.

"Where the hell is it?" he muttered until his hand closed around a beige cord. "All right!" He followed the cord until he reached the wall. "Damn!" Backtracking, he finally found his phone inside a drawer. Cradling the receiver between his ear and shoulder, he punched out a series of numbers. "Hi there. What I'm going to tell you is going to get me in a mess of trouble with a certain very stubborn lady we both know. Luckily, I'm not afraid of danger."

"I CANNOT BELIEVE the cleaners could lose something of mine again," Stacy muttered, walking into the office building. This time she had parked much closer to the building and kept a careful eye out for strange cars as she scurried across the lot. "If I was smart, I would just change cleaners."

"Except there's times you're not too smart, are you?" A familiar male growl intruded on her thoughts.

Stacy's scream came out more like a squeak, and she dropped her purse.

"That kind of scream wouldn't get you any kind of help." Mac stooped to gather up her purse and the belongings that had fallen out. "I'd work on my lung power, if I were you."

"Dean told you, didn't he?" Stacy watched him, feeling the anger build up again. Then embarrassment took over as she realized there were a few personal items in there. The moment Mac straightened up, she snatched the purse out of his hand. "I told him not to!"

"Better to tell me than to file a report," he said amiably. "He said it shook you up pretty badly." He scanned her face, noting the shadows under her eyes and her drawn features. She hadn't had a good night. "Are you sure you're okay?" His husky voice revealed just how much the idea of her being almost killed shook him up.

"I tore a brand-new pair of panty hose, which didn't exactly begin my day on an up note, but other than that I'm fine." She was unwilling to tell him just how upset she had been over the incident, nor how she'd barely slept all night. In fact she'd listened to what were probably innocent-sounding noises that hadn't bothered her before. But not for anything was she going to call anyone. Her independent nature wouldn't allow her to.

Mac looked her up and down with a more than interested eye. "You're into leather now?" He gestured toward her short, brown leather skirt and matching bomber jacket with a dull gold silk T-top. "I didn't realize conservative business owners dressed like this for the office."

"Only if they're visiting one of their clients who happens to be a rock singer." Stacy unlocked the door and pushed it open. She turned. "I suppose you're coming in."

"You got it." Mac followed her inside and watched as she set up the coffee maker. She called the answering service to inform them she was in the office and to take any messages they had. He wondered if she realized how badly her hands were shaking.

When the pot was full, Stacy handed him a cup and walked into her office with her own. When the liquid sloshed a bit over the sides, she carefully set the cup down on her desk.

"They're right, you know," she whispered, leaning against a corner of the desk. "When you think you're going to die, you do see your life flash before your eyes." She wrapped her arms around her body, as if she suddenly felt a chill.

Mac put down his cup and walked over to her, drawing her against his warm chest. "How many hours sleep did you get last night?" His breath caressed her forehead.

"Hours? It was more like minutes." She closed her eyes and rested her cheek against his shirtfront, deciding once again that she enjoyed the sensation of feeling protected.

"Why didn't you call me? Dean said he gave you my number." He rested his chin against her hair and kept his arms loosely wrapped around her.

"There was no reason to. My lack of sleep was due more to my imagination and crazy circumstances than anything else. Two cats decided to have it out on my patio at 3:00 a.m. Then the paperboy threw the paper directly at my door at six. I never knew a place could creak so much."

"Lord, you're stubborn." His accusation was warm with affection. He unconsciously nuzzled the soft curls over her ear, inhaling her spicy floral fragrance.

"I'm told I inherited it from my father." Stacy rested her hands on his hips. "Should we be doing this?"

"What?"

"You know very well what." She decided she liked the way he smelled of soap and clean male.

The crooked grin that sent shock waves through her system appeared. "Nope. 'Fraid I don't. Give me a hint."

"You holding me." She gulped when he continued rubbing his chin against her hair. "And doing that."

"Doing what?" he asked absently.

She found it difficult to breathe. "That." She needed no urging to tilt her head back and open her mouth under his, feeling his mustache brush her sensitive skin.

Both knew this wasn't the time, but they were past caring. They needed this form of togetherness—Stacy, who'd been alone so long by choice, and Mac, because he hadn't any choice where Stacy was concerned. Mac rubbed his tongue against hers, inviting her to a sensual dance. Stacy wasn't going to allow this to be one-sided. She slipped her arms around his waist and hung on to the waistband of his jeans, slowly undulating her hips against him and feeling the full pressure of his arousal.

"Why, Officer, is that a gun in your pocket?" she crooned, nibbling on his lower lip.

"You're proving to be very dangerous." Mac drew back his head and stared up at the ceiling.

"Public Enemy #1, that's me," she quipped.

This time he pulled away from her completely. She found herself feeling bereft without his warmth against her. "I know, but I have a case to solve and I don't intend to see you hurt, because the time might come when I have to come down hard on you, whether I like it or not," he said harshly, rubbing his hands through his hair, leaving the salt and pepper strands tousled, but not unattractive, she thought.

"We're both adults. We'll both handle it if it does happen. Is there anything wrong in giving this a chance?" Stacy wasn't about to allow him to back down now. She could feel all her nerve endings tingling and couldn't remember the last time a man had made her feel so alive. She decided it was because no man ever had. Of course, she hadn't expected that the man to ring her chimes so effectively would be Frank McConnell.

He looked extremely frustrated. Why? she wondered. "Right now it could be. Especially if my superiors thought I was trying to shield you."

"If they thought that, they don't know you very well. I can't see you shielding anyone, even someone you might care for." Stacy looked down at her fingers. "Mac, I understand what you're saying, but is it right to deny whatever is happening between us?" She had a thought that wasn't very pleasant. "Or is it me? I mean, maybe I'm not—"

"That's not it at all," Mac cut in. "For the first time in my life, I don't feel as if I'm thinking straight, and I don't know how to handle it. I'm in the middle of a case you're a part of, I'm quite a bit older than you, and I'm not exactly the best material for a relationship."

Stacy was stunned. "Business and personal life can be kept separate if we work at it. And you're certainly not in your sixties, and I'm not some nubile nineteen-year-old." She held out her hands. "Mac, I may not remember it, but I do know all about Vietnam, the Beatles, when the word fab was something other than the name of a laundry detergent, the Monkees, Yardley makeup and Sassoon's geometric haircuts. I also think I tended to grow up a bit faster than other kids. And I don't think those are the real reasons for your reticence. I think it's because of my past. Because of my old boyfriend, Chad, and me running around with four other kids, breaking into houses and taking whatever appealed to us. That's why, not because there's a few years between us. If you want to lie to yourself, go right ahead," she said sharply. "Just give me some credit and don't lie to me."

Mac spun around. "You don't know anything about me, so don't try to tell me how I think or feel," he said in a gritty voice.

Stacy wasn't about to back down now. "I hit the nail on the head, didn't I?" Her laughter wasn't humorous at all. "I'm a better suspect than a prospective romantic interest. After all, you couldn't take me to any business functions, could you? What if someone remembered the kid you used to bust so often? That could prove embarrassing for your career, couldn't it?"

"I can't stop you, if you want to look at it that way. I had a wife who enjoyed telling me no woman in her right mind would want me. And the few women who floated through my life afterward turned out to be more interested in the badge than the man," he retorted. "So why should I think you'd be any different?"

"If you kept your mind and heart open you would," she shot back. "But you'd prefer to keep your mind closed to anything good. Because you've spent most of your time in the sewers of life, you don't want to look for anything decent."

Mac continued standing there, his fists clenched, staring at her with murder in his eyes. Stacy didn't avert her gaze. When the ringing phone broke the heavy silence, neither moved. On the third ring, Stacy finally picked up the phone.

"Harris Agency." Her voice was husky; she looked across the room at Mac. "Yes, speaking."

Mac composed himself as Stacy spoke softly into the phone. He didn't wait for her to finish her conversation before leaving. Without looking at her again, he walked out of the office.

When Stacy completed the call, she collapsed into her chair before her knees gave out.

"Mac McConnell, for a man in your line of work, you're a coward when it comes to real life," she murmured.

Chapter Seven

"Oh, my, are you here to interrogate me, Detective?" the fluttery Mrs. Coffman tittered nervously, greeting Mac as the maid guided him into the drawing room.

He looked at the delicate French furniture that was probably antique, then spied a nasty-looking Pekingese, sitting royally on a pink silk hassock. The small dog took one look at this inferior human, lifted his black nose in the air, and turned away.

"Would you care for some tea?" Mrs. Coffman asked, after gesturing him toward a fragile-looking brocade love seat. "Or perhaps some coffee?"

"Ah, no, thank you." Mac managed a brief smile. He had a strong hunch that coffee or tea here was served in china cups, and he wasn't about to take any chances. "I'm sure you're aware that the Dorans' home was broken into two nights ago."

Mrs. Coffman's artfully made-up face showed distress. "Yes, I heard about it. Such a terrible thing to happen. Poor Olivia is just heartbroken that her emerald necklace was stolen. You see, it was an anniversary gift from her husband. I was planning to travel with my husband and now I'm afraid to go, but I'm also afraid to stay here alone." She looked at Mac as if he had all the answers.

"Do you use a house-sitting service when you're away?" he asked, though he already knew the answer to the question.

"Oh, yes. I use the Harris Agency," she replied. "Stacy Harris, the owner, is such a sweet girl. And my Tito loves her." She gave the dog a glowing smile. He merely scowled back. "Tito has a very delicate constitution, and many people don't understand my little darling. Stacy is very good at screening the people for me, before I see them, so no one unacceptable to my little boy is ever left with him. He's very sensitive to people who don't like him."

Mac privately thought that a majority of the world wouldn't like her sour-faced pet. "Did you ever use anyone else within the past, oh, six months to a year?"

Her small chin quivered with indignation. "Oh, yes. I once made the horrible mistake of using the Kramer agency. I would not recommend them to anyone."

His interest perked up. "Mistake? In what way?"

"They are just terrible people," Mrs. Coffman went on, fussing with a large blue topaz and diamond pendant she wore with her eggshell silk dress. "You see, one of Stacy's employees was just perfect for staying here, but she moved away. And I was a bit peeved because she couldn't house-sit for us a few months ago, so I called the Kramer agency. The woman they sent out was not sympathetic with my Tito at all. In fact, he was accosted by another dog while she was taking care of him. It traumatized my little baby. I must tell you I will not call them again. Luckily, dear Stacy forgave me for my little tantrum and found someone new for me. I've had to conduct more than one interview, since Tito also has to approve, but we soon agreed that a lovely lady named Edna would suit us perfectly." She smiled broadly. "Tito adores her."

Mac just nodded, wishing he had given Dean this assignment. "Do you also engage a security system?" He glanced at his notebook.

She gazed upward, as if the answer were written on the wall. "I believe it's Leonard Security Systems." Mrs. Coffman beamed. "Very lovely people."

"Of course," Mac murmured, looking through his notes on the security companies. "And you're obviously happy with them?"

"Ronald, my husband, is. He knows more about that kind of thing than I do. Is there anything else I can help you with?" Mrs. Coffman asked, clearly wanting nothing more than to please the dark-haired man sitting across from her.

"No, not really, although I do have a request." Mac stood up and pulled a business card from his pocket. "If you and your husband leave town before we're able to clear up this case, would you please notify us first?"

Her eyes grew even wider. "You don't think that horrible person might break into here, do you?" she asked in a horrified whisper, clutching her chest. "Why, I don't know what I would do. And my Tito is so sensitive."

"Mrs. Coffman, the thief has never harmed anyone. In fact, he's known to break in only when the owners are gone for the evening," he assured her. "Although if you're worried about your jewelry, I would suggest you start keeping it in a safety deposit box."

"Oh, I'm not worried about any of my jewelry. Ronald has an excellent safe that no one can break into, and the jewelry is insured," she explained airily. "What I would worry about is my little Tito." Her fingers rested on the champagne-colored, furry head. The aristocratic dog ignored his mistress.

Mac eyed the necklace, matching bracelet and two rings the woman wore, not to mention the diamond-studded beige leather collar of the bad-tempered Pekingese. The jewelry was undoubtedly real.

"Yes, ma'am," he muttered.

She offered her hand along with a warm smile. "I wish I could have helped you more, Lieutenant McConnell. I've heard rumors that the police think one of the house-sitting agencies is behind the robberies. I want you to know that I don't believe Stacy could be behind something so horrible."

Mac couldn't help but return her smile. "I'm glad that Ms. Harris has you for a champion, Mrs. Coffman. Not that many people would be so vocally trusting during an investigation like this."

She looked up at him, all trace of the fluttery woman erased. "Lieutenant McConnell, Stacy has a good heart. I'm sure to some she appears to be very cool and aloof, but deep down she's not. I feel as if she's a young woman with a very old soul. A soul that has suffered more than anyone knows." As if realizing that she might have said things she shouldn't have, she looked away.

Mac changed his first opinion of the silver-haired lady. "Goodbye, Mrs. Coffman. Thank you for taking the time to see me. And if you see anything suspicious, please call us."

"Oh, I will," she promised, walking with him to the door. "I'm not a very brave woman, you see. Goodbye, Lieutenant."

"Mrs. Coffman, you're a braver woman than you know," he murmured, walking to his car.

"My old man came back again," Tania, a beautiful sixteen-year-old girl with dark chocolate skin, said woefully, looking around at the group.

"And?" Stacy prompted.

The dark-haired girl sighed. "He says he's sorry and he'll never drink again or hit us, but I don't believe him. Man, the first time he gets a bottle, he'll do it. He only came back 'cause he knows Mom has a good job. I told her she should throw him out 'cause we're better off without him, but she said she still loves him. She don't know nothin' about love." Her bleak voice echoed the sorrow she had lived with for so long that she felt she had no choice but to accept it. Stacy worked hard to teach the children that they could do anything they wanted, but it wasn't easy for them to believe.

"Everyone looks at love differently," Stacy observed, thinking of her own parents and their unorthodox marriage.

"I don't want to fall in love with a loser like my dad, and in my neighborhood, I don't have much choice," Tania said vehemently.

"Thanks," Cal sneered. "I live two streets over from you, and you're saying all the guys you know are losers? Hey, baby, some of us are looking for more than what our folks have, you know. You're not the only one."

Tania didn't bother to answer him. She merely turned to Stacy. "I rest my case."

The boys immediately started defending their sex, while the girls loudly sided with Tania.

"Hey! Hey!" Stacy held up her hands. "This is a discussion period, not a free-for-all, okay?"

"She's sayin' we're all creeps not worth a girl's time!" shouted Artie, one of the newer members of Stacy's group. "Who the hell does she think she is?"

"Someone who can offer her own opinion," Stacy replied. "Just as you're allowed yours. Go ahead. Tell us what you think of what Tania just said."

He straightened up. "Okay, her old man's a drunken creep, but not all of us are like him."

"No, the rest of you guys are into drugs," Maria jeered.

Artie shot her a deadly glare. "Hey, I've been clean for three months," he informed her with a maturity greater than his fifteen years.

"Tell me that ten years from now," Maria countered.

"We're getting off track here," said Stacy, hastily intervening before a full-blown argument began. "Tonight, we're here to help Tania cope with having her dad back. Any suggestions?"

"Go out at night."

"Yeah, all night," one of the boys snickered.

"I'm doing my homework at the library now," Tania explained. "But I've got my brothers and sisters to consider."

"They're all old enough to help themselves," Maria pointed out. "You got to help yourself, Tania."

Stacy glanced at the clock on the wall, noticing that they had gone over their time again. "I guess that's it for tonight." She stood up. "Is the fact we have to do this a different night a problem with you kids?"

Everyone said no and agreed they'd be there on the new day.

"We've accomplished a lot tonight, and I'm proud of you." Stacy smiled. "See you next time." She noticed that Artie approached Tania and asked if she'd like him to walk her home. Stacy was pleased when Tania accepted. After gathering up the papers she had asked them to write about their future dreams and stuffing them into her denim tote bag, she walked out of the center.

"Great," she muttered, noticing the light pole she usually parked her car under was flickering, as if it were ready to burn out at any moment. Since the center was still crowded with kids and adults involved in other activities, she wasn't too worried about her safety.

She had just reached her car when she sensed she wasn't alone—and that the company wasn't exactly friendly. Since the center was housed in a less than desirable neighborhood, Stacy had always kept herself on guard when she had to walk outside alone. Most of the time there was someone to walk with, but tonight she had left later than usual. Now she regretted not asking one of the male counselors to walk with her to her car.

"Look what we've got here, guys," a sneering male voice called out. "Looks like the girl is in the wrong neighborhood, doesn't it?"

Stacy slowly turned, unobtrusively keeping one hand near a pocket just inside her bag. If she was uneasy about facing four boys in their late teens, she didn't look it. She knew she couldn't show any fear to them, or they would be on her like a pack of wild dogs.

One boy, dressed in black leather pants and a leather vest over his hairless chest, swaggered closer. "You're one pretty chickie for a place like this." He leaned over until she could smell the whiskey on his breath and see, even in the dim light, that his pupils were dilated. "Why don't we go someplace where we can party? Whaddya say?"

"I say you have the wrong chickie," she replied coolly. "So why don't you move on?"

He laughed. "Hey, me and my friends aren't so bad. You'd have a lot of fun with us. Wouldn't she?" He continued his suggestive study of her body.

Stacy's skin was crawling, and something told her she could be in for a lot of trouble, unless she handled the situation very carefully. If not, well, she had a few other options.

"Why don't you and your friends go back to your party and you find another chickie more to your taste?" she suggested, still keeping her voice bland and even.

The youth grinned, revealing nicotine-stained teeth. "But I like *you*, baby." He moved closer and reached for her breast.

Before anyone realized what was happening, one of Stacy's hands moved swiftly. A flick of a finger—and a steel blade snapped out.

"Try it—and you just might lose something very important," she warned, her eyes now ice-cold. "Now back off." Her gaze whipped momentarily toward his friends, who stood there apparently stunned by her action. "Trust me. I know how to use this and I won't hesitate."

The boy slowly backed away, his hands held up. "Hey, baby, we just wanted to party, okay?"

"Not okay." She held her hand steady, aware that any sign of weakness would be her downfall.

For a brief second, he looked as if he wanted to rush her, but wasn't sure if he might end up on the wrong side of the lethal-looking blade.

"Take the lady's word for it," they heard a man's voice say. "She'll cut you into very tiny pieces."

The boys turned. "Hey, you're a cop, man. You're supposed to protect me from psychos like her," their leader called out in a deceptively innocent tone, as if he were the wronged party. "All I did was ask her a question, and she pulls this blade on me."

Mac's smile held no humor. "I don't see any knife."

Muttering, the boys walked away, glaring at both Stacy and Mac.

"You better be careful, baby! You might not get off so easy next time, when your precious cop isn't around to back you up!" the leader yelled at Stacy.

Stacy was smart enough not to reply. She leaned against her car, looking as though being accosted by a gang was an everyday occurrence as she watched Mac walk toward her. He didn't appear to be very happy with her.

"You sure like to attract trouble, don't you?" he groused, standing over her. His eyes flickered toward her knife. "You would have used it on him, wouldn't you?"

"It would have been strictly self-defense." She tried to act as if seeing him were a matter of course, but failed miserably. "You'd think these punks would pass the word or something. I'm beginning to think I'm a part of some kind of macho initiation test."

Mac felt the bile rise into his throat. "This has happened before?" he asked in a hushed voice.

Stacy nodded. "Only once or twice." She looked at him curiously. "What are you doing here?"

"Dean and I coach a basketball team when we get some free time. He mentioned that you do some volunteer work here and on what nights, so I thought I'd see if we could 'accidentally' run into each other. After your performance, I'm glad I didn't try to surprise you."

She smiled, pleased that he had taken the initiative. "In this neighborhood it's best to be on guard and ready to fight back if necessary. I hold rap sessions for the kids. They talk about their problems, and we try to come up with reasonable solutions. We don't always succeed, but we try." Stacy closed the blade and dropped it back into the small pocket inside her bag.

Mac shook his head and held out his hand, wiggling the fingers in a "give it to me" gesture.

She hesitated for a moment, then pulled it out, dropping it into his open palm. "Not fair."

He pushed it into his jeans pocket. "Carrying switchblades is illegal, which I'm sure you already know. By all rights I should run you in for having one."

Stacy held out her hands, palms closed as if waiting for him to slap on the handcuffs. "Go ahead."

He grinned. "You're lucky I don't. And I happen to like this shirt with its pockets intact."

She bit her lip to keep from smiling, although her eyes danced with laughter. "Darn." She draped her bag handle over her shoulder.

Mac looked around the dark lot. "How about a cup of coffee?"

"It sounds better than getting arrested."

"Why don't you follow me? I know a good coffee shop not too far from here."

"Don't you mean a donut shop?" she teased.

He grimaced. "I've heard every joke known to man about cops frequenting the donut shops, okay?"

"I figured it wouldn't hurt for me to try." She unlocked her door. "Lead on."

Within ten minutes they were sitting in a rear booth, and had steaming cups of coffee set in front of them by a friendly waitress, who greeted Mac by name.

"Just out of curiosity, where did you get the blade?" Mac asked, sipping his coffee.

"I went to Tijuana with some friends last summer. They're real easy to get down there."

He nodded. "Yeah, too easy. I should warn the border patrol about you."

Stacy sobered, cradling the warm mug between her hands. "I was scared, Mac. Real scared, but I knew I couldn't show it to those creeps, or they would have been all over me."

"He didn't think you'd use it, but he wasn't going to take the chance that you might. The leader's name was Mario, and he can be mean when he's crossed," he replied. "I'd watch myself carefully the next time you go back there. He's going to be looking for you."

She was surprised. "You mean you're not going to order me to not go back?"

"Would you listen to me if I asked you not to?"

Stacy slowly shook her head. "No. Those kids have come to count on me, and I can't let them down."

Mac frowned, recalling something he had once heard. "Is Cal in your group?"

She chuckled. "Oh, yes. Cal makes the group."

"He's talked about the fox in charge of the group he sits in on, but he never said your name."

"Plus you didn't figure me for this kind of work," Stacy added.

"No, I didn't," he admitted. "But then you don't like to fit in any particular mold, so I guess I shouldn't be surprised."

She began fiddling with the sugar and artificial sweetener packets, piling one on top of the other in a neat stack. "Amanda was the one to get me into it. She thought it would help me to talk to kids who're in similar situations as mine. In the beginning they didn't trust me, and when they did show up, they would do everything to throw me off base. To them I was an adult, and since I probably had money, they thought I wouldn't know anything about their lives. Admittedly, I wasn't the best of counselors," she told him ruefully. "Finally, one night I blew my stack at them. I told them money and a nice home didn't mean beans, if your father didn't give a damn about you and your mother drank herself into a stupor every day. I told them about the gang I ran with and what we pulled. I don't think they believed me at first, but they soon came around. We still have our shouting matches, but I like to think we also accomplish something positive," she said shyly.

"Does it help?" His quiet voice somehow wrapped itself around her, she realized.

Stacy shrugged. "It got a lot of the poison out. And I learned that my problems were nothing compared to those of some other kids. In fact, it downright humbled me." She drank the rest of her coffee and looked up with a smile when the waitress paused to refill their cups. "What about you? How did you get started working at the center?"

"Dean roped me into it." He leaned over and stared at Stacy. "How come you're not married or have any men in your life?"

She was startled by his abrupt question. "How do you know I haven't or don't? Ah, your investigation, of course," she continued, answering her own question. "I was engaged once."

He wished he didn't hate the idea that she had once been involved with a man. "And?"

She stared into her cup. She didn't want to see his look of pity when she told him. "I decided I should come clean with him about my past. He couldn't handle the idea of his future wife once having been a thief, so he oh, so politely explained that he was afraid we had too many differences to make a good marriage. Six months later he married someone with an impeccable background and the personality of a turnip. A match made in heaven."

"Then you didn't lose anything," Mac told her. "If a man loves a woman enough, he'll accept her the way she is and not care about what happened in her past."

"It still hurt," she whispered, staring at the heavy, off-white mug cradled between her palms before moving it to one side. "I sat around feeling sorry for myself. That was when Amanda pushed me into working at the shelter."

"To get you to forget about it," he guessed.

"Yes." Stacy shuffled the sugar packets as if they were a deck of cards. "And because she felt I would understand their anger better than some of the other counselors."

"Stacy." When she still refused to look at him, he reached across the table and took her hand, turning it over and lacing his fingers through hers. "It's a trite saying, but you're probably better off without him."

She managed a weak smile. "That's what I keep saying. Too bad I don't listen to myself." She tipped her head to one side and regarded him soberly. "Ever since I can remember, I've lived my life day by day. I think I was always afraid to look to the future. But now I want to have more than just the agency and working at the center. And whether you like it or not, the change is due to you."

Mac shook his head. "Stacy, don't give me credit where it isn't due," he warned, shifting uncomfortably.

Her smile was soft and wistful. "Oh, but my friend, it is most certainly due."

Within moments they left the coffee shop and walked back to their cars. Stacy stood with her back against her door, while Mac leaned over her, his arm draped on the car top.

"I was right to call you a dangerous woman, Stacy Harris," he said quietly, picking up her hand and kissing the knuckles. "Now I want you to get in your car and lock your door."

She slipped inside and locked the door. Mac stood there, watching the taillights of her car disappear, feeling as if a part of himself had left, too.

Instead of driving directly home, he headed for Dean's apartment.

"Hi," Dean greeted his partner. "Want a beer?"

"Sure, why not?" he mumbled, walking inside. He looked at the overflowing laundry basket, and the closet that stood open because it was too full of clothes. "Your cleaning lady quit again?"

Dean laughed. "She wasn't here long enough to quit. She walked in, took one look at the place and said I couldn't pay her enough money to clean this place." He pulled two beer cans out of the refrigerator. "What's up?"

Mac held out the switchblade. "This, for one."

"Wow, who'd you pick that up from?"

"Stacy."

Dean's eyes grew larger. He gestured toward a chair. "This is one story I want to hear."

Mac told him everything, from the episode at the shelter's parking lot to the one at the coffee shop. The only thing he didn't tell him about was Stacy's declaration, which had sounded very much like a declaration of love. The idea scared the hell out of him. He just wasn't sure if he knew how to love. He had thought he loved his ex-wife, but that hadn't worked out. And the last person he wanted to hurt was Stacy.

Dean pulled the tab off his beer can. "She certainly has guts."

"Yeah, the kind that could get her badly hurt, if not killed, one day," he said glumly. "She just won't back down."

"My friend, whether you like it or not, you've got the hots for a lady who knows how to take care of herself and how to handle you. Hmm. This could prove real interesting. No wonder you're so worried about her." Dean smirked, enjoying his old friend's discomfort. "And she certainly doesn't look at you as if you're the friendly neighborhood cop."

"She's part of an investigation. If I get involved with her, I could end up as Henderson's breakfast," Mac argued, resting his elbows on his knees, clasping his hands tightly around the beer can. Silently he admitted that he was already involved.

"And when the case is over? What about then?" Dean pressed. "She's a good-looking lady, Mac. She's got a decent IQ, and for some crazy reason she seems to like you. What more can you want?"

"For all I know she could be out for revenge," he blurted out, draining the last of his beer and crushing the aluminum can in his hand.

Dean shook his head. "From what I've seen she's not the type. She's too up-front to play mind games. Okay, it's rough right now because of the case, but don't let it ruin something that could turn out to be the best thing you've ever had."

"Dean, you of all people know I'm not the best with relationships. My lousy marriage is the best example around," Mac pointed out, exasperated by answering questions he had already asked himself. "Stacy doesn't need any more pain."

"The fear of hurting her is just a cop-out on your part. Tell me something. When the case is finally wrapped up and you feel you have no legitimate reason to go see her, except for just wanting to see her, are you going to admit that reason? Or are you just going to brush her off like some lamebrain bimbo? You know, in the beginning I wondered why she seemed so angry about us, and now that I know I can understand. What you're afraid of deep down is she'll string you along, until you've fallen for her like a ton of bricks, and then she'll drop you. Right?"

Mac grimaced. "Right," he muttered, tossing the crumpled beer can into a nearby wastebasket.

"Nah. She doesn't seem the type to do something that rotten. As for your falling, I wouldn't worry, because I'd say you're already well on your way to that condition—and buddy, there's no known cure."

Chapter Eight

"I just want you to know that the police have questioned me in regard to my using your agency, Ms. Harris," said the portly woman facing her. "I do not like having my privacy invaded."

Stacy stifled a sigh. "I'm sorry if you were bothered by them, Mrs. Newton, but it's procedure for them. The Crenshaws had been robbed a few days ago, and they are going to talk to their neighbors." She glanced at the open file folder in front of her. The Newtons were one of her best customers, so she couldn't afford to upset the already irate woman.

Mrs. Newton adjusted her mink coat around her shoulders. She narrowed her eyes as she gazed at Stacy and threw out a question. "Then why was I asked about you specifically?"

Stacy reminded herself that patience was a virtue. She knew she deserved sainthood for dealing with this rude woman without doing her bodily harm. "Because the Crenshaws are clients of ours," she explained. "They need to explore every avenue, Mrs. Newton. I'm sure you can understand that."

"Yes, I certainly do. That is why we won't be needing you when we fly to Paris next month." Now she'd dropped her bomb, Stacy thought. "I don't like the police walking through my house, Ms. Harris. The best way for me to insure that won't happen again is to get rid of the cause."

Stacy stood up and planted her hands on her desk. "Then I suggest you also fire your gardening service, dog groomer, security system, household help and the man who comes to detail your car!" She took a deep breath, realizing she had just done the unforgivable. She had lost her temper with a client.

Mrs. Newton glared at her. "You can send the bill to our business manager." She stalked out of the office.

"Wow." Janet crept into the office after the front door had been slammed shut.

"Oh, Janet," Stacy moaned, burying her face in her hands. "I have never lost it with a client before. Why did I have to do it with Mrs. Newton?"

"Her only good point was that she paid her bills on time. Don't worry about it," she soothed. "Oh. Timothy called and asked if he could stop by for a minute."

"Only if he isn't looking for work." Stacy gazed at the stack of files containing names of clients who had canceled her services. It was growing at a slow but steady rate. She wet her dry lips. "Janet, I'm going to be honest with you. If this continues, I'll have no choice but to close the office."

"Don't worry about it just yet," Janet ordered. "They're going to catch the thief, and we'll be rolling again. You'll see. Everyone who left will come back with fervent apologies, begging us to take them back."

"Except Mrs. Newton," Stacy muttered. "I have a vague idea that she'll look elsewhere. Or she'll buy a Doberman pinscher."

"Why should she? She already looks like one," Janet pointed out. The two women looked at each other and burst into giggles.

"That certainly broke the somber mood," Stacy admitted, leaning back and propping up her feet on her desk. She smoothed her taupe wool skirt over her knees.

"Tell me something. Are you feeling sorry for yourself because Lieutenant McConnell hasn't been around in the last week, or because you don't know what else to do with yourself?"

"No, I am not feeling sorry for myself. And no, I don't care that Lieutenant McConnell hasn't been around for the past week." Stacy studied her nails as if they were suddenly of great importance.

Janet gave an unladylike snort. "Tell me another story, Mom."

"He doesn't think he's good relationship material," Stacy muttered. "I wanted to tell him that he's full of it."

Janet perched herself on the edge of the desk and idly swung one leg back and forth. "I don't know what he's worrying about. When the two of you are together, the air fairly sizzles! Didn't you once say he's divorced?" She leaned across the desk and opened the top drawer, withdrawing an emery board. Grinning slyly at her boss, she began smoothing a ragged nail.

"Some hardworking group we are," Stacy dryly observed, without altering her indolent posture.

"I'm not going to let you ignore my question." Now finished, Janet dropped the emery board onto the blotter that doubled as a calendar.

Stacy didn't like this subject at all. "I don't think this is because of his divorce. It's me."

"Then do something about it," her secretary advised. "Jump the man's bones. I know I would. There's something about that low, gravelly voice that sends shivers down my spine.'' She demonstrated her thoughts. ''Not to mention the way he fills out a pair of jeans.''

''Yes, he does that beautifully,'' Stacy agreed.

''What are you planning on doing this November? Hawaii again?''

Janet's boss shook her head. ''I thought I'd try something different. Maybe the desert.''

''Mmm, a big resort with yummy cowboys. Make that reservation for two. I'll stay out of your way, if you'll stay out of mine.'' Janet laughed.

''Do you mind if I come in?'' asked a shaky-sounding male voice.

Startled by the unexpected company, they looked up to see Timothy standing hesitantly in the doorway. He looked as if he'd run if he heard one wrong word.

Stacy greeted the elderly man warmly. ''It's about time you showed your face. Come in. Don't mind us. We're just sitting here, feeling sorry for ourselves.''

Timothy entered and took the seat closest to Janet. ''Yes, I heard about all the robberies. Do they have any clues?''

''Not a one,'' Janet said laconically. ''Would you like some coffee, Timothy?''

He shook his head. ''I just wanted to remind you that I am ready to work again.''

''I'll keep that in mind if anything new comes in.'' Stacy privately doubted it would happen, considering what was going on, but figured that she could always think positively.

The faded eyes behind the bifocals showed concern. ''Things are not going well?''

Stacy smiled. While she adored the elderly man, she didn't want to air all her worries. ''Things aren't going well for any of the house-sitting services. In fact, the police were here to talk to everyone while you were away.''

Timothy nodded. "Yes. I found the message from you on my answering machine. That is why I came here on my way to the dry cleaners. Was there a problem? You didn't say if you needed me to work for someone."

"No, it's just that the police wanted to talk to all of my people. In fact, would you be able to go down to the station and see them?" she asked, rustling through her papers to find his file folder. She was glad she'd kept track of the people who hadn't been able to make the meeting, those who'd made other arrangements and those who hadn't.

Timothy looked confused. "I don't know what I can tell them. I don't know anything about the robberies."

"Just tell them that," Janet advised. "And take something to wipe the ink off your hand after they fingerprint you. Talk about a messy procedure!"

His smile was beguiling. "I will take care of everything," he promised. Slowly he stood up. "I must go now. Things to do, you understand, since I was gone for so long." He nodded toward both women. "I'm sure everything will be fine."

Stacy was warmed by his assurance. "That's what we're hoping for," she replied lightly. "Have a good rest of the day, Timothy."

His eyes twinkled at her. "Oh, I will."

Stacy and Janet watched him make his way out of the offices.

"He is such a sweetie." Janet turned toward Stacy. "If only he was thirty years younger."

"If he was, you'd have to fight for him," she warned.

"Speaking of fighting, you're not going to give Mac up, are you?"

The look on Stacy's face was answer enough.

"IF THEY RAISE the price of food any higher, I'll have to quit eating," Stacy muttered, maintaining a tighter hold on the two plastic bags she carried. "Oh, great." She switched one bag to her other hand so she could unlock the door. Pushing the door open with her rear end, she backed into the living room.

The moment she entered, she found the room dark. Since she kept a lamp on a timer so that she would always come home to a lighted room, and she had just replaced the light bulb, she felt off balance for a second. Holding her breath, she edged her way toward the wall, looking for the switch, to see if it might have been somehow flipped off.

When she heard a faint sound coming from the bedroom she didn't think, but simply reacted. She opened her mouth and screamed—and kept on screaming. But Stacy wasn't about to be a passive victim when a dark-garbed figure rushed out of her bedroom. Without thinking of the consequences, she ran forward and kicked out. But the intruder was too swift and pushed her back, causing her to fall and hit her shoulder against the coffee table. Within seconds he was gone.

Stacy blinked, stunned by the events of the past few moments. Several of her neighbors appeared to see what had happened. She accepted one neighbor's offer of assistance, and he turned on the lights—to reveal cushions thrown around and broken dishes scattered across the kitchen floor. But her bedroom had suffered the most damage. The mattress and box spring were on the floor, and the contents of her closet and dresser had been tossed around the room.

"Oh, my," she moaned, looking at the destruction around her.

"I called the police," one woman told her, looking around with obvious interest. So that she could recount the details the next day to her friends, no doubt, Stacy thought wryly.

Stacy picked up her purse and searched its interior. "There's only one person who can help me." She picked up her phone and dialed a number scrawled on the back of a business card.

Mac arrived ten minutes after the uniformed officers did. He conversed with them for a few moments, then turned his attention to Stacy, who sat on the couch, looking as if she were encased in ice.

"You have a unique way of cleaning house." He sat down beside her.

"I never had that lock on the patio door replaced," she said in a monotone. "They said that's how he got in."

"Stacy, did you look around to see if anything was taken?" he asked gently, taking care not to touch her, although all he wanted to do was draw her into his arms and protect her.

She nodded. "Nothing. It doesn't make any sense, Mac. My jewelry is still in the chest, unless I came in before he could take it, and my stereo system wasn't touched. Correction. It was touched—it was deliberately broken. And the door to my microwave was broken." She stared blindly ahead. "A lot of my clothes were ripped." She glanced at the police officer who was taking notes. "They tried to infer it was a spurned lover. I told them they were nuts."

He tried to shake her out of her lethargy. "Could they be right?"

She turned her head and glared at him; her first sign of life, he thought. "There has been no one in quite a while. Are you happy to hear that?" She bit out the words in a low voice. "One also brought up the robberies, suggesting the break-in might have something to do with those. These guys remind me of a couple other blue uniforms from years ago.

They all have the same tender bedside manner,'' she said caustically.

Mac muttered a few choice obscenities. "Look, you can't stay here. Why don't you pack up a few things and I'll drive you over to Amanda's?"

She shuddered. "I don't want anything out of that bedroom."

"Okay, wait a minute." He got up and walked over to one of the officers and spoke to him in a low tone before returning to Stacy. "Get whatever you do want to take with you, and I'll drive you over there now."

"I can drive myself. My car escaped injury," she argued.

He stood fast. "I will drive you. Now, get what you need."

Too weary to argue, Stacy picked up her purse. "What about the apartment? Right now, it's ripe for anyone else who decides to avail themselves of my jewelry and what's left of my stereo."

"Bring your jewelry with you. Dean's on his way over here and will wait for a locksmith. Your door locks will be changed, and locks will be put on all the windows," he informed her.

"Oh, well, why didn't I think of that?" she said with a touch of her old spirit.

Before Stacy began to realize just how much Mac was taking charge, she'd been ushered out to his car.

"Nice car. I bet all the thugs can't miss you in this." Stacy stood back and studied the dark, nondescript four-door sedan. "What do you call it?"

"Generic." He unlocked the passenger door and guided her inside.

Stacy wrapped her coat more closely around herself and watched Mac switch on the heater; he directed the flow of warm air toward her.

"Thank you for coming," she murmured.

He smiled at her ultrapolite tone. "You're very welcome." He turned on the engine and backed out of the parking space.

They drove in silence for several minutes. "Mac, do you think that officer was right? That this was somehow connected with the other robberies? And don't give me the runaround. Tell me what your gut instinct is. Please?" She half turned in the seat.

He took pity on her. "Let's just say I wouldn't be surprised. Mainly because nothing was stolen. The word will be that you surprised the burglar before he had a chance to steal anything. The broken appliances can be for any of several reasons. Let that story stand, all right?"

She nodded reluctantly. "But that doesn't solve it, does it?"

"Only if they find any fingerprints. I'll look over the report in the morning and see what it says."

"Mac," she said in a small voice that bordered on tears.

He immediately pulled to the side of the road; the moment the car was parked, he drew Stacy into his embrace. With her head cradled against his shoulder and his arms around her, he could feel the tremors moving through her body.

"This hasn't been too easy for you, has it?" he murmured, rubbing her back with slow, soothing strokes.

"I'm beginning to think my life is turning into a never-ending Friday the thirteenth," she wailed, curling her arms around his waist under his jacket. Just the comforting warmth of his body and familiar scent of his skin was enough to make her forget her earlier fears. "I'm afraid, Mac."

He closed his eyes. He didn't want to tell her that he wasn't feeling too confident about all of this, either. "Are you afraid it might happen again?"

Her laughter trembled as much as her body. "We both know something will happen, except next time it's not going to be a near miss on the street or just my apartment trashed."

Mac gently pushed her away, keeping hold of her shoulders. He lowered his head to look at her directly. "Why do you think that?" he demanded.

"Because I'm the one losing more business than the other agencies. One of my clients came in today, objecting to your people showing up. She claimed an invasion of privacy." She blinked furiously to stem the tears that again threatened to fall.

"Lenore Newton," he guessed.

"Exactly."

He carefully moved her back and turned to switch on the engine. Before he changed gears, he turned around again and kissed her lightly on the lips.

"You're not going to come out the loser in this battle, Stacy. I promise you that."

"I know." She sighed.

He cocked an eyebrow at this expression of her implicit trust in him. "I do have a hunch that whoever is behind this is trying to drag you into it."

"If that's the case, I wish I knew why."

Mac changed gears and slowly drove back onto the street. "So do I, honey, so do I."

Stacy mentally hugged the endearment against her as they finished the drive to Amanda's house.

Just as she'd predicted, Alice hovered over her like a mother hen, and Amanda insisted on making sure that Stacy hadn't been hurt when the thief pushed her against the coffee table. She calmed down considerably when Stacy was able to assure her that she had nothing more than a bad bruise.

"But I would like to go to bed now." Stacy smiled apologetically at Mac. "I feel drained."

"That's expected," he replied. "But I want to meet with you tomorrow, so we can go over a few things."

She nodded. "How about we meet for breakfast?"

"Fine. I'll pick you up at eight."

"Come on, lamb, I'm putting you in a hot tub," Alice insisted.

Stacy halted in front of Mac first. "Thank you for being there," she said softly, leaning down to kiss him. Then she followed Alice out of the room.

Amanda chuckled. "Alice isn't happy unless she has someone to take care of. When I had a cold last winter, she kept coming in with hot drinks and juice. I got better out of self-defense."

Mac grinned. "Sounds like my mother. She believes in the healing properties of mustard plasters."

"Oh, dear. Do your parents live around here?" She refilled his coffee cup.

"No. After my dad retired, they moved back to where he grew up: Tyler, Texas. He has a garden to putter around in, and my mom cans what he grows."

"It sounds as if they have relaxing down to a science." Amanda smiled and shifted her position in her chair. "Do you have any brothers or sisters?"

"One brother. He's married and has three kids." He hoped that would stop her questioning.

"And you don't."

Mac began to understand how it felt to be interrogated by an expert. "Cops and marriage don't mix." He settled on his old standby statement. "My own marriage and divorce are more than adequate proof of that."

"If two people love each other enough and are strong in that love, it won't happen. Surely not all of your co-workers are divorced?"

He sat back, beginning to enjoy this. "No. Many have never been married, such as Dean."

Amanda fixed him with a look that said she knew exactly what he was doing. "I get more information from my kids than you're giving me."

"Perhaps because I'm not exactly sure where this conversation is heading," he retorted.

Amanda poured herself more coffee. "You don't like having the tables turned on you, do you?"

"No, I don't."

She nodded. "At least you're honest."

"It's part of my job. Amanda, I'll do whatever is necessary to keep Stacy safe," he vowed.

She smiled. "I know that. Actually, I see you as the best thing to happen to Stacy in a long time. She's come a long way these thirteen years. When she came to live with Russ and me, she was still a rebellious teenager hell-bent on getting into more trouble." She ran her fingers over her gold wedding band. "It took a lot of patience and understanding to get through to her. I'm proud to say we finally did."

"That's one thing I can understand. How did you gain custody of her?" he asked, curious to hear what she would say.

"An associate of our clinic treated Laura Markham," she explained. "We had been friends of the family for many years, so one of us couldn't do it. Actually, Jonathan had asked us if we would be Stacy's guardians, if anything happened to him. This was about the time Laura had started drinking heavily. When Stacy started getting into trouble,

Jonathan insisted she come to the clinic for counseling, but she arranged in some very creative ways to miss every appointment.''

"I'm sure her old man didn't appreciate that," Mac murmured, easily remembering the cold-eyed man who'd had an even colder nature.

Amanda sighed. "No, it only brought on more battles. There are a few things I will tell you. Stacy did what she did, because she felt it was the only way she could gain attention from her father."

"She got that all right," Mac said dryly.

"Not really. At least, not the kind of attention she wanted. It wasn't until much later that she came to terms with the fact that, no matter what she did, he wouldn't have cared. He only required his wife and child to trot out in front of the public. Then they were to behave impeccably, as befits a politician's family. Otherwise, they were to retreat into the background until they were needed again," she explained.

"Yeah, I remember the newspaper pictures. I always figured he threatened her with bodily harm to get her to behave."

"Stacy could have been a model daughter with excellent grades in school and all the right friends, but Jonathan wouldn't have cared. All that ever mattered to him was his political career. He saw Stacy as a daughter who was doing everything possible to embarrass him. But he couldn't see the reasons she did it." Amanda shook her head sadly, recalling the past in painful detail. "He never loved her, Mac. The girl who came to live with us was sullen, unloved, and didn't care what happened to her. It was all because deep down she blamed herself for her father's death, and for her mother's having to be sent to a sanitarium."

Mac frowned. He leaned forward, swinging his clasped hands between his knees. "Yes, she told me about that, but she still hasn't worked it all out."

"That's something that's easier said than done."

He cocked his head to one side, eyeing Amanda. She was talking very freely about the woman who was slowly driving him crazy. "Amanda, you're a wonderful lady, and Stacy is certainly enough to get a man to sit up and take notice, but..." He let out a deep breath, wondering how to explain something he still didn't fully understand.

"But she's a part of your case, and you have to remain objective," she finished.

He nodded. "Exactly."

Amanda studied his face, trying to discover his innermost thoughts without him being aware of her close scrutiny. "And you're afraid to see where your feelings will take you when the case is over. You should see, you know. You'll regret it if you don't." She might have been holding the ever-present pad with her pencil poised as she waited for his reply. "Tell me. Is it the age difference, your previous marriage, the case or just you?"

Mac threw back his head and laughed, rubbing his head with one hand. "Do all psychiatrists talk like you?"

"Of course—it's one of our best points." Amanda's smile disappeared. "Don't sell yourself short, Mac. I watched the two of you at the restaurant, and while you both tried very hard not to notice each other, the sparks were definitely there. I have an idea you two are very good for each other."

"You're speaking like my mother," Mac said wryly.

"I'm speaking as Stacy's mother. I've seen and heard enough to know you two could have something special, if you want it. Don't blow it," she warned, as a warm smile curved her lips.

Chapter Nine

Stacy knew she was acting all too anxious by waiting near the living-room window to watch for Mac, but she didn't care. The moment she saw his car pull into the driveway, she smoothed her hands down her short denim skirt. Pulling at the hem of her dark gold cable knit sweater, she opened the front door and walked outside. She knew it might seem corny, but she hoped to look like a ray of sunshine for him.

"Are you in a hurry to leave or something?" he inquired in an amiable tone, leaning over to push open the passenger door for her.

"I didn't want to keep you waiting." She flashed him a bright grin and pulled the door shut.

Mac kept his eyes on her legs. "When it's you, I don't mind waiting one bit."

She wrinkled her nose and slipped on a pair of oversize sunglasses. "I just hope we're going somewhere that has good strong coffee. If I don't have a couple cups first thing in the morning, I tend to turn violent."

Mac snatched her purse off her lap and began searching through the contents.

Stacy grabbed it back. "What do you think you're doing?"

He held up his hands in self-defense. "Making sure you haven't done any shopping in Tijuana lately."

"Just drive, McConnell. You promised me breakfast, and I intend to see you keep your promise."

He chuckled as he backed the car down the driveway and waited for another car to pass, before pulling onto the street. "Yes, ma'am."

"WHEN YOU TOLD ME you were taking me to breakfast, I didn't expect such luxurious surroundings." Stacy picked up one of her strips of French toast and dipped it into the small container of syrup. She glared at him across the Formica-topped table, but he just ignored her. "I swear, McConnell, you take a lady to only the best places for a meal."

"They make great coffee here," Mac said, defending his choice and digging into his own meal with gusto. "That's all you mentioned you really cared about."

"That's the only reason you're still alive." She braced her elbows on the tabletop. "Mac, real restaurants serve breakfasts, and many of them generally serve great coffee. A real restaurant doesn't have large plastic clowns sitting outside, asking to take your order."

After he finished his egg and sausage patty, Mac picked up his coffee cup and drained it. "Just a minute." He got up to have his cup refilled and returned to sit down beside her. "Okay, to work. I'm going to pick your brain, Stacy. I want you to think back on anything, even the most innocuous happenings, within...oh, the past year or so." He pulled his notebook out of his shirt pocket.

She groaned. "Mac, the most innocuous happenings might include my going to the dentist and having my hair cut."

"Do you ever see any of the kids you used to run around with? Talk to them on the phone, socialize with them?"

Stacy shook her head. "None of the above. I think we all wanted to forget those times, and the only way we could was by not keeping in touch. Although I did run into Pam Ferris once."

His interest picked up. He quickly scribbled the name in his book. "Pam Ferris? Which one was she?"

"She thought she was another Cher. Since then she's cut her hair and doesn't wear so much makeup anymore. She looked very conservative—the ultimate suburban matron."

"When did you see her?" he asked.

She shrugged. "Oh, a few months ago."

Mac grabbed one of Stacy's French toast strips and munched on it reflectively. "Where did you see her?"

Stacy shot him a wry look. "Help yourself, why don't you?" She mentioned a nearby mall. "I saw Pam at the Galleria. She was coming out of Nordstrom as I was going in. We traded hellos. She told me she was married to a dentist and had two children. She was happy, and her husband didn't know anything about her past, since he'd grown up back East, and she'd pretty much severed all ties with us. Meaning, if I ever saw her again and her husband was with her, she would appreciate it if I didn't tell him exactly how we used to know each other. You would have thought I was Public Enemy #1," she concluded sadly.

"So you got on the defensive and proudly informed her you would go her one better and pretend to not even know her," Mac guessed.

Head downcast, she stirred her coffee, although she hadn't added anything to the black brew. "You got it."

He reached across the table and grasped her hand, lacing his fingers through hers. "Okay, we'll scratch Pam. Anyone else?"

Stacy shook her head. "I think some of them moved away. I heard somewhere that Chad Stone moved to New

York after he got out of that reformatory, but that's all I know." Her face flamed with color. "He and I, well . . ."

He understood what she was getting at: she and Chad had been a couple back then. "I'm surprised he never tried to contact you after he was released from the reformatory," he commented, now remembering the dark-haired boy who'd hated all authority and had appeared to want to draw his girlfriend, the young Stacy, into a life of crime.

"One thing Russ and Amanda asked of me when I came to live with them was that I not keep in contact with any of those kids, especially Chad. I have no idea what's happened to him over the years. And to be honest, I really don't care."

He shook his head. "Sorry, I can't see you giving in that easy. Remember, I knew you back then."

She tightened her jaw. "I did it because they asked. They didn't demand or order me to stop seeing them. They *asked*. Since they put so much trust in me, the least I could do was honor their request."

Mac made a note to see what he could find out about Chad Stone. "Would you say you've made any enemies?"

Stacy wrinkled her nose. "Other than Warren Kramer?"

He nodded, easily recalling the name. "He owns one of the other house-sitting services."

"Sure does." She idly noticed several uniformed officers seating themselves at a nearby table and glancing their way. "No wonder you know about this place." She gestured toward the occupied table.

He looked around and nodded to one of the men. "Okay. Enough fooling around, think hard," he urged. Mac moved his hand toward another one of her toast strips—only to have his hand slapped.

"Get your paws off my toast."

"You're assaulting a police officer, lady," Mac warned, but the twinkle in his eye said something entirely different. Looking into those eyes that glittered gold and green, he threw any doubts he might still have had out the window. Amanda was right; he couldn't walk away from Stacy when this was all over. Not if he wanted to have a real life. He wondered how he was going to tell her that he had changed his mind about seeing her in the future, without sounding like an idiot.

"Don't tell me, Lieutenant. You're using a new interrogation technique."

Mac closed his eyes and cursed under his breath. Keeping his arm around Stacy, he slowly turned his head and looked up.

"Morning, Captain," he greeted the older man, whose cold blue eyes moved over the two figures seated so closely together.

"I've come to learn that your investigative technique is most unusual, but this kind of behavior is not professional, Lieutenant," Captain Henderson observed. "I suggest we have a talk in my office when you're finished here."

"Are you Lieutenant McConnell's superior in this case, Captain?" Stacy asked in a pleasant voice.

The man looked her over as if she were some kind of loathsome insect. "What about it?" It didn't seem to bother him that he was treating her rudely.

She smiled ever so sweetly, which left Mac wondering what was coming next. "Then you should be proud of Lieutenant McConnell and Sergeant Cornell for working so hard on this case. We, the public, hear so many terrifying stories about the police that it's always gratifying to know that they're so diligent in seeking out the criminal element. I'm sure they learned this professional technique from your shining example."

The older man appeared completely disarmed by her compliment. "Yes. Well, we try our best," he mumbled, shooting Mac a suspicious look, as if Stacy were not to be completely trusted. "I'll see you in my office later, McConnell." He walked away quickly.

Mac saluted her with his cup of coffee. "Aren't you afraid you might have laid it on just a bit too thick?"

"If the man truly has political aspirations, he doesn't dare antagonize a voter, even one who's a suspect in a robbery case." Stacy fought him for the last piece of toast and won. "Are we finished with business now?"

"I guess so. Why? Do you need to get into your office?"

She glanced at her watch. "Not really. I called Janet to warn her I might be late. I wouldn't turn down another cup of coffee."

He caught her hint and rose from the table to get two more cups. Once again he slid in next to her, handing her one of the cups.

Stacy stared down into the dark brew. "When this is all over, what do you say we run away to a tropical island that has no idea what crime is?" she suggested whimsically.

"It sounds good to me. No one could hide a gun under a loincloth," he agreed. "I'll even make the reservations for our getaway."

She half turned, reaching for his hand under the table. "I mean it, Mac." Her tone took on a new urgency. "I wish we could be in a place where your case and my business couldn't interfere, and we could turn into brand-new people."

He squeezed her fingers. "I don't need a brand-new Stacy. As far as I'm concerned, the old one is just fine."

Her smile wobbled as she looked into his dark eyes. They spoke so eloquently when he cared to bare his thoughts. It hadn't taken her long to notice that Mac didn't reveal them to many people. "I'm glad we have this chance, Mac. In fact, if we can't have the desert island, I'll settle for the next-best thing. When it's over, I'll just have to kidnap you and take you to a place where no one will find us for at least fifty years."

Mac wished he could do more than smile at her. But he couldn't. He was aware of eyes watching them with great interest. While bringing Stacy here, among men who knew him, might have been a mistake, he didn't care. He was happy just to be with her. He mulled over her lighthearted suggestion of running away. The more he thought about it, the more he liked it.

"Tell you what. You do the kidnapping and I'll provide the getaway car."

She literally glowed. "You're on."

WHEN STACY entered her office like a whirlwind, Janet knew something was up.

"What happened to you?" She eyed her boss's less than professional clothing.

"My apartment was broken into last night, and I spent the night at Amanda's," she answered, opening file drawers and pulling out folders. "I have had more than enough incidents happen to me, and I'm now determined to take care of this myself."

"Meaning what?" Janet watched her boss dump the folders onto her desk and arrange them in a neat stack.

"Sit," Stacy ordered, dividing the pile into two and sliding one half toward the edge of the desk.

Janet did just that and stared at the folders. "Okay, I give up—what am I doing?"

"We are going over every employee background to see if we can find something the police missed. In fact—" Stacy leaned over and pushed the folders together "—we're going to take turns reading the files and discussing the person, to see if they might have said something that doesn't go with what they wrote down on their application."

Janet stared at her boss as if she had lost her mind. "You have got to be kidding."

"No, I'm not." She attacked the first file with grim determination.

"Can I get some coffee first?" Janet begged, standing and moving toward the door.

Stacy glanced up, surprised by the question. "Of course."

"You want some?" Janet asked.

"Hmm?" Stacy was already immersed in her reading.

Janet returned with two cups of coffee and seated herself once more. "Who first?"

"Lauren."

Janet slumped in her seat, sipping her coffee. "I knew I should have made a dental appointment for this morning."

"WHAT THE HELL did you think you were doing?" Captain Henderson yelled. He walked around his office, waving his arms like a madman.

"I was having breakfast."

Mac's calm reply only fueled the other man's ire. "Having breakfast with a prime suspect? What else have you had with her?"

Mac's black eyes glittered with fury. He pushed himself out of his chair. "You're getting out of line...."

"*I'm* getting out of line? You're the one who's jeopardizing the case, not to mention your career."

Mac wasn't about to count to ten. He could have cared less if he lost his temper or not. "Ms. Harris's apartment was broken into last night."

"I know. I have a copy of the report here." Captain Henderson picked up several sheets of paper and shoved them under his nose. "How do we know her accomplice didn't get greedy and ransack her apartment for money? Or perhaps for her share of the stolen goods?"

Mac would have suggested that was a bit farfetched, considering there were still no concrete clues, but he knew that that kind of statement could get him thrown off the case. Right now, he knew he had to remain there for Stacy's sake. The next detective might try and convict her on her past alone. He was even prepared to eat a little crow....

Someone knocked on the door and opened it. It was an excited Dean.

"We got a clue," he announced triumphantly. "Not a big one, but a clue."

The two men turned, their previous fury now forgotten.

Dean strutted in, looking proud of himself, one hand hidden behind his back. "Gentlemen, our thief is getting a little careless. Probably because the other robberies have been so successful. Ten to one he's feeling cocky, which can only make him sloppy." He brought out his hand and held up three clear plastic evidence bags.

Mac took them from him. "Is this from the Crenshaw break-in?"

Dean nodded. "The lab says the hair in envelope #1 is dyed and doesn't match anyone's in the Crenshaw household. And they haven't had company in the last couple months. The button is the kind you find on cheap flannel shirts—also nothing you'd find in Mr. Crenshaw's designer wardrobe. The third is a corner torn from a business card. There's only a few letters we can see, but we're working on it. The paper used for the card is expensive, and since we have a few letters on it to see the ink color and kind of print, we should have little problem in tracking it down." He smiled confidently, but his look in Mac's direction told another story. There were many print shops in the Los Angeles area. Although they would be able to rule out some of them because of the paper alone, it would still mean a lot of legwork.

"Then what are you standing around here for?" Captain Henderson glared at both men. "Find out where the card comes from. I want some answers by the end of the day." He turned to Mac. "As to earlier this morning, I trust that will remain confidential business."

Mac knew exactly what he meant; Stacy's disclosure. "Of course, Captain."

"Then get out of here and do your job!"

They exited and returned to their desks. Dean opened a drawer and pulled out a telephone directory.

"The man is all heart," he declared.

"Yeah, I wonder how he ever passed the department physical without one," Mac muttered absently. But his mind was clearly elsewhere as he studied the three bags, staring the longest at the last one. Something about it scratched at the back of his mind and left him feeling uneasy. He was certain he had seen this kind of card before. He just wished he could remember where.

THE DAY PASSED all too slowly for Stacy and Janet; they discussed each applicant in full detail, picking each other's brains for the tiniest scrap of information that might help. The phone remained silent, so when lunchtime came, they were more than happy to leave the office. By midafternoon they were bleary-eyed and battling full-blown headaches.

"If I look at one more application, I am going to scream," Janet announced, standing up and stretching her arms over her head. "Stacy, we have to stop. My brain is turning into oatmeal."

"We can't. We're only up to the *H*'s," she argued.

"Stacy, either we stop or I'm going to forget how to read," she said slowly. "Better that than go blind."

Stacy threw the folder onto the desk and leaned over, bracing her elbows on the littered surface and rubbing her aching temples with her fingertips.

"Why does everything have to look so logical on paper?" she moaned, closing her eyes. "I had no idea so many people led such normal lives."

"Stacy, I don't want to sound like a pessimist, but I don't think we're going to find anything here. People with some dirt in their past aren't going to put it on a job application."

She nodded reluctantly. "You're right, but I guess I hoped something would suddenly appear to enlighten us." She looked up when she heard the outer door open and close.

"Detective McConnell," Janet greeted their visitor.

"Hi, Janet." He smiled at her before turning to Stacy. He dropped a small metal ring with two keys hanging from it. "Here's your new keys. I suggest the only person to have an extra be Amanda."

"Sounds fine to me." She picked up the ring.

"How about some dinner?"

Stacy mulled over his offhand invitation. "That's the best offer I've had all day." She pointed a warning finger at him. "But I want a real restaurant that doesn't have a clown in front or the orders yelled over a microphone."

"No matter what you say, they still have..."

"Yes, I know, the best coffee in town," she finished for him with a smile.

"Go ahead. Take her with my compliments," Janet urged fervently. "I'll lock up."

Mac looked at the desk covered with file folders. "Did an earthquake hit and no one told me about it?"

"No, we're just doing a bit of housecleaning," Stacy said breezily, looping her purse strap over her shoulder. "We don't want another misplaced file incident."

He sensed she wasn't telling the truth, but he wasn't about to push the issue just now.

"Any particular kind of food you're in the mood for?" Mac asked as they walked out to his car.

Stacy waited while he unlocked the passenger door.

"Italian," she decided.

He nodded. "Italian it is." He eyed her slyly. "How about Chuck E. Cheese? They have Italian food, so to speak."

She groaned at the idea of eating in the noisy pizza parlor. It catered to children with its video games and various other types of entertainment. She punched him in the arm. "No way. Something a little more sane and quiet, if you please."

Mac knew just the spot; a place where they could dine on excellent food, wine and indulge in quiet conversation.

"You rarely talk about yourself," Stacy commented, after they had given their order to the waitress. "Why?"

He shrugged. "Why should I, when you know me so well?"

"I don't know as much as I'd like," she pointed out. "I know that you care more about people than you want to admit you do. That you prefer to hide behind a gruff exterior, trying to let people think you're some grizzled old cop no decent person would dare associate with. And I, for one, know better. I'd hazard a guess that you divide your time between playing by the book when it suits you, and making up your own rules the rest of the time. And I would say the only one to get behind that facade of yours is Dean," she concluded triumphantly.

Mac steeled himself not to shift uncomfortably under her knowing smile. "You think so, huh? You seem to be doing a pretty good job of digging into my thoughts."

"You used to call my father first, instead of throwing me into jail, which I'm sure wasn't standard procedure. You didn't have to call him. There was plenty of proof that I wasn't exactly the smartest kid around, but I did know you bent the rules where I was concerned—and for a couple of the other kids. I also knew you didn't like or respect my father. That was the easiest to tell, since I wasn't too fond of him myself."

"That wasn't hard to guess. You weren't exactly polite to him the times he picked you up." He took a calming sip of wine.

"Ah, but that was expected of me." Her voice grew lower. "I once overheard someone saying that you thought Jonathan Markham was a real jerk for putting up with his bitch of a daughter, and should have just put her over his knee for a good, old-fashioned spanking."

"It might have straightened you out," he observed.

She shook her head. "Come on, McConnell. We both know I needed a full-time father back then, instead of a full-time politician. It took time, but with Russ's help I was able to understand my father's obsession for power. Maybe that's why I used to hope if anyone busted me, it would be you. You tried to understand me. He never did."

"Perhaps because you never gave him a chance," Mac argued.

Surprisingly, instead of arguing back, she nodded. "You're right. I never did, and we both suffered for it."

Then the pizza arrived.

Stacy was furious with herself for bringing up a dead subject instead of concentrating more on Mac. Since the restaurant was filling up and their waitress hovered over them a bit too much, they hurried with their meal and asked for their check as quickly as possible. As they waited for it, she mustered a wan smile and excused herself. After checking to make sure the ladies' room was empty, she pounded her fist against the wall.

"Good, real good, Stacy," she muttered, resting her forehead against the wall. "Some kind of date material you are. You have the man willing to listen to you, and you can't even talk about anything but this stupid case and the past. You better shape up, before you ruin everything beyond repair. After all, you finally discover someone who raises your blood pressure just by looking at you with those dark eyes of his, and has a voice that takes you right to the melting point, and you do something stupid. It will serve you right if he takes you straight home and makes sure to never see you again." Hearing the door open, she hurriedly straightened and moved back to the mirror, where she freshened her lipstick and spritzed on her favorite cologne, including a quick mist under her sweater and between her breasts. She ran her hands through her hair, took a deep breath and sauntered out. Mac was waiting for her near the front door.

"Sorry to keep you waiting." She produced her brightest smile.

He didn't return the smile. "No problem." He held the door open for her and they walked outside, to find it dark; the streetlights were just coming on.

"I understand you live in Sierra Madre."

"That's right."

"Do you have a house or an apartment?" She was determined to get him to talk to her and not retreat, as he was clearly trying so hard to do.

He wondered where her questioning was leading, and decided to go along with it. "A house."

"In one of the canyons?" She meant one of the canyons in the area that was dotted with homes, many built against the hillside, where people couldn't have garages for their cars. They climbed up the hill to their front doors.

"No, just below it."

Stacy nodded. "That's a lovely area up there. It has a very small-town feeling."

As Mac unlocked the car door, something caught his attention. "I want you to do something for me," he said in a low voice. "There's a car at the far end of the parking lot—over your left shoulder—I've noticed it several times before when you and I've been together. Unfortunately, I didn't think anything of it before, because the car isn't unusual. No, don't look around just yet," he ordered urgently. "Play it casual. Drop your purse or something. Then only turn your head just enough to see it, and tell me if you might know the person. Okay?"

Stacy had to resist the urge to stiffen. "All right. Why don't you open the door, and I'll take it from there?" Mac did so, and Stacy pretended to bump into it, dropping her purse in a manner that would cause some of the contents to spill out. Uttering a cry of dismay, she bent to pick them up, shaking her head as if rejecting Mac's offer of help. As she scooped up her lipstick and wallet, she carefully moved her eyes to the side and without looking too obvious, she hoped, caught a view of the parked car. "There's someone inside it," she said softly.

Mac crouched beside her. "I know." He took her arm and helped her up.

Stacy sat back in the seat, forcing herself not to turn around as Mac drove out of the parking lot.

"It's crazy. I'm sure I've seen that car before, but I don't know where." She sighed, feeling frustrated over it all.

"Could it have been the one that tried to hit you that night?" Mac asked, glancing now and then into the rearview mirror. But the darkness and the headlights of the other cars weren't any help in his attempt to determine if they were being followed.

Stacy bit her lower lip and chewed off her lipstick. "It is a dark color," she conceded. "But other than that I couldn't tell you. Did you get the license plate number, so you could run a check?"

"It didn't have a front plate," he replied. "I didn't think it would be a good idea to walk over and see if there was a rear plate. I wouldn't worry too much. I don't think we're being followed."

Stacy made an instant decision. "One good way to find out. Let's go to your place."

Mac was grateful they were at a red light, so that he could stare at her as if she had lost her mind. "What do you think that would accomplish?"

"We'll see if anyone might be following us," she pointed out.

"I can take you home and still find out if we're being followed," he argued.

"Not if the person lives nearby," she told him. "Besides, Sierra Madre isn't as crowded as Pasadena. You'd be able to pick the car out much easier, wouldn't you?"

Mac let out a breath, feeling himself fall deeper. "You watch too many cop shows, you know that?"

Stacy's face broke into a broad smile. "Then I'm right, aren't I? Besides, who knows what would happen if you took me straight home?"

He sighed, hating to listen to logic that sounded way too good. Still, he didn't want to take her to his house; that was his only refuge from the real world—one he'd shared with few people since his divorce, none of them women.

"We'll stop somewhere for a drink to see if the same car pulls in behind us. If it does, I'll confront the driver. If not, I'll take you home. I'll check out the area around the apartment complex first."

Stacy settled back in the seat. She wasn't pleased with Mac's decision, but couldn't think of a good enough way to convince him otherwise.

Mac drove several blocks before turning into the lot of a small lounge. He headed for the far end and immediately switched off the headlights. They sat silently for about ten minutes. Only one car entered the lot.

Mac pushed open his door. "I'm going to take a look around in case the car's parked in front. Keep the doors locked, and if anyone bothers you, honk the horn and don't stop until you see me, understand?" He turned his head.

"I will."

He might have only been gone ten minutes, but to Stacy it was more like a hundred. She huddled in the seat, whipping her head around at the slightest sound. When a dark figure appeared near the car, she started to panic and had reached over to punch the horn button when she realized that this visitor was friendly.

"Did you see anything?" she asked as Mac slid inside.

"Not a thing. Let's check out your neighborhood, then I'll see you inside." He switched on the engine.

"I never realized how dark this place was," Stacy whispered, walking behind Mac as they approached her front door.

He scanned the area. "Don't you have a light over your door?" He frowned at what he saw.

"Yes, but the bulb burned out a couple days ago. Actually, I think there's something wrong with the wiring, because the bulbs keep burning out." She resisted the urge to grab hold of the back of his jacket, reminding herself that she was an adult—an adult who was rapidly becoming afraid of the dark.

"I'll fix it for you before I go. Where are your new keys?" Mac kept her behind him as he entered her apartment.

Stacy viewed the grayish film over her furniture with dismay. "You've got to be kidding."

"They were looking for fingerprints," Mac explained.

"Don't tell me. All you found were mine." She collapsed onto the couch. She hadn't gotten a good night's sleep the night before, and the events of the day were catching up with her.

"Where do you keep your spare light bulbs?" Mac headed for the kitchen.

"In the pantry beside the refrigerator."

He smiled as he found the boxes next to cans of fruit juice. "Strange place to keep them," he commented.

"Not so strange if you used to keep them in the cabinet over the refrigerator, and had four new boxes of bulbs fall on the floor during our last earthquake." Stacy yawned.

"Did you lose anything important?" he asked, choosing the appropriate wattage.

"A glass pitcher of orange juice and my favorite crystal candlestick holders. How about you?" Stacy curled up on the couch and pulled off her loafers.

Mac walked out of the kitchen. "Four bottles of Dos Equis beer and a brand-new, open can of coffee."

She arched an eyebrow. "Interesting. My floor was sticky. Yours was gritty and foaming."

Stacy watched Mac reach up and unscrew the burned-out bulb and replace it with a new one.

"Keep this on all night," he ordered. "And don't forget to use the peephole if anyone comes to the door. If it isn't someone you know, ignore them."

"This is getting scary, Mac." Stacy wrapped her arms around her body in the hope of chasing away the chill in her blood. "I only thought this kind of stuff happened in books or in the movies."

"Not anymore." Mac walked over and enveloped her in his arms. Stacy snuggled as close as possible.

"Mac, I don't say things very well." Her voice was muffled against his shirtfront. "What I tried to say at the restaurant was..."

"I don't want to hear it."

She tipped back her head so that she could gaze into his face. "You will, because it needs to be said. What I was trying to say then was that I felt as if someone gave a damn about me. Even though I was as stubborn as they come back then, and I did my share of inflicting wounds on you, you never really lost your temper with me. I was pretty self-centered back then, but I still noticed that some of the other kids got pushed around and sworn at for their less than impeccable behavior." A tiny smile tugged at the corners of her lips.

His lips echoed that smile. "Less than impeccable, huh? You had ripping my uniforms down to a science. A flick of the wrist, and my pocket was torn off, or I was missing a couple of buttons."

She chuckled, then buried her face against his chest. "It's fate, you know. We're meant to be together, Frank McConnell, and I'm not letting you get away."

"Meaning I should just give in gracefully?"

Stacy's smile grew wider. "You yourself said I'm a very stubborn woman, so you might as well."

Mac lowered his head. "Then I'm more than willing to discuss it."

Chapter Ten

"Are we going to clear the air?" Stacy asked, once they had seated themselves on the couch and she had curled up against his side, her chin propped on her crossed arms.

"This isn't something I'm comfortable with," Mac admitted ruefully.

"No one is, but I learned how to do it at the clinic. Admittedly they said you felt better when you confessed all. I didn't believe it, but when I learned to express my feelings more I did feel freer." She half turned and placed her crossed arms on his shoulder. "The problem is still the case, isn't it? As long as the case is active, ethics tell you the more distance you put between us, the better."

"What's so wrong with that?" he argued, setting his jaw in the stony lines she was getting very used to.

She traced the line of his jaw with a fingertip. "I don't see anything wrong with it. In fact, I think it's very admirable of you." His laughter was strangled in his throat at her feather-light touch. "What's wrong, Mac?" Her voice echoed concern, but her eyes glittered with wicked lights.

"Nothing."

Stacy moved closer, which wasn't as easy as it might have looked, she reflected briefly. "You have an interesting face," she mused, studying him as carefully as an artist studies his subject.

"It wouldn't win any awards." With every breath he took, he inhaled the unique floral scent of her perfume.

"You're too hard on yourself." She continued her tactile exploration, enjoying the sensation of the rough skin under her fingertips. "You have very strong features—the kind that tell a person you might be hard as a rock on the outside, but you're really taffy on the inside." Her nail skimmed the edge of his mouth.

Having had enough, Mac whipped around and grasped her wrist, holding it up between them. "You're playing with fire, Stacy," he rasped.

She looked far from afraid. "God, you're slow, McConnell," she whispered.

"No. I just don't want to screw this up," he said sharply.

"Seems to me I've heard that before, along with how you don't feel we should see each other when this is all wrapped up." This time she didn't look upset, merely interested in his reply. "I'm glad you changed your mind about that."

"Stacy, right now I'm the guy who's keeping you safe from some kind of nut who seems to enjoy frightening you. I have to keep my mind on my work, and when I'm with you it's not all that easy to do," he told her.

She slipped her hand out of his grip and settled it in her lap. "Has that happened to you before?"

"No, but it's happened to others."

A tiny smile appeared. "Ah, but Mac, we go back a long way, remember? I admit you weren't high on the list of people I would have cared to see again, but now that I have, I'm more than willing to take a chance on us."

"I'm sure I wasn't."

"But I didn't throw you out of the office that day, either," she pointed out.

"Let's get back to the subject at hand," Mac interjected, taking her hand once more. "I do want to keep on seeing you, Stacy, but I will ask one thing of you." His expression was pained. "I want you to be honest with me when the time comes, and if you'd prefer not to see me again, you'll say so."

Seeing how serious he was, she swallowed her flippant reply that she couldn't imagine that happening. "I promise, just as long as you give me the same kind of honesty. And that you won't think about our ages or the positions we're in because of the case. Deal?"

Mac nodded. He only wished he could make Stacy understand that it still wasn't going to be as easy as she thought it would be. In so many ways the case lay between them, what with his investigating it and Captain Henderson still wanting to lay the blame at Stacy's door, even if there was no hard evidence. Mac had to be careful to not let anyone think they had a relationship that could seriously endanger the case or Stacy's credibility, not to mention his job. Still, when he looked at her, he hated to admit that he didn't want to be away from her if he didn't have to be. And if that meant tempting fate, well, so be it.

HE STOOD in one of the unlit doorways, watching the detective put in the new light and walk back inside. The orange light once again beamed brightly over Stacy's front door. So far, the policeman had been there for over an hour.

He wondered if it wouldn't be an appropriate punishment for the cop to be taken down, too, along with the high-and-mighty Stacy. He kept smiling. Yes. The more he thought about the idea, the more he liked it. He'd see what he could do.

"I HATE PEOPLE who spend the day smiling like an idiot," Janet grumbled.

Stacy continued doodling absently on a piece of scratch paper. "Why shouldn't I smile?" she asked. "We got two new clients, thanks to dear Mrs. Coffman, and it's sunny outside, even though the weatherman said it was going to rain. What more could a person ask for?"

"That you'll decide to give up the idea of going through all the files," the secretary finished with a relieved sigh. "Tell me something. Does this puppy-dog look have something to do with a certain police lieutenant?"

"Maybe," Stacy sang out, spinning around in her chair. With a broad smile she playfully ran a finger across her lips, as if zipping them closed. Mac had ended up spending more than two hours at her apartment. She'd begun to better understand his reticence regarding them as a couple, and had even conceded that they weren't in an enviable position, thanks to the overzealous Captain Henderson. He would like nothing more than to throw Mac out of his department. Nothing had been said about what exactly would happen later on, but there was no mistaking the fact that both really did want to spend as much time as possible with each other. In fact, Mac was going to come by this evening and drive her to the shelter. Stacy sneaked frequent glances at the clock, but the hands moved too slowly for her satisfaction.

"Well, look who's here." Janet pretended surprise when the door opened, then closed behind their visitor. "Hi, there." Her smile disappeared when she noticed his grim features. "If you don't mind, Stacy, I think I'll get back to my work."

"Stay," Mac ordered without looking at the secretary.

Stacy looked up, surprised by the underlying anger in his voice. "What is going on?"

Mac dropped a clear plastic bag onto the desk. "Just look at it, don't open it," he rapped out before she could pick it up.

Feeling confused by this sudden turn of events, Stacy held the bag between her fingers. "I don't get it."

"What does it look like to you?" His craggy features could have been carved from stone as he stood over her.

Stacy examined the piece of paper. "To be honest, it looks like part of some kind of card. It's too heavy to be stationery."

"It's a business card." Mac looked grim. "In fact, I checked it out. It's from your agency."

"COME ON, Ms. Harris, why don't you make it easy on all of us and tell me what really happened?" Captain Henderson suggested in an unpleasantly oily voice. "We're only here to help you."

Stacy sat in the metal chair, looking at him with no expression on her face. Only the opaque darkness in her eyes indicated that the happy young woman of that morning had retreated from the scene.

"Why don't you give me a hint?" she invited icily.

The older man walked around the desk and perched his bulk on one corner. He ignored Mac, who remained standing behind Stacy, leaning against the door frame. With his arms crossed over his chest and no expression on his face, Mac was giving no one any idea of his thoughts.

"Ms. Harris, we're talking about a very serious crime here," Captain Henderson insisted, his own posture clearly revealing his anger. It was obvious that he had hoped she would break down immediately and confess. He shot Mac a dirty look. The younger man looked back blandly.

"She was apprised of her rights, wasn't she?" the captain snapped at Mac.

He didn't move a muscle. "Yes."

"Don't worry, Lieutenant McConnell did his job strictly by the book," Stacy said flatly. "The only reason I don't have an attorney present is because I don't feel I need one, and that's because I haven't done anything wrong. Unless you want to count my being late in mailing in my car registration last year. Don't worry. I paid the penalty fee." Her brain was rapidly digesting information and trying to figure out why the agency's business card had been found where it shouldn't have been. She hadn't liked receiving the news one bit. "But the moment something is said I don't agree with, I will call my lawyer and keep my little mouth shut until he arrives. And believe me, he hates to make police station calls."

Mac turned away to hide his smile. It was clear that Stacy wasn't going to give the captain the kind of information he had hoped for. When he'd first learned the piece of business card had to be one of Stacy's, he'd felt as if someone had slammed a lead weight into his gut. He didn't want to believe that someone from her agency might be behind the robberies. One thing he knew was that if that was the case, she had nothing to do with it. His instincts screamed out that information, and they hadn't been wrong yet. So instead of worrying about Stacy having to deal with his boss, he sat back and listened to her play Captain Henderson for the fool Mac already knew he was.

"How long have the Crenshaws been your clients?" the florid man asked, quickly changing tactics.

"They haven't used the agency for the past year," she replied.

He pounced on her reply. "Why not?"

Stacy stared him squarely in the eye. "Mr. Crenshaw made a pass at one of my house-sitters," she replied in an even tone. "I contacted him and explained they should find another agency."

"And?"

She shrugged. "End of story. He promptly paid our bill and was smart enough not to call us again. I believe they're using the Clark agency now, but of course, you'd know about that better than I would."

Mac coughed into his closed fist rather than burst out laughing. He still received a look fit to kill from his boss.

Stacy stood up. "Captain, it doesn't seem we're getting anywhere here. If you have any further questions, I suggest you call my attorney." She opened her purse and dug out a business card case. Flipping through it, she retrieved a pale gray card and dropped it onto the desk. "Good day." She turned around and glared at Mac until he roused himself.

"Ma'am." He figuratively tipped his hat.

Stacy sailed by, her head held high.

Captain Henderson took several deep breaths to keep his temper under control. "Did she drive down here by herself?"

"No, I brought her."

"Then take her back to wherever she wants to go, and on the way, see if she'll say anything to you," he ordered brusquely.

He nodded. "Yes, sir."

By the time Mac caught up with Stacy, she was outside, stalking down the street.

"Do us both a favor and get the hell out of my way," she said sharply, brushing none too politely past him.

"Hey, look who came to visit us," said Dean, greeting them with a broad smile. It didn't waver under Stacy's stormy glare.

"Don't say one more cheerful word if you want your head to stay on top of your body," she warned, holding up her hand. "Your partner is already in danger of losing his life if he doesn't leave me alone. I suggest you join him, or I'm going to scream like you've never heard me scream before."

"That's what you think." Mac grabbed her arm and led her toward his car. He pushed her inside and walked around to the other side.

"I hope to see you again when you have more time," Dean called after them. "And may I say, Ms. Harris, you look lovely today."

Mac was the first to break the silence that followed. "You have every right to be angry. Henderson isn't one of the most tactful people around."

"I bet he hated it when the Spanish Inquisition went out of style," she muttered.

"It did ruin his day."

Stacy compressed her lips into a thin line. "Don't you dare make me laugh."

"I wasn't trying to. That's the way he is." He chewed on his inner cheek. "Stacy, I didn't take you down there because I wanted to. Henderson ordered me to bring you down, because of the business card found at the Crenshaws' house. There was no reason for it to be there, since they haven't been your client for so long. You have to admit it's suspicious," he added, glancing into the side-view mirror before making his turn. "One other thing. Do you know anyone with dyed, dark brown hair?"

"More women than I'd like to count. Why?"

"One of the other pieces of evidence was a strand of dyed hair that didn't belong to anyone in the household," Mac told her. "We figure it belongs to the thief."

"And Captain Henderson assumes I dye my hair before every job," she said tartly. "My, the man is a regular Steve McGarret, isn't he?"

"Stacy, I don't like the man any more than you do, but unfortunately, he's still my boss." Mac parked his car next to Stacy's.

She grabbed her purse and opened the door, then half turned. "You have my pity. If you find yourself out of a job, give the agency a call. We might be able to use you—if you pass our new, stringent requirements, that is." She climbed out and slammed the door shut.

"And she was so certain we wouldn't have any more problems," he muttered, watching her get into her own car and roar off. "If you get a ticket, don't come to me to get it fixed!" he yelled out his open window.

"HEY, STACY, did you know the Man was asking when group was over? I think he wants to talk to you," Cal teased, sauntering into the room where the group session was being held. "What'd you do—rob a bank?" He laughed at his own joke.

"No, I just murdered a member of my group who refused to get here on time," she said acid-sweetly.

"I got a good excuse." He dug into the frayed pocket of his denim jacket and pulled out a piece of paper, handing it to her. "I had to see my counselor at school."

"Don't tell me he wrote you a tardy slip," she said skeptically, opening the folded note.

"Yeah, I told him how you didn't like us to be late, so he said he'd write a note to tell you why I was late. See, I didn't want to talk to him 'cause I figured I was in trouble again."

She examined the note. "Hmm, the handwriting is much too neat to be yours, not to mention the words are spelled correctly." She read the neat script and grew more excited with each word. "Cal, he writes here that you have a very high IQ," she said enthusiastically, waving the paper around. "You try to come off as some kind of an idiot, and your school counselor says you are too smart for your own good. I should murder you for trying to act so dumb all the time!"

He ducked his head, his face a bright red. "So what do all those tests saying I'm smart do for me?" he muttered. "It won't get me out of here or let me do what I want."

The others settled back, realizing where the focus of their talk was taking them that night.

"What do you want to do after you graduate, Cal?" Stacy asked. "What do you really want to do?"

The boy looked down at the concrete floor, shuffling the feet shod in beat-up running shoes. "I want to learn to fly."

She leaned forward. "I didn't hear you."

Cal frowned. He knew Stacy couldn't help but hear him. He also knew she wanted him to admit it to the entire group, not just to her.

"I want to learn to fly!" he yelled, his face contorted with pain.

The others looked at him in disbelief.

Maria spoke up first. "You want to fly planes?" She looked at him with new respect. "You mean you want to work for some airline flying all over the world? Cal, that sounds so neat!"

"I don't want to fly for some airline. I want to get into the air force academy and learn to fly fighter jets."

"Man, you saw *Top Gun* too much to think you can do somethin' like that," Artie jeered. "Do you honestly think the government would trust *you* with a jet?"

Cal ignored his taunts and turned to Stacy. "I want to be more than my old man, Stacy. I don't want to work in some factory and get drunk on payday and beat up my wife and kids 'cause there's never enough money in the house. Or join a gang and either get killed or end up in prison for killing somebody." He straightened up and looked at her with none of his previous teen machismo. "I want some respect."

She stared into his eyes, for the first time seeing more than the anger she usually saw there. She jumped up and threw her arms around him.

"Congratulations, Cal, you've realized there's more to life than running around with a gang," she murmured into his ear. "I'm going to tell you what I'm sure your counselor told you. Work hard in your studies, and we'll find a way to get you in. I promise."

"Hey man, a fancy place like the air force academy ain't going to take someone like you," Artie sneered. "They want guys with class. You don't have any."

Cal spun around, his fists clenched. "What do you mean, someone like me? I can be anything I wanna be."

Stacy intervened. "Okay, guys, remember the rules. I'm not into mopping up the blood and gore if there's a fight. As for you, Artie, we look for the positive here. Why don't you sit down and come up with something positive about yourself?"

Artie didn't move closer to Cal, who remained frozen with his fists clenched at his sides, but he didn't back down, either.

"He's startin' to think he's too good for the rest of us," Artie muttered, finally returning to his chair and picking it up from its fallen position before sitting down.

"Cal's looking to the future," Tania pointed out. "What's so wrong with that? I know I don't want to be like my mom and have a kid every year. Stacy said the only way we'll get anywhere is if we do it ourselves. Who says Cal won't make it to the air force academy?"

"I heard, if you want to get in you have to have connections," Maria tentatively pointed out. "What kind of connections can someone like us have?"

Stacy smiled at her. "You'd be surprised." She motioned for Cal to be seated. "Are you absolutely serious about wanting to go to the academy?"

He nodded, obviously afraid to look too hopeful. "I've wanted that for three years. I just never talked about it before. I figured everyone would laugh at me."

"Then we'll see what we can do," she announced. "I can't make any promises, but there's no reason why you can't fight for what you want."

The rest of the time Stacy talked about the need to think positively. She invited their input. Everyone knew the reason for her speech and spoke up, sometimes helpfully, but not always.

"Hey, if he wants to be a general, there's no reason why I can't be president," Artie argued.

"I didn't say I wanted to be a general. I just wanna fly!"

"If Artie was president, I'd leave the country," said Ronnie, one of the other boys.

At the end of the session, Stacy asked Cal to remain behind for a moment.

"Did you tell your counselor you wanted to attend the academy?" she asked, gathering up the papers she had asked them to write for her.

He shrugged. "No. I figured he'd laugh at me."

She grinned. "Cal, if you could stand there and tell this group, telling your counselor would be a snap. But I will suggest you start working on those grades. I don't know what their requirements are, but I have a pretty good idea that good grades are a part of it." She accepted the stack of papers he handed her. "Do me a favor and talk to your counselor. He can advise you better than I can. And do yourself a favor. Work on a more conservative hairstyle."

He rubbed his hand over the lacquered bush of hair. "No problem. I can handle short hair," he said cheerfully.

Stacy shifted her weight from one leg to the other, studying him carefully. "The earrings will have to go, too."

"Okay, I get the hint." As he walked out the open door, he glanced toward Mac, who stood there waiting. "Now you know why I don't come to basketball practice anymore, Coach."

Mac smiled. "I'd drop basketball, too, if I had someone like Ms. Harris to deal with. But there are other nights, you know."

He nodded. "I'll see what I can do."

Stacy stuffed the papers inside her tote. "Sorry, Officer, I left my brass knuckles at home tonight." *How can a man look so sexy, wearing such disreputable jeans and a dingy gray sweatshirt with the sleeves hacked off?* she thought. His jaw was dark with stubble and his eyes appeared slightly bloodshot from lack of sleep, and yet he still looked good enough to eat! She hated him.

"Pity. I was hoping to have the chance to conduct a more thorough search." He leaned against the door frame, his hands pushed inside his jeans pockets. "You do very well with these kids. I'm used to Cal acting like your typical hoodlum instead of a real human being. How did you do it?"

"I treat him like a real human being." Stacy forced herself to keep her eyes away from Mac's lean form. She reminded herself that her earlier thoughts about him had been less than charitable, but it wasn't his fault, right? Right? She breathed deeply several times.

"If you can't decide whether to string me up by my toes or kiss me, why don't you go for the latter?" he suggested. "I wouldn't suffer as much."

She dipped her head to hide her smile. "You sound as if you've been taking lessons from Dean."

"When you've been partners with him long enough and listened to his phone calls with various ladies during that same time period, you pick up a few pointers." Mac watched her put several chairs back into a neat semicircle before gathering up her tote bag and slinging the handles over her shoulder.

"I guess your boss wasn't too happy that he couldn't throw me in jail." Stacy and Mac walked out of the room and down the dull, green-painted hallway. Sounds of voices filtered from various rooms and the basketball court, along with the thump of balls hitting the floor and shouts and curses from the boys.

"He's like the rest of us. He wants to see this case closed. Trouble is, he's in a little too much of a hurry to close it."

"Aren't we all?" she said dryly, flipping off the light switch. "After everything that's happened, I'm beginning to think this all has something to do with me."

"If it did, we would be a little bit closer to a solution. Or it might be some crazy coincidence." Mac walked with her to the parking lot, his senses working overtime, making sure there wasn't anyone lurking in the shadows. Most of the time he spent with Stacy, he felt there was always someone watching them. He didn't like the feeling one little bit. He had a horrible fear that Stacy just might be right—the case might indeed have something to do with her. After all his years in police work, dealing with more oddities than he could count, nothing seemed strange.

WATCHING from his spot in the shadows along the side of the building, the man laughed softly. He was certain the cop sensed he was there, and he liked the idea. His plan was working out much better than he'd expected. With luck it would soon be all over, and Stacy Markham Harris would get exactly what she deserved.

Chapter Eleven

"McConnell, you take me to the most interesting restaurants for lunch," Stacy said, as they returned to her office.

"They've got the best hot dogs in town," Mac argued amiably.

She rolled her eyes. "Next time I'm treating you to lunch. Of course, I would hope you'd wear something a bit more conservative." She eyed his beat-up jeans and equally battered leather jacket. "You know, even during my most rebellious phase I had better taste than you."

"You only shoplifted at the best stores."

She threw back her head and laughed. "You know, I never thought I would be able to laugh about those days."

"Glad I'm good for something." He pushed open her door and waited for her to enter.

"Thank God you're back!"

Stacy faced her wild-eyed secretary. Since Janet rarely overreacted, Stacy wasn't sure she cared to hear the news she had to impart. "What's wrong?"

Janet handed her the phone. "It's your mother."

"Amanda?"

She shook her head. "Laura."

Stacy froze. She had to force herself to pick up the receiver and punch the flashing light.

"Mother?"

Mac couldn't help noticing the wariness in her voice.

"Darling, I'm so glad I could talk to you. It's been so long since you've been up to see me," the low, husky voice murmured into her ear.

She licked her dry lips. "Mother, where's Mrs. Collins? I'd like to speak to her."

"She's off doing whatever. The woman is not reliable at all as a companion. Please, dear, tell me you're coming up to see me soon. Oh, did I tell you your darling boyfriend was up to see me?" Stacy's eyes flew upward to meet Mac, silently accusing him. "He hasn't changed a bit, Stacy. He's still a nice polite boy. I know they used to say horrible things about him, but I couldn't believe them. He was always so polite to me," she said.

Stacy felt an icy chill run through her veins. "Mother, who exactly are you talking about?"

"Honestly, Stacy, haven't you heard one word I've said? You haven't changed in that respect at all. You never seemed to have time for me before, and you certainly don't, now that you have your precious business to run. All you want to do is keep me here among all these horrible people who don't understand me!" All of a sudden the tone coarsened, as did the language.

Mac grabbed the receiver out of Stacy's hand and listened for a moment. *Finish this conversation, now,* he mouthed.

"Mother, I have to go. No, I am not trying to put you off. I'll be up there to see you. Goodbye, Mother." She hung up and walked into her office, collapsing into her chair and burying her face in her hands.

Mac lost no time in following her, with Janet close behind. "What in the hell is going on?"

Stacy pulled her phone toward her and started dialing. "I'm not sure, but I'm going to find out." Her grim features indicated that what she was about to say wouldn't bode well for the person at the other end of the line. "Yes, Beverly Collins please. This is Stacy Harris." She tapped her fingernails on the desk surface as she waited.

"She's Stacy's mother's private nurse," Janet explained to Mac in a low voice. "Mrs. Markham isn't supposed to make any unsupervised phone calls, so I have an idea Mrs. Collins is in a lot of trouble. When Mrs. Markham is on one of her tirades, she tends to call her old friends and tell them how horrible her daughter is. Needless to say, when it first began, the phone company had a great demand for new unlisted phone numbers."

Stacy continued speaking into the receiver. "Mrs. Collins, I just received a phone call from my mother. Two things. How did she get to a phone, and who came to see her?" She listened to the other voice. "What do you mean, you don't know exactly who he is? How could you allow someone you didn't know to visit her? For all you knew, he could have been a reporter using my name!" She frowned at the reply. "She insists she knows him? If something like this happens again, I would appreciate it if you would call me immediately." She sighed. "And would you please tell her I'll be up day after tomorrow to see her? Thank you." She slammed down the receiver and turned to Mac. "A man has been up there to see my mother, saying he was my boyfriend. There's a very short list of people who can see her, and there's no boyfriend on that list."

"Then how did the so-called boyfriend get in?" Mac questioned.

She shrugged. "Who knows? But he somehow got past the front desk and found Mother's room. She recognized him and has said he can come back anytime. Mrs. Collins didn't think to contact me about it, since Mother greeted him like a long-lost son." Her lips twisted in a pained grimace.

Mac sat on the edge of the desk. "What's his name?"

"Mother wouldn't tell her. She's acting as if she's playing some bizarre game. I'm going to have to drive up there and see what I can find out."

Mac shook his head. "*We're* driving up there."

"I think I sense a battle coming on," Janet murmured, discreetly backing out and closing the door.

Stacy glared at Mac. "This has nothing to do with the case, so there's no reason for you to go along."

"If someone is up there, claiming to know you, it very well could have something to do with the case. The same as that piece of your business card showing up at the Crenshaw house."

"You know, maybe I should confess now," she said sarcastically. "He's really my partner, and I send him up to see my mother, so he can hide our loot somewhere in her room. I have a map of the hiding places somewhere."

"This is not a laughing matter," he warned darkly.

"I can't honestly see Captain Henderson letting you go."

His next words effectively erased her smirk. "He will, if I tell him it has a strong bearing on the case."

"I will not have my mother upset over all this," she said, punching out each word with an icy clarity.

"I don't intend to."

Stacy still wasn't about to give up. "I don't like to drive back the same day, so I generally stay overnight."

"I'll pack clean underwear."

She bowed her head. She knew she had lost before she had even begun. "Fine. I'll pick you up around ten, so we can miss the rush-hour traffic."

Mac grabbed a notepad and scribbled on it, then handed it to her. "I'll be ready."

Janet came in after Mac left. "He might be right, you know. Maybe this does have something to do with the case."

Stacy brushed away that idea. "How? Not that many people know where she is."

"Still, Mac's been a cop for a long time. Maybe he senses something you don't, because you don't want to."

"Or maybe I don't sense something, because there's nothing there."

Janet looked at her with pity in her eyes. "You're getting stubborn again. Just give him a chance to do his job, okay?" She turned when the phone rang. "I'll get that."

"I'm sick and tired of being accused of being stubborn," Stacy muttered.

STACY STOPPED THE CAR in front of the single-car garage and got out, looking down the steep street. It was lined with tiny, bungalow-style homes and old-fashioned houses with deep front porches. She turned to look up at the hills that began at the top of the street. From her position she could see the hiking trails etched into the earth and wondered if Mac ever took advantage of them. If it hadn't been for the brown smog smudging the blue sky overhead, she would have thought she was in a small mountain town away from the rest of the world.

She moved the sleeves of the taupe, cream and black plaid blazer and adjusted the cuffs of her orange silk blouse before closing the car door.

"This does not fit the man," she murmured, walking up to the front door and hearing melodic chimes ring through the house when she pushed the doorbell. She stepped back a pace when the door opened, revealing a bare-chested Mac rubbing a towel over his damp hair. For one wild moment, she seriously thought about taking a bite out of the muscled chest that was liberally covered with dark hair. The round gunshot scar and thin line bisecting one nipple didn't detract from his masculinity at all. His smile lighted his face as he leaned over and dropped a gentle kiss onto her lips, then lingered for a second one. She inhaled the musky scent of clean male mixed with after-shave, and knew there couldn't be any better way to start the day than by kissing this man.

"Better than morning coffee," he murmured, stepping back and allowing her to enter. "Come on in. There's coffee in the kitchen." He gestured to the rear. "I'll only be a minute."

She passed through the tiny but neat living room filled with comfortable furniture in beige and green colors, into an equally small kitchen.

"I thought bachelors were typical slobs," she called out, as she poured herself a cup of coffee.

"I was for a while after my divorce," he called back. "Then I got a good look at Dean's place. That was a more than good enough reason for me to clean up my act."

She chuckled. "If he's that bad, why doesn't he get a cleaning lady?"

Mac appeared in the doorway, buttoning a pale blue shirt and tucking it into his tan slacks. In keeping with the more formal wear, he had on brown loafers instead of his usual beat-up running shoes or scuffed boots.

He grinned. "He's had six. They keep quitting on him. One walked in, took one look and walked right out."

Stacy finished her coffee and rinsed the cup in the sink. She turned, leaning back against the counter. "I'd like to set up a few ground rules first." The expression on her face told him this was no joking matter. "My mother knows nothing of what's going on down here, and I'd like to keep it that way. Her emotions are very fragile, and she's easily upset. I don't want you questioning her like some heavy-handed cop.''

His features darkened. ''Have I ever done that with you?''

''Not exactly, but you do have a hard edge when you question people.''

''If so, it's because I need to. But I'm not the kind of man to do it to a woman who's gone through as much as she has,'' he snapped.

''I'm sorry. I guess I'm just edgy.'' *Edgy, because we're about to take an overnight trip, and I don't know what's going to happen during this time. I want him, and if I had any brains at all, I wouldn't even think about it.*

''Aren't we all?'' he said cryptically, turning away. ''I'll get my bag.''

With Mac's overnight bag thrown into the back and Mac himself buckled into the passenger seat, Stacy started up the car and headed for the freeway.

''Where we're going is not your typical sanitarium,'' she told him once they were heading west. ''Actually, it's set up more like a country club.''

''Meaning they charge hefty fees to go with the image,'' he commented.

She nodded. ''Yes, but the medical care there is excellent, and the patients have many advantages.'' She winced. ''Oh, oh. I just sounded like a snob. I don't mean to. It's just that my mother has been pampered all her life, and after what's happened to her, I couldn't have her put into just any sanitarium.'' She drew a deep breath. ''She isn't the same woman I remembered when I was a little girl.''

''Alcohol will do that.''

''My father abandoning us for his career did that. The alcohol was just her means of escape.''

Mac glanced at the dashboard. "I don't see a radar detector."

Her smile delighted him. "Radar detectors are illegal, Lieutenant."

"So are switchblades."

"Ah, but that was for self-protection."

"I'll teach you judo."

She shook her head. "I don't think so. That's such a violent activity."

Mac's reply was decidedly blunt.

"I have a thermos with hot coffee and some commuter mugs in the back," Stacy told him, as she maneuvered a quick pass around a slow-moving van. "There's also a cooler with Cokes and snacks. Once I get on the road, I don't like to stop unless I have to."

After moving the seat as far back as it would go, Mac stretched his legs in front of him. "You make yourself sound like quite a traveler."

"I do enough to make it interesting."

"Such as?"

Stacy thought for a moment. "I took two weeks off last spring and drove through Arizona and New Mexico. I spent part of last November in Bermuda, and in Hawaii the year before."

He couldn't resist asking. "Alone?"

"You're the detective. You figure it out."

Mac watched the way Stacy whipped onto the next freeway, heading up the coast. "You must keep one eye constantly on the rearview mirror to make sure you're not being followed by the highway patrol."

She chuckled. "I once saw a bumper sticker on a California Highway Patrol motorcycle that said Smile, I Might Be Behind You. I swear it!" she told him when she saw his look of disbelief.

"Someone once said to beware of those with a sense of humor. He was right." He paused. "I've done some checking around again with my contacts. So far, none of the stolen items have been fenced around here. Not even any loose gems that were set in some of the custom design jewelry have surfaced."

"I may only be a layman, but I would think that a thief would fence some of the goods for money," she commented. "Or do you think he's waiting until things cool down?"

"Beats me. Since he's mainly taken jewelry and small pieces that can easily be gotten rid of, it is unusual for those kinds of items to be held this long. Obviously, our thief isn't all that money-hungry." He reached around the seat and retrieved the thermos and two mugs, filling one mug only halfway and snapping on the lid. He held it out for Stacy. He then filled the other one for himself.

"How long did it take you to come up with this little bit of information?" she asked, sipping cautiously before setting the mug in a portable carrier.

He grimaced. "About a week."

"A week? I hate to tell you this, but from what I've seen, your line of work can be very boring."

"Yeah, we don't have all those shoot-outs and high-speed car chases the public thinks we have. When I worked undercover in Vice, I wore out more pairs of running shoes just walking."

Stacy wrinkled her brow. "Vice? That means being around hookers and pimps and con men, doesn't it?"

"Yeah," he said slowly, thinking of some of the people he'd met and the things he'd seen that he could never speak of. "I also worked in Narcotics for a while."

"After working Vice and Narcotics, I would think Robbery would be a step down," she said.

Mac winced. "When you happen to offend certain people, you tend to be moved into a less threatening department."

"I don't think Captain Henderson looks upon you as being nonthreatening."

"Captain Henderson has trouble finding his pants in the morning."

The drive passed faster than usual for Stacy, and pretty soon the little red car was moving up the winding streets in the hills overlooking Santa Barbara.

"It's definitely out of the way," Mac said, glancing at the adobe walls and wrought iron gates guarding the occupants' privacy as Stacy turned down a narrow road marked Private.

"That's the way they like it." She stopped at a guard shack and gave her name to the man. She nodded when he indicated she could enter.

"How did your 'boyfriend' get in past that guard at the front?" Mac turned his head right and left, noticing people strolling across lawns or seated on benches. Because there were no white uniforms, he couldn't tell the attendants from the patients.

Her lips tightened. "Something else I'd like to find out. This place charges a small fortune to maintain the patients' privacy. Cheer up. Maybe I'll let you act the part of the typical heavy-handed cop while we're here."

He shot her a wry look. "One thing I've never been is typical."

"That's true." She pulled into a side parking lot and slid between two Mercedes sedans. "So wing it."

Mac climbed out of the car and walked around to help Stacy out. He eyed her legs below her straight, black wool skirt that finished off her professional, not to say formidable image.

"Very nice."

She flushed and turned to pick up her black leather clutch purse. "My mother doesn't believe ladies should wear pants."

"So you dress to please her."

Stacy led the way toward the building marked Administration. "It's the least I can do."

Mac's sharp eyes missed nothing as they entered the luxuriously decorated lobby. Stacy formally greeted the receptionist and explained that she had an appointment with the director. Within a few moments they were ushered into a front office with a bay window overlooking the grounds. A tall, silver-haired woman, wearing a black silk dress rather than a white uniform, smiled at Stacy and offered her hand.

"Ms. Harris, it's nice to see you again." She nodded at Mac. "Please be seated. Now how can I help you?"

"Just tell me how a complete stranger got in here to see my mother, and why I wasn't notified the first time it happened."

The woman's carefully made-up face didn't display a trace of emotion. "I'm afraid I wasn't aware of such a thing happening," she said clearly. "But I will get to the bottom of the matter and ensure it won't happen again. You can be certain of it."

"I don't want your promises, Mrs. Leonard. I just don't want this to happen again," Stacy said coldly. "My mother was brought here because she required long-term care, and because her privacy would be assured. That privacy has been breached, and I am not happy that I was not informed immediately."

The older woman looked uneasy. "Ms. Harris, this is the first time this has happened in all the years your mother has been with us. Plus you must remember she did allow him to return."

Stacy wasn't about to let her off easily. "You had also told me she has trouble making sound decisions. This is only the first time that we know of. I just want to inform you that if it happens again, I will have my mother discharged and find another hospital for her, where I know something like this won't happen."

"Of course," Mrs. Leonard replied, tight-lipped.

Stacy stood up, silently indicating that their talk was over as far as she was concerned. "Now if you don't mind, I'd like to see my mother."

"Talk about one tough lady," Mac murmured as they left the building. "You're very impressive."

"With these people you have to be," Stacy said. "They seem to think they have all the power, and all you can do is remind them who writes the checks. It's a bitchy attitude I don't like, but it's the only one that works around here—the only kind they understand."

"Are you sure we're in a hospital?" He studied another lobby just as well decorated as the administration building. "Their carpet is better than mine."

"You should take a peek at the rooms. They're decorated more like royal suites. Hello, Sylvia." She smiled at a young woman dressed in a pink print dress.

"Ms. Harris." She smiled back. "Bev said you'd be coming in today to see your mother." She gave Mac a questioning look.

Stacy knew why Mac was regarded with curiosity. During all the years she had traveled up to see Laura Markham, this was the first time she hadn't come alone.

"She just returned from the dining room. If you'd like to wait in the solarium, I'll let her know you're here."

"Thank you." Stacy smiled and turned away, adding in a low tone, "They have a rule here that only the bedridden patients can see their guests in their rooms. The ambulatory meet visitors in the solarium or one of the gardens. They like to keep their 'guests' away from their rooms as much as possible, so they are not made to feel ill.''

"I'll send some coffee out for the two of you." The nurse smiled more at Mac than at Stacy.

"They even serve coffee here?" he asked under his breath as they walked down a carpeted hallway to a large sun room. "Something tells me it won't be instant."

"Everything to keep the paying guests happy," she said wryly, leading the way.

The glass-enclosed room was empty.

"I'm surprised they don't have plants in here," Mac commented, walking over to look out the window, where a swimming pool dominated the view.

"They did. One of the patients insisted on eating them, so they had to be taken out. They put silk ones in after that, but he tried to eat them, too."

Mac just shook his head, unsure what to say. When he turned around, he discovered a silver tray with a carafe and three cups on it, along with another serving tray covered with Danish pastry and frosted brownies, all sitting on a drop-leaf table.

"Darling, look at you!"

They turned at the sound of the melodious voice. Laura Markham appeared. Wearing oyster-colored raw silk slacks and a sage-green, tailored silk blouse, her age was not at first apparent. Her expertly tinted golden-brown hair was drawn back in a French twist. It wasn't until she drew closer that Mac noticed the very fine lines around her eyes and the faint tremor in her hands. The woman floated over to them and pressed her cheek against her daughter's.

"Let me look at you." She grasped Stacy's hands and stepped back, looking her over carefully. "Very lovely.

You've grown up so well. I only wish I had been there with you." Her eyes, hazel like her daughter's, dimmed.

"I'm here now," Stacy said hastily, sensing imminent disaster. "You don't look as if you just finished your exercise class."

"Ah, but you didn't see me a half hour ago, sweating horribly." Laura Markham laughed, then turned to Mac. "And who do we have here?"

"Frank McConnell, ma'am," he said politely, taking her hand. "I'm very pleased to meet you."

She arched an eyebrow. "Stacy has never brought anyone up here with her before." She eyed her daughter. "Does this mean something I should know about?"

"I never dared bring anyone with me, because you ask too many questions."

"What does Amanda think of him?" Laura asked Stacy, talking as if Mac weren't standing next to them.

"She thinks he's acceptable."

"But what about Chad? He never said anything about you seeing anyone else. Did you two have an argument?"

Stacy's eyes flickered toward Mac, whose interest immediately sharpened. "Chad?"

"Yes, Chad. Such a nice young man. He was up here about a week ago, you know," she chattered on. "He brought me a lovely bouquet of flowers in a crystal vase."

"Mother, did Chad talk about seeing me recently?" Stacy tried to keep her voice casual, to choose her words carefully. She knew from past experience that one didn't push Laura without dire results.

Her mother frowned. "I don't remember, dear. He talks of seeing you, but never exactly when. Why?"

Stacy hid her frustration. "I guess because I can't remember the last time I had seen him, that's all."

"What does he talk about when he's here, Mrs. Markham?" Mac interjected.

The older woman turned to him. "Why would you want to know?" Suspicion colored her tone.

His careless shrug was a piece of art in Stacy's eyes. She knew he didn't feel that way at all. "Curiosity."

"Are you still taking those needlework classes? I'd love to see what you've done lately." Stacy took her mother's arm and led her away. She knew, more than anyone, that Laura Markham could not be pushed without throwing a tantrum typical of a three-year-old, and right now, Stacy didn't want the mood ruined before she could find out what she needed to know.

Mac listened to Laura ramble on about the needlepoint pillow she'd been working on, and decided it might be a good time to take a look around. He let Stacy know in a few quiet words and slipped out of the solarium. He only hoped she would try to find out why Chad had been here. The simple fact that the elusive man had been here would eat at him like an acid until he found a reason. His own instincts told him that he might not like it.

Most of the room doors were closed, and one of the few open ones revealed a sitting room with period furniture. He noticed that the attendants wore street clothing with only name badges to differentiate them from the patients.

"May I help you, sir?" asked a young woman wearing a badge saying her name was Julie. She looked at him curiously.

"I'm just giving Mrs. Markham some time alone with her daughter." He smiled at her. "One thing Ms. Harris did wonder about. Her friend, Chad, had been up here last week. Did you happen to see him? I'm sorry, I don't recall his last name." Especially if the man had decided to use a different last name, he reflected wryly.

Her eyes lighted. Obviously Chad had made quite an impression on the female sex. "Oh, yes, I remember Chad. He comes up here every couple of weeks or so to visit Mrs. Markham. He really knows how to cheer her up. Mrs. Markham said she's known Chad for years, although he never started coming up until a couple months ago. He once said something about living out of the state until then."

"Did he happen to say why he hadn't?" Mac tried to sound casual.

She thought for a moment and shook her head. "No, he never did. He was more interested in what Mrs. Markham and Ms. Harris had been doing, especially Ms. Harris." She appeared to realize she was probably discussing something that she shouldn't. "Excuse me. I have to see to someone." She quickly brushed past him and hurried down the hall.

After taking a turn around the grounds and casually speaking to several attendants and patients, Mac returned to the solarium to find Stacy and Laura seated in a far corner. Judging by the tight-lipped expression on the older woman's face and the exasperation on Stacy's, the conversation was not going well.

Laura's voice rose. "I don't understand why you don't want Chad to visit me. After all, he comes more often to see me than you do." Her tone was sharp with accusation.

"I'm not saying that, Mother," Stacy said slowly. "I just don't want you to feel tired out from too many visitors."

"How can I be tired, when I hardly ever see anyone? After all, you only show up to gloat how well you've turned out under Russ and Amanda's supervision, since the honorable Jonathan Markham didn't feel I was a fit parent. Even in death he wouldn't even give me a chance. He thought he knew so much. That so-called knowledge didn't save his life, did it?"

"Mother, you know very well why Russ and Amanda were given guardianship of me. You weren't feeling well back then, and he wanted to spare you the stress of taking care of me. After all, I wasn't exactly a model child during those years." Stacy chose her words carefully.

"I felt just fine until you put me in this hellhole! You only sent me here because you didn't want me around, while you did all those horrible things. Your father was right in leaving you in that jail that night. I only wish he had left you there forever!"

"Laura, there you are." A woman of similar age glided into the solarium. She appeared oblivious of the visitors as she approached the angry woman, speaking in soothing tones. "Are you attending the lecture this evening? You know, I can't believe how fast this year has flown by. Do you realize it will be Thanksgiving before you know it?"

Laura spun around. "Thanksgiving?" she screamed, advancing toward the unsuspecting woman. "That day does not exist for me. I have nothing to be thankful for, when my daughter killed my husband on that day!"

"Mother!" A stunned Stacy grabbed hold of her arm, and Mac was immediately on the other side.

As if by magic, another woman appeared in the doorway and hurried in. "Come along, Laura. Why don't we lie down for a while?"

Laura's face twisted with fury. "Why don't you? Don't you understand? My daughter killed my husband as surely as if she had put a gun to his head! If it wasn't for her, I wouldn't be here now!"

Stacy's face whitened. "You know that's not true."

Laura snatched her arm away. "No? Is that why you tell everyone how horrible I was as a mother? Chad told me what you've said about me. I heard it all. You just want to keep me here until I die. You don't want me to see anyone but you!'' Her voice rose with every word. "I'm nothing more than an animal in a cage!"

"Come on, Mrs. Markham, why don't we go back to your room? If you'd like, I'll call Dr. Rankin, so you can speak to him," the other woman, obviously a nurse, soothed. She barely glanced at Stacy as she applied all her attention to Laura. Within moments she had skillfully led her patient away.

Stacy shuddered. "Come on," she said to Mac in a clipped voice. "One more stop."

Dr. Rankin proved to be a man probably in his late thirties or early forties.

"What is going on here?" Stacy demanded. While anger held her head high, strain was evident in the lines etched along her mouth and around her eyes. "I brought her to be helped, and she's only getting worse. Unauthorized people are getting in to see her, telling her lies. You told me the mention of Thanksgiving didn't upset her any longer. She would have torn that poor woman into ribbons, if we hadn't been there to stop her. I want some answers."

"Ms. Harris, your mother's many years of drinking have greatly impaired her mental capacity," he said calmly. "All we can do here is keep her away from alcohol and work on the problems that prompted her to drink. As for Thanksgiving: that hasn't been as easy, but yes, she has been doing better with that particular problem."

"Her problem has been dead for many years," she said bluntly.

"Ms. Harris, you're asking for miracles, and we can't promise those here." Mac had to admire the man's patience. He knew if he had been in a similar situation, he would have told Stacy off in no uncertain terms, although he realized she had to be tough in order to get her answers. "But your mother is healthier than she has been in a long time and she is certainly happier. Still, she has all those memories to live with, and many of them are not pleasant. If I were you, I would think about looking to myself, to see if some of those problems might not be discovered within.''

Stacy stiffened. ''I've done that, thank you. I just want her well taken care of. I think that's a small enough request. I'm also requesting that a better watch on her visitors be taken. A man claiming to be my boyfriend and an old friend of hers is showing up. He's lying, and I don't want him here, upsetting her. I want to know immediately if he does show up again.''

''Actually, Doctor, I would appreciate it if you would contact me the next time this Chad shows up.'' Mac handed him one of his cards.

The physician read the card and glanced up. ''Why would the police be interested in one of Mrs. Markham's visitors?''

Mac smiled. ''We just need to talk to him. Your help would be taken kindly.''

The doctor said nothing. Mac sensed there would be no phone call.

Stacy stalked out of the building, not waiting for Mac as she made her way to the car. She reached the driver's door and paused. ''Would you mind driving?'' She held up the keys, her fingers trembling from the strain of the past hour. Her face was paper white, and her eyes were dark with anguish.

''Not at all.'' He took them from her and steered her to the passenger side.

Stacy stared straight ahead as Mac headed down the hill and through the town. She didn't rouse herself until he turned north.

''Now maybe you know something I don't, but this isn't the way back to L.A.''

"You said you generally spend the night up around here."

"Around here, yes. Not San Francisco. In case you've forgotten, that's about another four-hour drive, and I don't think either of us is up to that."

"Just relax. There's a place not all that far from here I've always wanted to stay in. This might be a good time to try it. It appears to be a very relaxing atmosphere, and after today I think we both need it," he explained.

She stared out the window. "If it is Chad, why is he coming up here to see her?" She spoke more to herself than Mac. "What can he hope to accomplish from it? It doesn't make any sense."

"Not now maybe, but we'll figure something out," he assured her. He glanced to his left and apparently seeing what he was seeking, flipped the turn signal and pulled off the freeway.

Stacy looked up at the Victorian-style hotel that stood before them. She had often seen it from the freeway, but had never thought of stopping here even to eat. She waited until Mac parked the car before turning toward him.

"We're a few hundred miles away from our real selves," she murmured, touching his arm. "Let's be very, very selfish, and let tonight be just for us."

Mac's craggy features softened. He leaned over and grazed her cheek with his fingertips before following the same path with his lips. "Welcome to our new world."

Chapter Twelve

"I must say this doesn't look like the Holiday Inn," Stacy said, as she climbed out of the car and looked at the sprawling white outbuildings that resembled the houses of the late nineteenth century. The gingerbread trim was echoed on the main buildings that housed the registration desk, restaurants and gift shops.

"I've passed by the Madonna Inn on my way to and from Morro Bay many times, but it didn't seem to be a place I would stay in by myself," Mac explained. "I've heard it's always busy, so we'll probably have to take whatever we can get."

She looked into his eyes and knew he meant more than just getting a room. He was also giving her an out if she regretted expressing the wish she'd made earlier. "See if you can get something with a view. I'm going to stretch my legs."

Stacy wandered over to a Victorian-style rose garden and walked around, feeling as if she had been transported into another century. She had stooped to examine one rose when she happened to glance up. Mac was approaching her.

"How do you feel about a room all in blue, with a wrought iron stairway leading to a small viewing tower?" he asked, stopping beside her and holding out a color photo-graph postcard of an ornate bedroom.

She studied the picture as she considered his question. "I've always felt I looked good in blue."

"If you're hungry, we can live it up a little and eat in the dining room. The clerk told me they don't have a strict dress code," he told her.

"Sounds good to me."

Mac grinned. "I figured you'd say that. Of course, if you'd prefer, there's a Carl Jr.'s down the street."

She linked her arm with his. "Oh no, you don't. I'm not letting you get out of it that easy. All I usually get out of you are hot dogs and greasy hamburgers. For once, we're going to sit down to a beautiful meal. All I ask is a little time to freshen up."

"Fair enough."

"When you said the room was blue, you meant just that, didn't you?" Stacy looked around the large bedroom with its blue walls, carpet and furniture. She glanced up at the chandeliers, whose gold Cupids held the candle-shaped lights, and peeked into the blue floral bathroom. "I love it!" she exclaimed with a laugh, spinning around. "It's a very campy version of a French bordello."

Mac chuckled and dropped their two overnight cases into a chair. "When were you ever in a French bordello?"

"Never, but I'm sure this is what one of the rooms would look like." Stacy opened her bag and rummaged through the contents. She pulled out a cosmetic bag. "I shouldn't be more than ten minutes." She disappeared into the bath-room. "Oh, Mac, there's flowers painted along the rim of the sink! It's beautiful!"

Mac headed for the phone. Within minutes he was con-nected with Dean.

"So how's your impromptu trip?" Dean asked. "Are you back?"

"I got what could be a very promising lead." Mac ignored his second question. "Somebody's been visiting Stacy's mother, and it looks like the visitor is Stacy's old boyfriend, Chad Stone. He was the leader of the gang Stacy ran around with years ago. Dig around and see what you can find out about him in the present tense. He's supposed to have lived in New York for several years."

"If he hasn't gotten into any trouble, it won't be all that easy," Dean pointed out.

"Just do a little nosing around and see what you can scare up. Also see if the Santa Barbara cops will help us check out the visitors to the hospital Mrs. Markham is in. I talked to a few members of the hospital staff, but didn't get very far. They're pretty protective of their patients."

"Okay, I'll see what I can do. Anything else?"

"Nothing I can think of. What's happening on your end?"

"Nothing much, although we did arrest the kids who've been ripping off ladies' purses in the malls."

"I bet that made Henderson happy."

"You know him. Any arrest is a good one. If I need you, where can I find you?"

"I'll be in touch." He disconnected before Dean could say more.

"The bathroom's yours, if you want to freshen up also." Stacy walked into the bedroom.

"Sounds good."

"Mac." He turned. "You called Dean, didn't you?"

He nodded.

"Did you tell him where you were, and with whom?"

"No."

"Then he doesn't know we're still together," she said softly.

"No."

Her face broke into a sunny smile. Their time was still their own. "Why don't you clean up? We can enjoy a leisurely dinner in this new world of our own."

He kissed her gently on the lips. "Give me ten minutes and I'll do you proud."

THE INN'S RESTAURANT turned out to be even more than they expected. While casual dress was allowed in the dining room, the decor was more formal. They were seated in a private booth with a candle on the table. Balloons floated over tables in several booths, proclaiming a happy birthday, honeymoon or anniversary.

"How sweet." Stacy looked at one of the pink balloons. "It is a perfect place to celebrate a special occasion."

Mac watched as their wine was poured. He held up his glass. "To our newfound world."

She picked up her glass and touched his, her eyes on his the entire time. "Yes, to our world," she murmured, then sipped her wine.

Mac continued to hold her gaze. "No matter how it looks, I'm not trying to rush you into something you don't want. All right?" Her orange blouse picked up the golden lights in her eyes, he realized.

"Hmm, seducing you could be quite fascinating. But first, we have to find out those cute little tidbits about each other, don't you agree?" She smiled.

He looked wary. "Such as?"

She tapped a fingertip against her lips as she thought about it. "Oh, such as... When did you first decide you wanted to be a policeman?"

"Ever since my dad gave me a toy police kit when I was eight," he replied promptly. "I thought that badge, handcuffs and gun was the best thing I had ever seen. From then on I preferred playing cops and robbers over Cowboys and Indians. I applied to the police academy as soon as I was old enough, and I never looked back. What about you? No offense. I can't see you wanting to run a house-sitting agency when you were eight."

Stacy shook her head. "Actually, I first wanted to be a prima ballerina. My mother had taken me to see the *Sleeping Beauty* ballet, and after that I wanted nothing more than to learn how to dance on my toes. And since I used to be such a klutz at that age, my father suggested I take lessons, in hopes I'd also learn some grace." She smiled at the memory. "Mother bought me a pink leotard and tights and said I was the cutest ballerina she had ever seen. I never balked when Thursday afternoons came around and I had to attend ballet class. Unfortunately, after six months of lessons, the instructor told Mother not to waste her money. I just wasn't ballet material. I was still a klutz, but from then on I tripped gracefully over my feet." For a split second she looked pensive.

Mac took her folded hands between his and pressed his mouth against her knuckles. "By the time I was twelve, my feet had grown more than I had, and I tripped over them practically every time I took a step. Luckily, two years later I shot up in height to go with my shoe size. I dread to think what would have happened if I hadn't." His crooked smile lifted the corner of his mustache in the endearing way that caught Stacy's heart.

She studied the rugged lines of his face. In the back of her mind lingered thoughts of reality waiting for them in Los Angeles; she vehemently pushed them away. She was determined to keep this night for just themselves, no matter how melodramatic it sounded. To judge by the expression on Mac's face, he was thinking along the same lines.

"Since I couldn't be a ballerina, I thought I could try being a singer," Stacy told him. "There was only one problem: I was tone-deaf, so that took care of singing or playing a musical instrument. So I was eventually sent to charm school, where I learned how to walk correctly, set a proper table and how to be the perfect hostess. I did pretty well at that. We put on fashion shows at ladies' club luncheons and other social functions. My mother was so proud of me." She stared down at her plate. "She didn't drink then." She took a deep breath and pasted a broad smile on her face. "So tell me, were you football or basketball?"

Mac shook his head. "Baseball, varsity to be precise. I was a pretty hot pitcher."

She laughed. "And all the girls ran after you?"

"Yes," he said without modesty.

"And you loved it." It was more a statement than a question.

"I was seventeen. Of course, I loved it."

Stacy's spirits were considerably lifted by the time they retired to the adjoining lounge for a brandy and to listen to the live band.

She had barely taken a sip of her drink before she jumped to her feet. "Let's dance."

Mac winced. "If you think you were bad at ballet, you haven't seen me on the dance floor."

"No problem. Even with these tunes all you need to do is shuffle your feet convincingly. I'm sure you're great at faking things." She held out her arms.

He soon learned that Stacy was right. With the press of people on the dance floor there was little that could be done but move slowly in a tiny circle to a well-known tune from the 1940s. She looped her arms around his neck, while he kept his at her waist.

In her high heels, Stacy came to Mac's chin. Relishing the feel of his body against her and the spicy scent of his after-shave mingling companionably with her perfume, she didn't want this time to end. She was amazed that she was now falling in love with the man she had hated for so many years. After denying the emotion for so long, she found that she now cherished it. But she also feared it; there was still so much between them because of the robberies. She only hoped they would be able to go on when the worst was over.

As they danced, Mac could see how her hair shimmered with gold highlights under the dim lighting. The way they moved together, looked at each other and spoke with their bodies said a lot about a couple who shared more than a passing fancy for each other. What they had was indeed special, he felt.

Mac sensed that Stacy was still hurting inside. He knew it from the way she held her body, from the darkness in her eyes and her forced smile. He wondered if they wouldn't have been better off driving back to L.A. that night instead of stopping here. Still, she shouldn't be left alone tonight to brood over the day's happenings. And while he wanted nothing more than to make love to her, he wouldn't rush her into it—not when so many obstacles still lay between them. Right now he just wanted to hold her in his arms and chase the hurt away. For now he'd take what he could and be there when she needed him. He had an idea that what he felt for her was something lasting, but all he could do was curse the timing. All the same, if it hadn't been for the case, they never would have met again. He had finally stopped worrying about their age difference, but what about the rest of the problems that were hovering over them? Could they be as easily dismissed?

"I'm sorry if I've been a wet blanket at times," Stacy said, as they climbed the steeply inclined driveway to their building. "You've given me such a beautiful evening, and I did enjoy myself, even if there were times I might not have looked like it."

"You haven't been a wet blanket at all. I learned you were a klutzy eight-year-old ballerina. After all, how many people know that kind of dirt?" He kept her tightly against his side.

They slowly climbed the two flights of stairs, stopping at the railing just outside their room.

Stacy looked at the lights dotting the surrounding buildings. Since the inn was just off the freeway, she could also see the lights of the cars and hear the sounds of tires racing over the pavement.

"We didn't have to create a new world just for us. This is a whole other world," she murmured. "Did you see all the people in the restaurant who were here on their honeymoon or celebrating their anniversary? I almost feel as if we don't belong—that we're here for all the wrong reasons. Then I want to argue with myself that we have just as much right here as anyone else!" She flexed her jaw. "I'm right, aren't I? I'm not just lying to myself, am I? Can we honestly forget? What if the timing isn't right for us? What if fate wants to punish us for some past misdeeds? *My* past misdeeds?"

"You've done nothing to be punished for." He took her shoulders and gently shook her. "I told you before. This has to be right for both of us. I won't be angry if you change your mind."

She tilted back her head to look up at him under the dim lights strung across the gingerbread trim. "This case brought us together, and it could also tear us apart by the time it's ended. Yet you've done so much for me, and I've grown greedy for more. I want to reach out and grab as

much as I can. And I want you so badly that I cry about it."
Her eyes shimmered in the soft overhead lighting.

He guided her toward the door. "Then, my love, we feel
exactly the same."

Mac didn't bother turning on a light when they entered
their room. Once the door was closed, he pulled her gently
into his arms and traced the outline of her face with lingering kisses. "I have something to say before we go any further," he murmured.

"If you tell me that you've changed your mind and prefer to play the part of a gentleman, so help me, I'll inflict
bodily harm." She ran her fingertips over the lapels of his
jacket and pulled it off his shoulders.

He chuckled, the sound rusty. "No, far from that." He
pulled back a short distance. "Just as you said once before, I never looked into the future, because I never felt
there was one for me, either. And when I'm with you, I'm
also greedy and want to look ahead. What I'm trying to say
in a clumsy way is that I'm falling in love with you."

Her breath caught in her throat. "Oh, Mac," she whispered, flattening her hands against his shirtfront. "We were
both wrong about thinking we couldn't have more in life.
We can have it all, because I love you so much, I'm not
going to allow anything to tear us apart."

"After tonight, nothing will be able to." He eased off her
jacket, allowing it to fall to the plush carpet. While Stacy
slowly pulled his shirt over his head, he was busy unzipping
her skirt. Once his head was free of the confining material,
he returned to kiss her. He hunted for the buttons of her
blouse and found the one at her nape. He stepped back long
enough to pull the blouse over her head and dropped it to
the floor. He groped for the switch that controlled the
chandelier over the bed and stared at Stacy, now wearing
nothing more than a soft mocha, lace-trimmed chemise. The

cold air had caressed her nipples into taut points. He wrapped his arms around her waist and pulled her up until their faces were at the same level. "You are so beautiful. Are you sure we're not under a spell that will disappear any moment?" he inquired.

Her smile was like sunlight as she draped her arms around his neck. "If there's a spell, it's one we cast ourselves." She brushed her lips several times against his, teasing him with the tip of her tongue, whispering to him in the nonsensical language lovers use.

Mac carried Stacy to the bed, collapsing with her and rolling so that her weight fell onto him. They weren't aware of pushing back the covers, only that cool sheets now caressed their flesh. Mac only pulled away long enough to dispense with his shoes, socks and slacks, then returned to Stacy.

"Why would anyone do this to you?" she whispered, tracing the profile of a knife scar on his shoulder.

"If you want to look at a more interesting scar, try this one," he suggested, holding out one wrist.

Stacy stared at a set of tiny white marks that looked suspiciously as if they had been made by teeth. "Who would do this to you?" she cried, looking up. The expression in his eyes gave her the answer. "No, you're joking. I did this?"

He nodded. "Even back then you left your mark on me."

She picked up his wrist and caressed it with her lips. "No more pain for either of us." She ran her hands over his chest, feeling the crinkly hair under her palms, the small brown nipples hardening under her touch.

Not to be outdone, he enlisted her help in drawing the chemise over her head, and slipped her lace bikini pants down her legs. He slid his hands over her calves, moving them slowly up her legs to her thighs, while his mouth mated hungrily with hers. When his hands gripped her hips, she moved under his touch. And when his lips fastened on her nipple and drew it deep into his mouth, she arched her back, moaning softly at the pressure she felt deep inside.

She felt his heated body against hers and knew she needed all of him to feel complete. Her open mouth against the smooth skin of his shoulder conveyed her feelings.

Mac trailed his hands over her breasts, feeling them swell even more, then moved over the soft curve of her belly and even farther; she was ready for him. A harsh breath hissed between his teeth; he realized how much he loved her and wanted this time to be as perfect as possible.

"Look at me, Stacy," he urged.

She opened her eyes. Their gold flecks swam in the hazel depths as she showed him all the love she held for him. When their bodies became one, so did their souls. There were no more shadows surrounding them as they flew upward, upward, until they blazed together.

When they finally returned to the present, they lay on the damp sheets, feeling more complete than they had in a long time.

Mac nuzzled the moist skin of Stacy's neck, inhaling his own scent mixed with hers. They were one at last. The thought made him feel ten feet tall.

Stacy lazily rolled onto her side and placed one hand on his perspiration-slick chest. "Everything felt so right," she said softly, as if afraid she might break the spell. She stared at the drawn curtains. "I don't want dawn to come."

He instantly picked up the new tension in her body. He left the bed, smiling at her tiny sound of protest as he walked to the windows and made sure the drapes were tightly closed. He was glad their room was high enough; no one could look in. "It won't. Not if we don't want it to." He moved over her once again and showed her just how he planned to keep the broad light of day away—until they were ready to face it.

MAC HAD NO IDEA what woke him up, unless it was because the other side of the bed was ice-cold. He sat up, blinking rapidly so that his eyes would adjust to the darkness. No Stacy. The bathroom door stood open, the room dark; he knew she wasn't there. Something prompted him to climb out of bed and head for the winding stairs that led to the small viewing tower. He found Stacy at the top, with not even a robe to protect her from the night chill. He quickly descended the stairs and grabbed a blanket from the tiny closet.

"Standing up here in the cold air is a good way to get yourself sick," he said gruffly, draping the blanket around her shoulders and pulling it closed in front of her, holding her body in his arms to keep the blanket in place.

She didn't move. "My mother was right. I did cause my father's death," she said woodenly, continuing to look out the window at the nearby freeway and mountains beyond.

He rubbed his hands up and down her arms in slow motion. "Stacy, you didn't kill him. He had a stroke."

She shook her head. "No, it was more than that. I deliberately picked an argument with him. I told him things that upset him, and he grew so angry that a vein in his head burst and he died instantly. I wanted to goad him. To make him angry. Dammit, I wanted him to notice me! Instead, I killed him." She rested her head against his chest, hot tears sliding down her cheeks. "Why did I have to be such a monster then?"

"You had no control over what happened, Stacy. Keep remembering that," he said quietly, aching at the idea that she had suffered with an unnecessary guilt for so long. He recalled Amanda telling him it was something Stacy still had to deal with on her own and that not even he could help her.

"Russ and Amanda explained that he could have had that stroke at any time. Something about a weak vein. The logical part of me understands, but another part says that he would have lived longer if I hadn't started the argument during dinner. I've hated Thanksgiving ever since. You see, I threatened his political campaign by telling him things he didn't want to hear."

"You were at the age when rebellion was in. You weren't any different than a lot of other kids I dealt with those years," he pointed out.

Her laughter held no humor. "I wanted to hurt him. All during dinner he droned on how he was going to run for state senator, and Mother and I were to turn into the perfect family, or else. He was going to send her to a clinic to dry out, and I was to straighten up. If not, I would be sent to a European boarding school. I told him I'd make sure no boarding school would accept me and besides, I wasn't exactly the pure-as-snow daughter the public would like." She took a deep breath. "I reminded him of a few of my extracurricular activities, and he told me that was taken care of. So I started laughing and asked if he was also going to see my virginity restored. That's when I started screaming at him that his precious daughter wasn't a virgin, and wouldn't the public just love to hear about that?" She shuddered. "I screamed horrible, hateful things to him that day because I wanted to ruin his day. That was my only reason. Just to ruin his day. How immature I was back then."

Mac's arms around her tightened their hold. "And you accomplished your purpose."

"I guess so. I do know I got his attention. He started screaming back at me that I was nothing more than a slut and I would be shipped off the following week to a boarding school, where I would be whipped into shape or pay the consequences. Then he started screaming at my mother that if she hadn't been drinking all the time, I wouldn't have turned into such a monster. He told her she was pitiful and that I was the worst kind of child around. He also said that I couldn't be his. He couldn't have *spawned*—that was his word—such a devil." Mac saw her eyes grow glassy as she remembered that time. "It was odd. He suddenly stopped in midsentence, looked at us as if we had changed before his eyes, and fell over. The maid started screaming and Mother fainted. I just stood there looking at him, thinking that we were finally free."

"But you weren't. You kept all this inside and never allowed yourself to be completely free."

She nodded. "The only thing we were free of was Dad's physical presence. Otherwise he still ruled our lives. His will stated that Russ and Amanda were to have guardianship of me, if he died before I turned eighteen. It also stated that if Mother was still drinking, she wouldn't inherit any of his money, but a trust fund would pay a clinic for her care." She leaned back into his warmth, desperately needing his comfort. "And I was to be given nothing but a trust fund to cover any expenses I might incur while I lived with Russ and Amanda. If I turned out to be another Bonnie Parker, I could just sit in jail or be sent to the strictest boarding school in the world. The rest of his money was set up for scholarships at his law school. The lawyer holding his will said it wouldn't do any good for me to contest it, because it was written so tightly, it couldn't be broken. Dad may not have been the warmest person in the world, but he was an excellent attorney. That's when I learned how much he really hated me. By then I didn't care. I never cared about the money. I had my grandmother's legacy, which wasn't a lot, but enough to begin the agency and allow me to invest money that I use for my vacations and emergencies. All I ever wanted was something he didn't know how to give.''

Mac rested his chin on top of her head. "Yes, you did. You just didn't want to admit it, because you hurt too much. Stacy, the little I saw of your father showed me how cold he was. I admit, at first I saw you as a bratty kid, out to make as much trouble as you could and embarrass your father, but my partner back then kept saying how cold-blooded he seemed, and how obvious it was he didn't care for you.''

"It still left scars," she murmured. "To this day I cannot celebrate Thanksgiving. I usually go away for the long weekend. Luckily Amanda understands, and since Russ's death even goes with me sometimes.''

"Be thankful you came out of this a whole person," he told her. "I just wish I had known some of this back then.''

She turned her head, rubbing her cheek against his rough skin. "No sparing the rod as far as you were concerned?''

"No way.''

"You should have children, Mac," Stacy murmured, turning and sliding her arms around his waist. "You should have a dozen children to give love and attention to, so you wouldn't be cynical about the world.''

He chuckled. "Couldn't I start out with one first, and see how it goes?''

"Mac?" Her voice was tiny as she rested her cheek against his chest. "Our time is running out.''

He knew she meant more than the coming of dawn. He'd bet his badge that Chad had something to do with the robberies, and he had a horrible feeling that the man was trying to make some kind of connection through Stacy's mother.

"No worries." He combed her tangled hair with his fingers. "We'll pretend to be Scarlett O'Hara and think about it tomorrow. Okay?''

She tilted back her head and smiled. "Okay." Then her smile dimmed as she thought of what was still ahead of them. "Mac, we have to find Chad as soon as possible. He's somehow tied up with the robberies. I can feel it, and I know you can, too. What worries me is that he's seeing Mother."

"How could he have found out where your mother was?"

"Not very easily. While it wasn't exactly a state secret, it wasn't something I talked about, either. And we never ran around in the same circles, except for the gang. I'm sure I would have recognized him if I had seen him again."

"Unless he's changed a lot," he mused. "Come on. Let's get back to bed before we both freeze."

Stacy allowed him to lead her down the steps. He tucked her under the covers but before pulling them over her, grasped the ankle circled by the gold chain.

"Didn't you wear one back then?"

She smiled, even though she knew he couldn't see it in the darkness. "Yes, as a sign of rebellion. My father said good girls didn't wear ankle bracelets. I told him I wasn't a good girl. Now I wear it as a reminder."

He lightly touched the line above her eyebrow. "The same with your scar?"

"Yes."

Mac climbed in beside her and curved his body around hers in spoon fashion, letting his body heat warm her. "No more reminders, Stacy. It's time to move on."

She turned in his arms. "You're right. The best way is to make our own memories," she breathed, her mouth feathering over his.

"BUT I'VE TOLD YOU everything I remember! You're talking about thirteen years ago." Stacy glared at Mac.

She should have known his extra-attentive manner during breakfast was leading up to something—the way he'd made sure her coffee cup was refilled, that her eggs were cooked correctly and the bacon was crisp enough. Not to mention having the thermos filled with coffee and a few Danish tucked away.

"In case one of us gets the munchies," he had explained with a broad smile.

Now she knew it had just been a way of buttering her up. The moment the car entered the freeway, he passed her several pieces of paper.

"Write down everything you can remember about good ole Chad that might help us in tracking him down. Names, places—anything—no matter how trivial you think it is."

Stacy drew lines for a ticktacktoe game and began marking in *X*'s and *O*'s. "Mac, I already told you everything I remember."

"Tell me again. Just write it down this time."

She seriously thought about tossing it all out the window, then doing the same with Mac.

"All right. Just remember you asked for this." She tapped the pen against her cheek, stopping every so often to jot something down. "Isn't it enough you've talked to all my employees? It's a shame that Timothy had to go down to your office, though. He's a very sensitive man. No wonder I haven't heard from him recently. Your questions probably scared him off."

Mac frowned. "Who?"

"Timothy Foster. He was out of town when you came to my office, so the next time I saw him, I told him to contact you at the station. He said he would."

Mac looked puzzled. "Give me a little more information."

Stacy shrugged. "Well, he's in his seventies, wears bifocals, has old-fashioned manners. Not at all pushy, like some people I know." She shot him a pointed look. "He's a very sweet man. Believe me, you wouldn't have forgotten speaking to him."

He took his eyes off the road for a moment to catch her gaze. "I never spoke to anyone like that, and I'm sure Dean or the others haven't either, or I would have heard about it."

Chapter Thirteen

"What do we do now, Sherlock Holmes?" Stacy turned to Mac when she dropped him off at his house.

"You do nothing. I'll check into it myself," he informed her, climbing out of the car and walking around to retrieve his overnight bag.

"I don't see how you can even imagine that someone as sweet as Timothy would be involved in the robberies. After all, he's an old man. He's not the type." She followed him to the front door. "If he didn't contact you, it's because he forgot, that's all."

He pulled his key ring out of his pocket and unlocked the door. "Age has nothing to do with it. If he's competent enough to work for you, he wouldn't forget to see us."

Stacy felt like stamping her foot, but realized in time that stamping one's foot in Reeboks had little effect.

Mac pulled some letters out of his mailbox and walked into the house. Stacy entered on his heels and kicked the door shut.

"Stacy, I've got to check out every idea. I just wish I had known about this one sooner."

"I'm telling you right now."

"The next time you see Timothy Foster I want you to call me immediately."

She looked confused. "Why? Because he hasn't contacted you? Mac, he's an old man. He wouldn't have anything to do with this."

"Promise me you will call me the moment you hear from him," he insisted in a hard voice. "Until I can check him out further, I don't want you to be alone with him."

She exhaled. "All right. I promise I'll call you if he calls or comes around."

He dropped his bag onto a chair and turned. "Look, Stacy, Dean and my butts are on the line with this case, because it's taking so long for us to wrap it up. I can't afford for you to get in the way, and I can't afford to overlook the tiniest point."

She faced him squarely. "I'm good enough to give you all the information I can, but not to help you in any other way. Are you afraid I'll somehow solve it?"

"No, I'm afraid you'll get hurt!"

Stacy subsided. "Okay, but the least you can do is tell me what's going on."

He wrapped one hand around the back of his neck and massaged the tense muscles. "Stacy, I've told you more than I should have. And you've done plenty already to help us. Let it rest for now."

"Does this mean I'm not under suspicion any longer?" she asked.

He sighed. "That's up to Captain Henderson, but as far as I'm concerned, you're not, which I've basically told you before."

"But you're in charge of the case."

Mac threw up his hands in a gesture of despair. "Stacy, it's been a long drive, thanks to that accident on the highway holding us up for more than two hours. Right now I'd love nothing more than to stand under a hot shower for the next hour.''

She nodded. "Good idea. A long soak might soften that thick head of yours!" She stalked out, slamming the door behind her.

Mac closed his eyes. "That woman is making me crazy, and as soon as everything settles down, I'm going to do something about it."

HE SAT IN HIS CAR across the street, watching Stacy slam her way out of the cop's house. He smiled. It appeared the two lovers had had an argument. He enjoyed the idea of their parting. Especially since he had set the rest of his plan in motion. He was proud of his timing. Did she think he wouldn't hear of her seeing her mother and what she had said? It had paid to make friends with a couple of the nurses up there. Especially the little blond one who'd called him last night to tell him about Stacy and Mac's visit to the clinic. What would that scruffy police detective think of the high-minded Stacy Harris when it all hit the fan? Not to mention what his superiors would think of the way he obviously bungled the case. He smiled. He always enjoyed seeing a job well done.

"MMM, NO," Stacy mumbled, rolling over in bed and sticking her head under the pillow to drown the ringing of the phone. "Leave me alone," she groaned, when the phone rang for the tenth time. "'Lo." She squinted, trying to read the digital clock.

"This is a wake-up call you're not going to like."

She frowned. "Mac? Do you know what time it is?"

"Yeah, time for your funeral," he retorted. "Do you get the *Times*?"

"Yeah, but I don't think the paperboy is up this early to leave it at the door."

"It's not that early. Go take a look. Page 3 of the first section. Go now, I'll wait."

"Okay, okay." She stumbled out of bed and groped her way to the front door. "Doesn't he realize some people sleep past dawn?" she grumbled, opening the door and gathering up the folded newspaper. "Page 3, page 3." She opened the paper and glanced over the headlines until one washed over her like a cold shower. "Oh, no!" She ran back to the bedroom and picked up the receiver. "How did this happen?"

"I don't know," he said grimly. "But whoever leaked that story is going to be taken apart."

"My records are supposed to be closed!"

"They are, but if someone remembered you, it would be easy enough to dig back for information on your father, or talk to people who knew you back then."

Stacy felt sick to her stomach. "This will ruin me. I may as well close up the office right now, because no one will trust me now. The reporter might just as well have said that I was behind the robberies. Listing my past crimes certainly makes it look that way."

"You're going to have to fight back," he advised. "Call and arrange an interview to give your side of the story."

She cradled the receiver between her chin and shoulder and rubbed her aching temples. "Captain Henderson is having another litter of kittens about this, isn't he?"

"More than that."

"All right. I'll do as you suggest and give the press the truth."

"Good girl," he said softly. "I'm here if you need me."

All Stacy heard was the soft click of the line on the other end. She couldn't remember ever feeling so alone. She jumped when the phone rang again. She picked it up before it could ring again.

"Hello?"

"Stacy, have you read the paper?" Amanda asked.

"Yes, Mac just called to tell me about it." She sighed. "He suggested I contact the paper and offer my side of the story."

"Excellent idea, and he's right. Don't sit there and worry about it. Just call," Amanda urged.

"I will," she promised, sure that she sounded as if she were waiting for her turn with Madame Guillotine. "But that doesn't mean I'll like it."

When she reached the office, she found Janet sitting at her desk, already looking harassed.

"I turned on the answering machine out of self-defense," Janet explained. "The service had a ton of messages for us. Very few positive ones, and the phone wouldn't stop ringing."

"You saw the article, too?"

She nodded. "Stacy, I sensed there was something about your past you didn't want to talk about, but I figured that was your business."

Stacy's eyes filled with tears. "If you want to get out of this situation now, I won't blame you, Janet."

"Hey, what did I tell you before? We're in this together, boss. You just tell me what to do, and I'll do it."

Stacy held up the newspaper. "Then would you mind calling the reporter who wrote this article, and ask if she wants to hear my side of the story? Go ahead and keep the answering machine on, and just screen all the calls. If a reporter happens to sneak through, just tell them 'No comment.'"

"Have you talked to Amanda?"

She nodded. "She said she was surprised this hadn't happened sooner, and to basically tell them my side of the story."

Janet winced, obviously unwilling to give bad news. "We've had six cancellations so far. Mrs. Coffman called and said that she's never believed anything the *Times* has to say, and she still wants to use us."

"Bless Mrs. Coffman," Stacy said fervently, walking into her office. "Oh, I'm willing to see that reporter anytime she's willing. *If* she's willing. Just to be on the safe side, I'm going to put a call in to my attorney. I may as well cover all my bases."

Luckily, the reporter was more than willing to talk to Stacy that day. Within an hour Irene Rand, a woman in her forties, sat in Stacy's office; a tape recorder lay on the desk.

"First of all I'd like to warn you that I don't want to hear anything you prefer to be kept off the record," the journalist said crisply.

Stacy managed a brief smile. "I checked on you and learned that you're fair with everyone, and you don't beat around the bush. That's just fine with me."

Irene turned on the recorder. "Shall we start with your nefarious career of thirteen years ago?"

"Sounds fair." Under Irene's questioning, Stacy soon relaxed and gave her answers as honestly as possible. She spoke of her father's neglect, her mother's fragile emotions and a child's need for her parents' attention—and the only way Stacy had discovered she could get it. She also talked about Mac and his partner, merely mentioning the police officers who had been more than patient with such a rebellious teen. She spoke of her guilt over her father's death and how she'd learned to work it out with Russ and Amanda's help. By the time she reached the present, she felt drained.

Irene turned off the recorder and sat back. "You've told me quite a bit."

"I've told you the truth," Stacy declared, looking the reporter in the eye.

The older woman nodded. "All I can do is write it up and see what the readers have to say."

She barely smiled. "I understand. I want to thank you for allowing me to tell my side."

"Honey, I wouldn't have missed it for the world." She stood up and the two women shook hands. "You won't mind if I question your secretary, will you?"

"I don't mind, if Janet doesn't."

After the reporter had left the office, Stacy and Janet looked at each other. Both appeared exhausted.

"Most of the calls were from reporters," the secretary said apologetically.

"And the rest from unhappy clients," Stacy guessed.

She nodded with a miserable air.

Stacy pulled her checkbook out of her desk and wrote rapidly. "The best thing I can do is close up, before the police do it for me." She tore out the check and handed it to Janet.

"I'm considering this my vacation pay," Janet warned. "Once this is cleared up, you're going to need me to field all those calls from clients eating crow."

Stacy felt her smile wobble. "It would be nice, wouldn't it? Thanks."

They glanced up when two men entered the office. Stacy didn't need to see their badges to know they were from the police department. She'd hoped that Mac would be doing the job she was certain they were here for.

"Ms. Harris, we have a warrant to confiscate your records." One of the men held out a sheet of paper and showed her his badge and identification.

She nodded. "Of course." She got up and pulled open every drawer. "Be my guest." She stood back and watched them fill boxes with file folders and miscellaneous papers. All emotion drained away as the contents of her office were carried off. She could see that her life was falling apart for the second time—and knew she was powerless to stop it.

"As Lieutenant McConnell is in charge of this case, I'm surprised he didn't come here personally to close my office," she commented in a voice devoid of inflection.

One of the men hesitated. "He's been taken off the case, ma'am."

She stood still, refusing even to clench her fists. "Thank you for not making a mess in here."

The other man looked at her as if he'd already tried and convicted her. "Captain Henderson would like to see you down at headquarters as soon as possible."

"Am I under arrest?"

"No, ma'am. He'd just like to talk to you."

Stacy nodded. "Yes, I'm sure he would."

Both men nodded jerkily and left with the boxes.

"This is ridiculous!" Janet huffed, looking around at the now-empty file drawers. "Why aren't they out there looking for the real thief, instead of harassing innocent people?"

"Because it's easier to accuse the most likely person around, and right now I'm their best bet," Stacy said wearily. "Let's go. I can't stand to look at all this."

"Do you want me to call the service?"

She nodded her head. "Would you, please? Just have them tell the callers that the office is closed until further notice. Thanks for being such a rock during this time." She hugged Janet.

"Hey, we'll be back in business before you know it. You'll see." Tears brightened her eyes.

Stacy just wished she could feel as positive. As she left the building, she found herself fending off a couple of reporters as she rushed to her car.

She was quite relieved to get into her apartment without any mishap, and the first thing she did was call Amanda.

"How are you doing?" the woman asked before Stacy even got out a hello.

"Better than I thought I would be doing. The reporter came by and was very nice. I was so honest about everything, it hurt, but I knew it was the only way I could do it. The police also came by and took all my records, and I've been asked to go down to police headquarters to see the captain."

"You call that attorney of yours before you do anything," Amanda ordered. "Don't you dare go down there alone."

"Oh, I intend to." Stacy closed her eyes against the headache that was pounding behind her temples. "Amanda, I wouldn't be surprised if they decide to search my apartment next."

"Let them. You have nothing to hide."

"Not unless you count all the dust bunnies under the bed." Her laugh ended on a sob. "I'm sorry, I can't talk any longer." She carefully hung up and stretched out on the bed, where she could indulge in a good long cry.

"HE'S NOT going to do this." Mac's dark expression boded ill for the world.

"Don't screw this," Dean warned in a low voice, taking his friend and partner aside.

"He took me off the case, because I believe Stacy isn't behind the robberies and I want to handle this case right, while he just wants to make a quick arrest. Because of her past, he figures he can make it stick," he muttered.

Dean pulled him into a corner. "Just calm down and listen to what I've learned."

He smiled bitterly. "I'm not on the case, remember?"

"I'm picking your brains, nothing more." Dean lowered his voice. "I checked on Timothy Foster, and there's a few discrepancies."

"Such as?" Mac asked sharply.

Dean grinned, looking very proud of himself. "Such as: the social security number for Timothy Foster was issued to a Timothy Foster who died during World War II. I also found out a couple things about Chad Stone—that's his real name. Up until a year ago he worked in New York for a film company. He supposedly took a job out here about a year ago. There's only one problem. Chad Stone isn't working for any of the studios out here. One more thing. He left New York about the same time Timothy Foster appeared here."

Mac stared at his friend, his hopes rising. "Then Chad and Timothy could be one and the same."

Dean nodded. "I called the Foster apartment and there was no answer. I also called the agency and got the answering service. They said the office is closed until further notice, and refused to forward any calls to Stacy. I guess she didn't want to stay after Stan and Will picked up the records. Stan said that Henderson wants to see Stacy again. I'll warn you now, the man is talking about arresting her."

"I want to talk to Foster, or whatever he calls himself, before anything else is done," Mac insisted.

"You're not on the case anymore. If you show up, Henderson will string you up. He's already accused you of unprofessional behavior where Stacy's concerned."

"Let him. I want some answers," he said grimly, walking away. "Don't worry. I'll just happen to be in the neighborhood and run into Foster."

"Don't screw this up, Mac, just because you're mad," Dean repeated on an urgent note. "Emotions can't enter into this. They'll only mess you up."

"There's no way I'm going to mess this up. If this guy has something to do with the robberies, I want to see him convicted."

Dean watched him walk away and uttered a pungent curse. "I wonder what kind of jobs are available for cops who get fired?"

"STACY, IT'S ME, Timothy." The quavering voice could barely be heard through the door.

She thought about Mac's suspicions regarding the elderly man—and instantly dismissed them. "An old man couldn't do the things the thief did," she muttered, turning the dead bolt and opening the door. "Timothy, what a surprise! Come in," she said warmly.

"I called the office and talked to your answering service. They said your office was closed," he told her. "I didn't know if you were sick, and I thought I would stop by."

"Obviously you haven't read this morning's *Times*," she said wryly, gesturing for him to be seated.

"Oh, that." He dismissed it with a wave of the hand. "All lies, we both know that."

You call me right away if Foster shows up. Mac's words echoed in Stacy's mind, but she quickly banished them. She certainly wasn't in any danger from this kindly man.

"Thanks for believing in me. Very few people are." She smiled as she seated herself in a nearby chair.

"They just don't know you the way I do." He stared at her in an intense manner that somehow made her feel uneasy.

"Yes. Well, that's good to hear." She willed her hands to remain still in her lap. "By the way. Did you ever go down to talk to the police detective who wanted to see you?" she asked casually.

He shook his head sadly. "No, I am so sorry, but an old man like me forgets to do everything. I will see him soon. I tried to see you day before yesterday, but you were not here, and Janet would not say where you were."

The longer Stacy looked at Timothy, the uneasier she grew; she had an eerie feeling that the picture in front of her wasn't quite right. She was missing something very important, but couldn't figure out what exactly was wrong.

It's because of Mac's suspicions, she told herself. *He wants to suspect him, so now I'm starting to, when there's no reason to.*

"I'll be honest with you, Timothy, I don't know if I'll be reopening the agency. I hate to say it, but I'm not sure if any of the other agencies would use you, since you worked for me. I'm sorry if you wind up being a victim in all this," she apologized.

Timothy continued to watch her intently. "That is all right. Lately I have thought of moving away." He smiled as if he knew something she didn't. "With all of this turmoil going on, I realize Los Angeles is much too dangerous for an old man like myself."

Stacy nodded. She couldn't remember him ever talking of relatives living elsewhere or of a desire to travel. He'd always seemed to be content here. "I'll miss you," she replied finally, wanting to study him further but afraid of looking too suspicious. She kept asking herself what there was about him that seemed to keep her off balance, but couldn't seem to find the right answer.

As her eyes moved over his nondescript clothing—a worn brown suit, white cotton shirt with frayed cuffs, neatly polished shoes—she still sensed that the picture before her was out of focus. It was something she had never felt before when she was with him. If only she could figure out what was different.

"What will you do?" She hoped that by keeping him talking, she'd be able to work out what was puzzling her about him.

Timothy smiled—a feral smile, at odds with his kindly features. "I will make a new life for myself."

She felt confused, sensing that he was toying with her for some perverse reason. "A new life?"

Stacy finally became aware of something she hadn't noticed before. The seventyish-looking man sitting before her had the hands of a much younger person! While there were faint age spots on the backs, there were no prominent veins and no signs of knobby knuckles. She couldn't understand why she hadn't noticed it before. Was it because she wouldn't have thought there might be something wrong with him until Mac brought it up? She forced herself to continue smiling, and silently berated herself for not listening to Mac.

"Would you like some coffee or tea?" She hoped she sounded natural as she thought of the phone in her kitchen.

If she could just get word to Mac, she'd even endure the expected lecture for not calling him earlier.

"No, thank you." Even the eyes behind the bifocals suddenly didn't look like an old man's anymore. *Who was he?*

Stacy jumped when the phone rang. "I better get that." She forced herself to take her time walking toward the kitchen. She just prayed it was Mac. "Hello." She turned so that she would face Timothy as she talked, trying to look as if nothing was wrong.

"Stacy, Mac is on his way over, and I've got a warrant for Timothy Foster a.k.a. Chad Stone alias Chad Lawrence." Dean spoke urgently. "You stay put with all your doors locked. We think he was doing all this as some kind of vendetta against you."

"I'm really glad to hear from you, Donna, but I have company right now," Stacy said brightly. "Is it possible for me to call you later?"

The silence was charged. "Is Foster there?"

"Yes. I agree we need to talk about giving Karen a surprise birthday party." She felt sick inside. "So let me call you later, all right?"

Dean's reply was a string of curses. "Okay, I'll put out the word and get Mac on the radio. Just remain cool, honey."

Stacy hung up. " A girlfriend of mine wants to give a mutual friend a party," she explained, surprised to turn around and find Timothy standing behind her.

"When did you realize I wasn't Timothy?" His sharp tone struck her like spears.

She feigned amusement. "Well, if you're not Timothy, who are you?"

He suddenly appeared taller and very menacing. "You know very well what I mean. Come on, Stacy, we share a past. We used to have some good times, remember?" His voice held a deadly chill that transferred to Stacy. "How did you figure it out?"

"Your hands weren't like those of an old man," she whispered. "How did you manage to look so old?"

"I've been a movie makeup artist for the past ten years. This kind of disguise is a piece of cake, although I should have done a better job with the hands. I was in too much of a hurry today, because I wanted to get this over with." He grinned, the action ludicrous beneath the heavy makeup.

Her whisper barely reached him. "Why?"

His eyes were cold. "Because you sent me to prison, baby, while you lived it up on your old man's money. I had a lot of time to think about what you did and how much I hated you for sending me there."

"I never sent you to prison. You did that to yourself," Stacy protested, trying to back away, but the unyielding counter left her no escape route.

He advanced on her, taking her wrist in a bone-crushing grip. He tightened it until she winced.

"You and your little friends had the money and connections. I only had myself. Naturally, if anyone was going to take the fall, it would be me. You never even wanted me to meet your old man. You never wanted him to know you and I were a team. I was good enough to pull jobs with and to hang around with, as long as your parents didn't see me. If I hadn't come over to your house that one day, I wouldn't have met your mom. I bet she told you I've seen her up in that fancy hospital you've got her in. She thinks I'm a gentleman. I always bring her flowers and stuff, and I listen to her ramble on about how horrible you are for making her stay there. I kinda let her think we'll get her out, once we get married. That was smart thinking on my part.

Once she thought we were getting married, she told me anything I wanted to know."

Stacy looked into the gleaming eyes and realized she was not speaking to a sane man. *Oh, Mac, I didn't know. Why didn't I listen to you?* she silently cried, vainly trying to twist free from Chad's grip.

"What gave me away?" he asked conversationally.

"I don't know what you're talking about."

He twisted her arm painfully behind her back. "What do you know? I thought I did so well. You never guessed anything before now, so it must have been that cop who first got suspicious about me. Yeah, I remember him real well. He's the same guy who used to bust us years ago. I bet the two of you had a lot of old times to talk over, among other things," he said with a leer.

She refused to show him how frightened she was. "He's on his way over here."

He continued smiling coldly. "I'm not surprised. He's got the hots for you, Stacy girl. I've seen the way he looks at you. I bet he's going to feel real sorry when you're gone. Especially since the two of you had so much in common. You used to rob houses. He used to arrest you. The past really caught up with you, didn't it? I pulled the robberies, made sure suspicion was cast on you—and planting that article about your past finished the job, didn't it?" He appeared proud of his accomplishments. "And who would expect a little old man to be behind such daring robberies? It was perfect. You'll be in jail, and I'll be living very comfortably in Europe."

"You won't get away with it," she breathed.

He laughed as if her claim were a joke. "Of course I will, lover girl," he said, using the pet name he'd once called her. To her it now sounded almost obscene. "Your dirty past has been revealed to the public in such a way that even that cop won't be able to save you like he used to years ago."

She shook her head, trying to take it all in. She kept praying that someone would come soon. Seconds passed like hours. "I don't understand why you did all this."

"After I got out of prison I went to New York, took some courses and worked as a makeup artist for several film companies. I was well-known for heavy-duty jobs. This was child's play for me. Not to mention very amusing." He was playing with her, the way a cat torments a mouse, she realized. "How I enjoyed acting the doddering old man, and you were my adoring granddaughter. I knew my time would come soon. And so will yours."

Stacy's eyes widened. "What do you mean?"

He pulled a filled syringe out of his jacket pocket and used his thumb to pop the cap off. "You're distraught over all this, because you know the police will find some of the stolen jewelry you've hidden in your closet. And your secret lover who helped you with the robberies has disappeared. You have nothing to live for."

Stacy stared at the syringe with horror. She dreaded to think what the contents were. "You can't get away with this. No one will believe I used drugs to kill myself, when I've never used them."

"You've had an unstable emotional past. Your mother is one step away from a straitjacket most days. They'll believe it. Especially with the suicide note I typed on your typewriter at your office. I was able to secure a key through the cleaning crew. They never knew," he explained.

"You're the one who tried to run me down outside Amanda's," she guessed.

"Very good." He began pulling her out of the kitchen. "Let's make you comfortable, before I give you your little injection of heroin."

Now even more afraid, she dug in her heels as he dragged her along the floor.

Chad's expression grew ugly under the heavy makeup. "Don't make me force you, Stacy. You won't like it."

"If you think—"

"Stacy!" The door vibrated under the pounding blows.

"Mac, he's crazy!" she screamed, lashing out at Chad with her free hand; he quickly grasped it with his other hand.

"Get out of here, cop!" Chad screamed. "You're too late!" He now held both her hands in one of his and tried to stick the syringe into her arm with the other. He swore as Stacy struggled against him; at last she succeeded in knocking the syringe out of his hand. "No, I've come too far to stop now." He quickly tripped her up and straddled her thrashing body, pushing his thumbs against the hollow of her throat.

Stacy tried to scream, but the lack of air prevented any sound coming out. She concentrated on trying to live.

When Stacy was abruptly released, as Chad was pulled off her struggling body, she could only roll over and gasp for air. She turned her head—to see Mac pummeling Chad in the face.

"Hey, man, I give up!" Chad shouted, but Mac was past hearing any pleas for mercy. After seeing the younger man trying to kill Stacy, Mac was only intent on making Chad suffer.

"Mac, please don't kill him!" she cried weakly, her voice roughened by the abuse her vocal cords had just suffered.

Within seconds, the apartment was filled with uniformed officers, their guns drawn. Dean was on their heels.

"He admitted to everything," Stacy said, almost choking, still feeling dizzy as Dean helped her to her feet. Before she could steady herself, Mac pulled her into his arms and held her tightly.

"I was going through hell out there," he groaned. "I was afraid I wouldn't get in here in time. Dammit, I told you to call!"

"Mac, please don't scold me for not calling you right away and letting him in," she said weakly, grabbing his arms. She looked up at him. "He tried to shoot me up with heroin, then tried to choke me when I knocked the syringe out of his hand." She made a face at the pain in her throat. "The syringe is still on the floor. As for me, I think I'll do something I've never done in my entire life." She allowed the darkness to overtake her.

Chapter Fourteen

"You certainly look a lot better than you have the past few weeks," Amanda commented, as Stacy stretched out on a patio chaise longue next to Amanda's wheelchair.

"I feel more human, more like my old self," she admitted, extending her arms over her head and closing her eyes against the warm October sun. "Or maybe I should say the person I plan to be."

The older woman smiled. "And who exactly is that?"

Stacy opened one eye. "Are you playing shrink again?"

Amanda looked reproachful. "How many times have I told you not to use that term when you're referring to me? Are you going to answer my question or just ignore it, just as you ignore all my other questions these days?"

Stacy waved a languid hand. "Ask away."

"Why have you been avoiding Mac? You're not taking any of his calls, and you won't see him when he comes here."

"I wanted to make sure my head was on straight first," Stacy replied without hesitation. "I love that ornery man, and I know he loves me, but we've also been in a situation fraught with tension and danger. I wanted to assure myself my part of the attraction wasn't due to the situation we were in, and hope that he'll do the same and come up with the answer I did where we're concerned.''

"And?"

Stacy smiled. "I have finally come to fully realize my father couldn't help the way he was. I spent those years looking for something he didn't know how to give, and that was love. Unfortunately, I convinced myself I had found it with Chad. Luckily I learned the truth in time. My mother can't help what she is, because she's a weak person who buckled under my father's iron personality, instead of fighting to make a life for herself. They didn't make my life miserable for me, per se. I did that all by myself, and I have no one to blame for what I did back then but myself." She opened both eyes and turned to face Amanda. "You and Russ showed me what true parental love was, and Mac showed me what true love between a man and a woman is. We have a chance to share something very wonderful and very special, and I intend to make sure we don't lose it. By looking deep into myself and facing up to the past, the way I should have years ago, I know I'm more than ready to forge ahead and take that new turn in my life."

Amanda looked ready to cry. "My darling, you've done what I've prayed you would for years. You've healed."

"I KNEW life wouldn't return to normal easily, but I didn't expect this, either," Stacy grumbled, helping Janet return the office to its usual pristine condition. "Boy, they really made a mess of these files, didn't they? It's going to take us forever to straighten these out. I should make them come over here and help us put everything back together again."

"I can't believe that Timothy wasn't who we thought he was," Janet commented, opening file folders and making sure the information inside was for the same person as the label on the outside stated. "He must be a great makeup artist, because he sure fooled me. I know I never could see anything wrong in the way he looked. Have you heard when he'll stand trial?"

"When a doctor decides if and when he can." Stacy evened up the folders and stacked them in the file cabinet drawer. "It still isn't over. Not with the trial to come and my having to talk about my past. Unfortunately, quite a few people still feel I had something to do with the robberies, and others feel I somehow betrayed them by supposedly keeping it a secret," she said wryly. "No, it's far from over."

"Hey, we're both strong, we'll handle it," the secretary assured her in a bright voice. "Besides, we have important people on our side."

"Thank God for Mrs. Coffman and her speaking on our behalf." Stacy slammed the drawer shut. "You know, I always thought she was a little flighty, but when it came to standing up for us, she turned into a regular superwoman."

"She probably knew she couldn't find anyone else to take such good care of her little Tito," Janet quipped.

"You could always have volunteered."

"No way! I met that little monster of a dog once. That was more than enough for me, thank you." Janet placed her hands against the small of her back and arched to relieve aching muscles. "Can we go home now, boss? Of course, unless we get lucky, all this will still be here tomorrow."

Stacy smiled. "Boss. I never thought I'd hear that word again. It makes me feel very good."

"Since you're in such a good mood, I think it's the perfect time to hit you up for a raise."

"In your dreams."

"Can't blame me for trying. Now that things are cleared up, are you and Mac finally going to get together? No offense, but I don't think he believes me when I tell him you're either not here or in the bathroom, every time he calls. Even though I told him how hard you've been working in the field, trying to restore the business. Maybe that's why he hasn't stopped by.''

Stacy smiled. "Don't worry, you're off the hook. It's time for me to keep a promise," she said cryptically.

"HEY, ARE YOU going to stand there until the grass grows up around your knees, or are you going to pitch the damn ball!" Dean shouted from home plate, balancing the bat lightly on his shoulder.

"Fine. You want it thrown, you'll get it thrown," Mac growled, bending over and squinting against the afternoon sun. He wound up and pitched a perfect fastball over the plate. Dean swung and missed.

"The guy cheats!" Dean called, excusing himself to his team. "That has to be a trick ball from a magic shop!"

"This, coming from a guy who wears a shirt reading Trust Me, I'm a Cop," one of the other men scoffed. "Give it up, Cornell. You never could play this game. My wife bats better than you do. Hell, my dog bats better than you!" The other men burst out laughing.

"I don't even know why we're out here." Mac walked in from the pitcher's mound. "I could be home mowing the lawn or something else just as exciting."

"This is much better for you than mowing the lawn or wandering around your house, doing absolutely nothing. Besides, the grass will still be there. You're restless, old man," Dean told him. "Haven't you been able to talk to Stacy yet?"

Mac shook his head, aware that his frustration showed. "Not since the day she gave her statement at the station.

Since then she's hidden out at Amanda's, refusing to talk to any reporters except that woman who first interviewed her. When I call there, all Alice or Amanda tell me is that she can't talk to anyone just now. When I call Stacy's office, I get that damn answering service or Janet. I'm about ready to eat nails and storm the house and drag her out. To be honest, I'm more partial to the latter.''

"Don't worry, everything will turn out fine.'' Dean clapped him on the back. "You'll see.''

Mac glowered at his partner. "Easy for you to say.''

"Will you look at that?'' One of the men whistled under his breath. "Very nice.''

Mac and the others turned—to see Stacy crossing the field toward them. Dressed in skintight, faded jeans and a bright orange wool V-neck sweater, with brown leather boots covering her calves, she was a sight to behold.

Mac spun toward the men. "What's going on here?'' His suspicion grew as he saw the deceptive innocence in the others' eyes.

Dean shrugged. "Beats me. It looks like the lady has finally come out of hiding. Aren't you lucky? You won't have to drag her out, after all. She came out all on her own.'' He pushed him from behind. "Don't be shy.''

"Gentlemen.'' Stacy smiled at them. Unspoken communication flashed between Stacy and Dean before she turned to the man she'd really come to see. "Hello, Mac.''

He stood warily. "Stacy.''

She continued smiling, obviously knowing something he didn't. He grew uneasier by the second.

"If the rest of you don't mind, I'll be taking your friend away from your game now.''

"Take him,'' Dean said promptly. "With someone else pitching, I might get a chance to hit the ball.''

Mac's features expressed his frustration. "What the hell is going on? I better get some answers very soon." He couldn't believe he was just standing there, when he wanted nothing more than to haul Stacy into his arms and not let her go. How many nights had he walked the rooms of his house, unable to sleep because his thoughts were filled with the woman standing before him? How many times had he tried calling her, only to be put off? Doubts had begun to assail him that perhaps her words of love had been just that, after all—words, not truth. He ached for her, but he was afraid to touch her.

Stacy took his arm. "Come on, Mac. We have some unfinished business to discuss."

He stood fast. "Not until you tell me why you've been avoiding me for the past three weeks."

"All in good time." She spoke patiently, as if she were dealing with a small child. "Now come along, dear."

Dean addressed the others. "Guys, I don't think he's cooperating with the lady here. Maybe we should give her a hand."

Before Mac could say a word, six men surrounded him and steered him toward the bright red sports car, whose engine was running. He had no chance to defend himself and was pushed into the car.

Stacy jumped into the driver's seat and roared off before Mac could leap out. Deep down, she feared her plan wouldn't work if the other party wasn't amiable. She had held off talking to him, until she had worked out many things in her mind. Now she felt free to come to him. Without wasting time, she'd contacted Dean and with his help, put her plan in motion.

"What are you doing?" Mac demanded, holding on to the dashboard as he fumbled with the seat belt.

"I'm kidnapping you," she said cheerfully. "Just sit back and relax. We have a bit of a drive ahead of us."

He steeled himself not to break into a broad grin. Relief flowed through his body. "Kidnapping is against the law."

"So's owning a switchblade, but that didn't stop me from having one, did it?"

He laughed, feeling more alive than he had in days. "Lady, you're dangerous."

She flashed him a wicked grin. "Yup, the best kind."

Mac looked up. "Stop at the corner."

Stacy shook her head. "No way. I'm not having you escape me, now that I have you in my clutches."

"Escape is the last thing on my mind. Just go ahead and stop."

She slowed at the corner, where Mac gestured to a small boy standing next to a bucket of cut flowers. After a brief exchange the happy boy handed Mac all the flowers he had. Mac presented them to Stacy. She looked down at them, then up again. Her eyes were damp.

"They're beautiful," she whispered.

His reply was interrupted by a fierce honking from the rear.

"Cool it! You're disturbing police business here!" Mac yelled.

"I don't think he sees it that way." Stacy laughed, gunning the engine and quickly pulling into the briskly moving traffic.

"How come the theatrics? Didn't you think I'd go with you otherwise?" Mac asked, settling back into the seat, one arm draped behind Stacy's neck.

"Easy. I once told you, when it was all over, I'd kidnap you—and I intend to keep that promise."

He nodded, remembering the conversation well. "Why didn't you speak to me earlier?"

"I wanted to explore my feelings and make sure they were genuine."

For a brief second he felt a spurt of fear, then reassured himself. After all, she was here, wasn't she? "And?" he still forced himself to ask.

"And…" She drew out the word. "I've decided it's time for you to make an honest woman of me." She held up her hand to forestall his reply. "Now, you keep quiet until we stop. Just sit back and enjoy the ride."

A few hours later, Stacy parked in a small lot leading to the beach. She opened her door and swung her legs out, bending over to pull off her boots and socks. "Come on," she urged.

They lost track of time as they walked hand in hand down the empty beach. After about ten minutes Stacy guided Mac a short distance from the shoreline and sat down cross-legged. She picked up a handful of sand, watching it flow from her fist.

"I want a long romantic courtship with flowers and candlelight dinners. There is not to be one fast-food restaurant in the bunch. I don't care how good their coffee is." She didn't look at him as she spoke. "And I want the wedding to be held in Amanda's garden. And tell Dean he can only be best man if he wears something suitable. Naturally, Captain Henderson will not be invited, for obvious reasons."

Mac started laughing, feeling more lighthearted than he had in a long time as he hauled her into his lap. "You're pretty sure of yourself, aren't you?"

She looked smug as she looped her arms around his neck. "McConnell, I've been sure of you for a long time now. I just wanted *you* to be sure."

"Considering our position, I hope you don't expect me to get on one knee and propose to you. Or are you planning to do that? Anastasia Markham Harris, will you marry me?" he asked huskily.

Tears glittered on her lashes. "You're not just saying that because of what I said, are you?"

He shook her gently. "By now you should know that's not my style. No. I want you to give life to my house, not to mention to me. I enjoy the times we battle, and because I can't believe you'd love a grizzled old cop like me, and most of all because I love you so much, I don't intend to let you go for the next hundred and fifty years."

"Then I accept." Her voice dropped to a husky whisper as she buried her face against his neck.

"But no long courtship," he warned. "I'm not the most patient man around."

A tiny smiled curved her lips. "Yes, I've noticed that. Actually, I was thinking about having our wedding on Thanksgiving Day, if that was all right with you."

Mac stilled, realizing the meaning behind her suggestion. "I hope you're not talking about next Thanksgiving. I'm not into that long of a courtship."

She nodded. "To be honest, neither am I." She pulled away and reached down her leg. She unsnapped the clasp to her ankle bracelet and dropped it into his hand, closing his fingers around it. Words weren't needed then.

Mac knew then that Stacy was finally pulling completely away from the ghosts that had once haunted her; she was offering him the last link to the past.

"Oh, lady, I love you so much," he groaned, kissing her hungrily. "If you don't want to be ravished right here on the beach, we better find a place . . . fast."

She smiled. "I've already got that covered."

MAC LOOKED UP at the white Victorian buildings with their gingerbread trim and grinned broadly.

"So what do you think?" Stacy asked archly, tossing a key in her hand.

He shook his head. "I'm very impressed."

"I thought you might be." She led the way down the short hallway to the familiar room, where a cloud-shaped sign hung on the door.

Mac continued smiling as he followed her. "You must have gone to some trouble to get the same room."

"I've been calling every day to make sure I could reserve it." She unlocked the door and pushed it open, gesturing for him to enter. He smiled and inclined his head, indicating that he preferred she go in first.

Mac had barely walked inside and closed the door before Stacy pressed him back against it.

"You're right, McConnell. I didn't want to be ravished on the beach," she told him in a throaty voice. "I think we've wasted too much time, don't you?"

"Way too much. So what do you have in mind?"

"This." She pressed even closer, looping her arms around his neck and nipping the rough skin. "You're my prisoner, McConnell, so don't bother calling for help."

He felt his blood pressure shoot up sky-high. "That's the furthest thing from my mind."

She nibbled delicately around his ear, listening to his groans. "Why McConnell, haven't you ever been seduced before?'' she murmured throatily, flicking her tongue into his ear.

His laughter was strangled in his throat as he felt her knee insinuate itself between his legs and rub up and down in a seductive motion. ''Not lately.''

Their mouths met in a hungry kiss that spoke of the time they'd been forced to spend apart; it was also a promise to never be apart again.

''It's not going to be easy,'' she whispered, once they had broken apart. ''We still have Chad's trial, and they're going to bring out every dirty detail of my past. It's going to be even worse, since we're involved.'' She showed distress. ''In fact, maybe we should wait until after the trial.''

He shook his head. ''No way. You're going to be my wife Thanksgiving Day.''

She inhaled the warm, musky scent of his skin. ''I wonder if our kids will realize how lucky they are to have us as parents,'' she mused.

He pulled back slightly. ''Do you know something I don't?''

''Not yet, but I don't want to wait too long, do you?'' she asked softly.

Mac was stunned; this woman was giving so much. ''Why don't you get the agency going again before we talk about it, all right? Although I'm all for the idea of a little girl just like you. Minus the switchblade, of course.''

''Then she better have an older brother to help keep her in line.'' Stacy's brain was whirling with all that had happened over the past few hours. Much more had happened than even she had planned. ''You're not at all worried about what may happen, are you?'' She ran her hands up and down his arms, needing to feel him, to feel the reassurance of his skin against hers.

Mac buried his face against her hair as he gripped her arms and hauled her against him. "Not one bit. We're going to make it, you'll see. We've got each other, don't we?"

Stacy felt joy filling every part of her body at his words. "Yes, we certainly do."

HARLEQUIN

American Romance

COMING NEXT MONTH

#329 BEST WISHES by Julie Kistler

Known as the Grande Dame of the Rockies, The Stanley Hotel had its share of legends. But when a mysterious stranger gave front desk manager Hayley Austin a golden apple, she didn't know she was about to make hotel history. When she met Mason Wilder, the man of her dreams, Hayley wondered if the apple was truly magic, or was it sheer coincidence?

BEST WISHES introduces a three-book series called ROCKY MOUNTAIN MAGIC. In March 1990 don't miss #333 SIGHT UNSEEN by Kathy Clark, and in April 1990 look for #337 RETURN TO SUMMER by Emma Merritt.

#330 SURVIVORS by Judith Arnold

Nursery-owner Paul Tremaine grew stately oaks and graceful birches—but the humid jungles of Vietnam plagued his dreams. Bonnie Hudson taught her son that his father was a hero, an antiwar activist who'd died for his beliefs. But it was the terrible truth about those years that challenged them to put the past to rest—and save their passion for living.

#331 OUTSIDE IN by Beverly Sommers

At twenty-seven, Jill was masquerading as a high-school senior to find the truth about her sister's death. She was also causing quite a commotion, snubbing the cheerleaders and hanging out with the jocks. And giving her Civics teacher the fright of his life. Poor Doug Lacayo had no way of knowing that his provocative, attractive pupil wasn't a teenager.

#332 MEMORY LANE by Vella Munn

Though she'd been brought back by duty and responsibility, Kim Revis had promised herself to enjoy her visit to her childhood home. But Kim's grandmother's handsome lawyer, Mark Stockton, had made promises of his own. His presence kept luring her away from the deceptive pleasures of the past and warning her of the danger of the present.

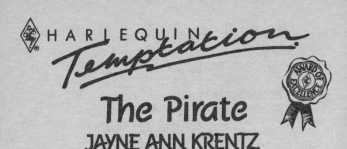

The Pirate
JAYNE ANN KRENTZ

At the heart of every powerful romance story lies a legend. There are many romantic legends and countless modern variations on them, but they all have one thing in common: They are tales of brave, resourceful women who must gentle and tame the powerful, passionate men who are their true mates.

The enormous appeal of Jayne Ann Krentz lies in her ability to create modern-day versions of these classic romantic myths, and her LADIES AND LEGENDS trilogy showcases this talent. Believing that a storyteller who can bring legends to life deserves special attention, Harlequin has chosen the first book of the trilogy—THE PIRATE—to receive our Award of Excellence. Look for it in February.

AE-PIR-1

You'll flip . . . your pages won't!
Read paperbacks *hands-free* with

Book Mate • I

The perfect "mate" for all your romance paperbacks

**Traveling • Vacationing • At Work • In Bed • Studying
• Cooking • Eating**

Perfect size for all standard paperbacks, this wonderful invention makes reading a pure pleasure! Ingenious design holds paperback books OPEN and FLAT so even wind can't ruffle pages — leaves your hands free to do other things. Reinforced, wipe-clean vinyl-covered holder flexes to let you turn pages without undoing the strap . . . supports paperbacks so well, they have the strength of hardcovers!

Pages turn WITHOUT opening the strap.

SEE-THROUGH STRAP

Reinforced back stays flat

Built in bookmark

BOOK MARK

BACK COVER HOLDING STRIP

10" x 7¼" . opened
Snaps closed for easy carrying, too

Available now. Send your name, address, and zip code, along with a check or money order for just $5.95 + .75¢ for postage & handling (for a total of $6.70) payable to Reader Service to:

Reader Service
Bookmate Offer
901 Fuhrmann Blvd.
P.O. Box 1396
Buffalo, N.Y. 14269-1396

Offer not available in Canada
*New York and Iowa residents add appropriate sales tax.

BM-G

A compelling novel of deadly revenge and passion
from Harlequin's bestselling international
romance author Penny Jordan

POWER PLAY

Eleven years had passed but the
terror of that night was something
Pepper Minesse would never
forget. Fueled by revenge against
the four men who had brutally
shattered her past, she set in
motion a deadly plan to destroy
their futures.

Available in February!

 Harlequin Books®

HPP-1A